Playing With the Hand I Was Dealt

PLAYING WITH THE HAND I WAS DEALT

NIKKI JENKINS

STREBOR BOOKS

NEW YORK LONDON TORONTO SYDNEY

Strebor Books
P.O. Box 6505
Largo, MD 20792

ISBN: 978-0-7394-8720-4

Cover design: www.mariondesigns.com

Manufactured in the United States of America

DEDICATION

I dedicate my first novel to...
The two that make me smile more than
they make me want to pull my hair out;
The one who gives me high highs and low lows.
(Can't have the yin without the yang);
Those who believed in my talent when
I wasn't sure if I had any;
Those who tried to bring me down because
they couldn't rise on their own;
and
Those who gave me a chance when no one else would.

ACKNOWLEDGMENTS

As I sit and write this acknowledgement, I wonder how many people will be hurt by not being mentioned. Please know that if you don't see your name it isn't because you aren't important to me. I love you all so very much!

Mommy, we've been through it all. What doesn't kill us, only makes us stronger, we're living proof. I love you!

Michael H., you love me like one of your own...thank you. You were right, after 25...

Grandmommy, I owe you everything. As long as I do, you'll never be broke. Big chocolate hugs and kisses!

Karen N.M., thank you for being my bestest friend. If I need to talk about it (or someone), I know you'll listen. Thanks for being there.

D. Brooks, it was a blessing to find you. We clicked right away. I look forward to working with you again.

LLPE, please know that I love you.

My family and friends are so important to me! Without all your support I surely wouldn't be here today. I am truly blessed to have so many wonderful people in my life who care about me.

K.L.S., remember in 2000 when I told you I was going to write a book? Can you believe I did it?

CHAPTER ONE
SATURDAY EVENING

Natalie had been working all day and by evening the exhaustion hit her hard. She collapsed onto the leather chaise that once belonged to her Gigi and Pappi, her father's deceased parents. The chair overlooked the garden she took such pride in. Natalie had to imagine the view from the window. Darkness had erased the beautiful landscape that was her backyard. It was a scene that she woke to each and every morning, the colorful hydrangeas, the graceful Jacqueline Kennedy roses and despite it being a common flower, Natalie loved the beauty and serenity of the rows and rows of black-eyed Susans. She smiled at the garden below, imagining what had started out as a means to calm her frazzled nerves and eliminate her twitching eye, but had evolved into a hobby and an art.

The master bedroom was dark except for the glow from the nightlight, an amenity courtesy of her son, Kendall. He didn't want his mother and father to sleep in the total darkness that night brings. He assumed that because he was afraid of things that go bump in the night that they were, too. Little did he know that it was the darkness that comforted his mother. She could hide from her reality and never have to admit that there was a problem under the cover of pitch black.

Natalie hoped and prayed that her son didn't lose that conscientiousness as he grew older. Lord knows most men haven't a clue as to what it means to care about other's feelings, especially the feelings of women. Natalie figured that if she couldn't find that perfect man, in terms of one who would be cognizant of and responsive to her needs, she sure as hell would make certain that her son was as close to perfect as possible. He was a work in progress, her work in progress, and by the time he started dating, he would be ready if it killed her. She swore on her grandparents' graves that her son would not be any other woman's headache, the same type of headache his father was to her.

It had been several hours since she had put her two small children to bed. The feeling was strong to check in on them, but comfort held her down, its grip tight. She had to push herself to rise from her seated position. The chaise eased her aching bones. Sometimes it seemed as if her children were growing up way, way too fast. She thought back to the day she gave birth. Despite the pain that accompanied their delivery, she decided almost instantly that she wanted to have more. But it was Anderson's insistence that they wait until their "lives were more stable" that caused her to have to put her maternal desire on hold. Something nagged at her that there were other reasons for his hesitance, but without concrete evidence she had to hold back her suspicions. Besides, she had two beautiful babies to occupy her time and that they did.

Natalie, moving slowly, rose from the comfort of her chair and made her way into the nursery. There they were–the two children she considered to be her life, her reason for living. And as far as she was concerned, they were her reason for waking in the morning. She could remember vividly having those same feelings for Anderson, and how the feelings for him were replaced the day she gave birth to her blessed twins.

She walked around the room, hanging clothes that had sat in a basket for days. The gentle snores of her children made her smile. She leaned down and kissed each one, brushing back the hair on Kayla's head. They smelled of baby lotion and powder.

She hated that her feelings for Anderson had waned after their birth. However, as far as she was concerned, they naturally needed her much more than he did, and he would simply have to deal with it. She could tell there were times he missed having her undivided attention. He seemed at times to even be jealous of his own children. But attempting to be an adult, he'd try to push past his childlike behavior, most times falling short.

"I miss you, Nat," he would whine while the twins cried for her in their room. She was torn about who needed her more.

Natalie found it difficult to juggle caring for her children and then having to cater to her husband. After they were born, for months she would fall into bed exhausted each night after having to care for two newborns and be attentive to Anderson at the same time. She cooked, cleaned, and washed clothes daily. She would cry at night when he would climb on top of her, have his way with her, and then fall off to sleep. He ignored her desire to rest. He ignored her request for help. And he ignored her pleas for a break. She hated him for it. She felt trapped, but didn't know what to do or how to fix it.

The twins were sleeping peacefully in their cribs. *Nat, girl, you are so crazy. Let those children be*, she reprimanded herself silently and smiled contently.

The telephone rang and forgetting how sound her children slept, she attempted to hurry through the nursery door. As she hastened through the room, she stumbled over building blocks and banged her knee on the closet door that sat ajar. Biting her lip to muffle the sound of her pain, she closed the door behind her and moved quickly back to her bedroom. Natalie reached for the handset, almost knocking the receiver onto the floor, and out of breath, she blew her greeting into the telephone.

"Hello."

Nothing.

"Hello?"

Still nothing.

"Hello!"

Dial tone.

That was the third time today the phone had rang and no one was on the receiving end. Or at least no one responded. Natalie placed the cordless phone back in its cradle and returned to the chaise, but her thoughts started to wander.

Who could have called the wrong number that many times in one day? Once, twice maybe if they were checking, but three times? What if it was another woman calling for Anderson? He'd say she was crazy, that she had an overactive imagination. Still, he had strayed from her once before. She might have forgiven, but she never forgot. Who could blame her for being a bit paranoid after that incident, after all?

The phone's ring jarred her from her thoughts. She let it ring three times before picking it up. Her concern now wasn't so much about waking the children. Instead, she worried about what she would or wouldn't hear on the other end. *If this is another hang up, I'll scream!* she thought to herself.

"Hello?" she questioned the person on the receiving end. Ah, a familiar voice. Her knee began to throb and she rubbed it to soothe the pain.

"Oh, what's up, Les?"

"Hey, can't talk long. I'm on my way out. Are you doing anything Monday?"

"Monday? No, I'm not doing anything."

"Meet me at the gym."

"Okay, I'll meet you there, but why?"

"Look, I don't have time to explain. Make sure that you meet me there."

"Leslie, this had better be good. You know how I hate surprises."

"Natalie, just be there."

"Where are you…" Before she could finish her question, Leslie had hung up.

Who knew what plan Leslie was cooking up now. Probably some scam to meet a man, using Natalie, her married best friend, as bait. Oh well, she was free then so why not show up and go along for the ride.

CHAPTER TWO

Natalie met Leslie Ann West their freshman year in high school. She was bused into the district in the school board's attempt to integrate the predominately white Sheridan Heights High School. Leslie's coal black, board-straight hair extended well below her shoulder blades, providing evidence of her Native American heritage. She had flawless, mocha-colored skin and a short, curvy body that attracted boys and men alike. Suffice it to say, the boys loved her and the girls scowled when they saw her coming. She took their dislike as a compliment and used their energy to drive her to reach her goals, which most of the time were to rob them of their boyfriends.

While in high school, Leslie lived with her two brothers, her sister, her mother and her grandmother in a three-bedroom apartment in an area of town most people talked about but rarely ever visited. But now Leslie had moved up and out of the projects. She had worked her way through college as an exotic dancer in local gentlemen's clubs. It was a fact she wasn't shy about divulging. In fact, she bragged often times of the fact that she had the type of body that made men cry and even made married men want to leave their wives, or at least forget about them for the night. Her erotic endeavors allowed her to earn enough money to put herself through one of the most expensive private colleges in the city and upon graduation she received the distinguished honor of magna cum laude.

Yes, she worked hard in all she did, even dancing. She didn't mind working hard and it paid off. She was now working hard as the Director of Marketing at a local wireless phone company. She brought home a six-figure paycheck and that, incorporated with the same curvaceous body, made her a magnet for every Taiquan, Devonte and Darshawn in town.

Since she was a little girl, Leslie had dreams of being a wife and a mother. She planned her wedding day down to the last detail and thought up names for the children she hadn't yet bore. Ignoring her biological clock, she went through her twenties jumping from one relationship to another and terminating two unplanned pregnancies. She rationalized to herself that she would have plenty of time to bring a few pregnancies to completion before menopause. But now that she was able to see the end of her thirties quite clearly, she began to panic about whether or not she would accomplish the only reason she had been put on earth as a woman, to procreate. Leslie had tried practically everything to meet men of substance. And so, hesitantly, she tried speed dating. She spent about an hour and half jumping from one table to another and it seemed as if her choices were going from bad to worse. Those brothers who seemed to have potential were flawed by bad breath, out-of-date clothing or both. The night was quickly coming to an end and when it seemed as if she was going to have to go home empty-handed, again, she met Reginald Warrington. R.W. was the director of a grassroots organization. He didn't have the cash necessary to make a woman like Leslie happy. Strike One. But he was more than handsome—he *was* something to write home about. And so the two cancelled each other out. R.W. had all the women breathing a little hot and heavy, and so he could pick and choose who he wanted to date this particular evening. And it was Leslie who came out the winner.

Leslie had agreed to meet R.W. on Saturday night at a new restaurant that had opened downtown. Leslie entered the restaurant and all eyes were on her. She could feel the energy from the men and it excited her. She knew that she had made the right choice when she wiggled into the black spaghetti strap dress and thong panties. She could feel it—tonight would be a good night.

"It's good to see you again, Ms. West." The voice came from behind her. Leslie had wished he would have entered through the front door. She wanted to see him before he saw her, in case she needed to make a mad dash for the exit.

She turned around and her face lit up. The view was as spectacular tonight as it had been a week ago.

"Mr. Warrington. It's great seeing *you* again."

R.W. leaned down and placed a kiss on her cheek. Leslie closed her eyes and envisioned the two of them walking together hand-in-hand toward their home with the white picket fence. She saw their dog, Sandy, frolicking in the yard and their son and daughter, Michael and Michelle, playing on the swings. It was all so vivid.

"Are you hungry? I'm starved. Today's been rough. Although it's the weekend, I'm always working." R.W. motioned to the waiter that they were ready. As they walked to their table, Leslie noticed that R.W. received as much attention from the women in the place as she had from the men. Leslie didn't know if she was secure enough to handle a man who was as pretty as she was.

"I'm starved, too," she agreed with him. Leslie hadn't eaten since she had grabbed a bagel and orange juice for breakfast. She felt his pain about having a rough day. There were no weekends for her either. It wasn't unusual for her to be found at her desk toiling away Saturday and sometimes Sunday. Today the entire office had to work and so she had gone from one meeting to the next, skipping lunch in order to accomplish all that had been put on her calendar. Leslie had instructed her administrative assistant, Molly, to give her at least an hour a day to nourish herself. However, the woman seemed to have a burr up her butt when it came to her boss and she most times neglected to do as instructed. Leslie swore Molly hated her and she wanted her fired, but the union rules dictated something different and so she was stuck with her.

Leslie perused the menu, her stomach growling with each entrée description she read. Selecting the meal that fit her fancy for the evening, she placed her order with the waitress. While waiting for their food, they conversed about work, their likes, their dislikes and the future.

"Well, Ms. Leslie, you're looking awfully beautiful this evening." No matter how many times she heard the compliment, she blushed with embarrassment. R.W. reached across the table and grabbed her hand. He caressed her fingers with his and she recognized that he had a tattoo on the inside of his right wrist. A shiver raced up her spine. His body art excited her, allowing her to believe that she had found the gentle thug she so desperately craved.

"Thanks." She lowered her eyes. "Well, Reginald, what type of work are you in?"

"Like I said the other night, I'm the director of a grassroots organization that works with homeless families, particularly the children. Children are my passion."

Bingo! Leslie thought. He loves kids and she would be willing to bear his; dozens of them, if he wanted. She felt her face light up.

"I want to have tons of them." He took a sip of his wine and smiled endearingly at Leslie.

Leslie felt her uterus perk up, her Fallopian tubes stand at attention, and her cervix expand, ready for the auspicious occasion. She smiled back at him.

Their food was served and they ate with little conversation. Leslie ate with thoughts of her night. She envisioned them in bed together preparing for the family that they would soon have. First they would have a boy. Leslie didn't like the name Reginald and so that she wouldn't offend her man, she would name him Reggie. Then her daughter. From the time she was a little girl, she loved the name Morgan. The next one she didn't care if it was a boy or a girl. But she ultimately wanted to have a Rebecca and then an Oliver. Her thoughts wandered until the waitress set the check down in front of R.W.

Staring Leslie in the eyes, he asked hesitantly, "Uh, Leslie. I'm a little short this month. Would it be a problem if we went Dutch?" He tried to smile to ease his request.

Leslie's whole demeanor changed. She couldn't believe that this man had the audacity to ask her to dinner and then ask her to pay for her own meal. Never before had she been asked out and then been told that she needed to pay her own way. He was more than broke, he had no class.

"You know what? I've got it." She grabbed her wallet out of her purse, picked up the bill to read the damage, and then threw $75 on the table. She pushed back her chair, picked up her goblet of wine and swallowed the last bit. She pushed her way through the crowded restaurant. For a moment she considered having her way with this man. Men did it all the time. They paid the bill and felt it was their right to bed the woman. Deciding that he wasn't worth the time it would take, she decided against it. Again, she would go home alone, to cold sheets. The idea depressed her. It would be the last time she saw R.W. and it would be the last time she would try speed dating.

CHAPTER THREE

Natalie treasured her fifteen-year friendship with Leslie. She felt blessed to have a friend as special as her. They were as close as sisters. But what Natalie felt the best part of their relationship was that Anderson liked Leslie as well. He considered her to be the little sister he never had despite the times he wanted to curse her for her stubborn behavior and brash personality. There were many times he would threaten to renounce their friendship while encouraging his wife to do the same. But ultimately, they were like family.

Natalie's thoughts drifted back to her childhood. She ran her fingers across the smooth leather of the chair she sat in, thinking back to when she would watch each grandparent take a turn relaxing in it. She could vividly picture the pea-green velvet material that used to cover it. It most definitely was a statement of the times—the '70s. Bellbottoms, big collars and afros. *What were they thinking?* Natalie thought with a laugh. The memories brought back warm feelings, distinctly different from how she felt now.

Natalie knew for sure that her grandparents' spirits were still present in that old lounge. Her belief in that was as strong as her belief that her husband would be late getting home that night. Her grandmother taught her to always have faith, "If you believe, therefore it is." That was the beginning of her religious education. From the very beginning, her beginning, it was instilled in her very core to believe, to have faith. "Just have faith, girl, and whatever you want, He will give it to you. He may not be there when you want Him, but He'll be there right on time."

Those were the good old days. Her thoughts floated from her past, which at times she so longed to go back to, to the present where she prayed that the wisdom and strength each grandparent possessed and attempted to pass down to their grandchildren would ooze from the porous leather material and permeate her body. She squeezed her eyes together as tight as she could and prayed that God would give her wisdom and strength.

Natalie thought about some of the deviant activities their other grand-children (particularly her older sister, Andrea) took part in. She decided that most of them missed their share of the family wisdom and as a result had the mental capacity, drive and conviction of street rogues. She wondered how such non-ambitious people could come from a lineage so strong, so fine and so well respected as her own. Her grandfather was the first presi-dent of one of the South's first Black colleges and her grandmother was envied and respected by all in the city for her community work, gracious giving and delicious Southern cooking. *We're all going to hell in a hand basket!* Natalie thought, sounding like her Gigi. She tried to shake the images of her family. She could not, nor would she deal with or think about their problems right now. She had two distractions of her own. Three, if she counted the man who was responsible for impregnating her with the two angels sleeping in the nursery down the hall.

She often asked herself where all the charitable groups were who normally knocked down the doors of parents blessed with a multiple birth. "So what," Natalie whispered to herself. "I only have two children to deal with at one time." She didn't want the money. Money was something they had. It was the help she needed. Sometimes she wanted to beg for help, if for nothing other than to have the companionship of another adult in the house with her. Especially at those times when her husband was missing in action.

Frustrated, Natalie looked around her bedroom. She let out a long sigh, releasing with it the tension from a long, hard day. Her room was never immaculately kept, but now that she had children, there always seemed to be more trucks, doll carriages and plastic toys in her bedroom than in the nursery. The disorganization that overwhelmed her room tonight was a sign that the twins were feeling better. Five days earlier, Doctor Schubert diagnosed Kayla with strep throat and Kendall with an ear infection. It took at least three days for the antibiotics to kick in and do their work. Those three days were shear hell! No rest for the weary! Except for Anderson Kelley, of course! She was up and down the stairs all day cleaning up vomit and diarrhea, dispensing medication and rocking children to sleep. It seemed as if more came out of the twins than went in. It truly was her reality. She knew for sure this qualified her for some type of sainthood.

It was like Anderson was taking sedatives. His ability to sleep through the insufferable shrills of two toddlers screaming, crying and complaining baffled her. His assistance during this trying time had been limited. Very limited! His excuse was that he had to maintain his strength so that he could go to work. Work—puh-lease! Natalie needed just as much strength to keep up with two active toddlers all day, every day. Still, his offers to help were futile; way too little; way too late. Natalie wondered to herself how she could love such a man.

She couldn't think of the exact words to express her disbelief in his behavior. She could only shake her head and murmur. "That man, that man, that man," were the words her Gigi would say when her grandfather got on her *last nerve*. And now Natalie could feel her pain. She couldn't call Anderson lazy. He was far from that! He would work all day, every day, to put food on the table or to purchase Natalie or the kids the luxuries that many were deprived. The many designer clothes, purses and shoes in her walk-in closet were a testament to that. But then, what was it? What was wrong with him? She knew it wasn't right. Something just wasn't right.

Natalie loved Anderson, she adored him, but sometimes it bothered her that her life had to change so drastically upon the birth of their children while he was able to continue to live the same life as before. He came and went as he pleased. He slept with little disruption. He could even finish a meal without it getting cold. She found it difficult to believe that he made the progression from ego to id. Or that he was even trying to. She wanted him to sacrifice for parenthood as she had to.

Sometimes it pained her that he was out schmoozing with those spoiled, overpaid athletes or at his gym, Hoop Dreams. His life seemed, to Natalie, to be so uncomplicated and undemanding. He had Natalie to do all the hard stuff, the hands-on work. The kids, she loved them, but they were a lot of work. Anderson had a wife, two children, Jenn-Air appliances—the perfect life. What else could a person ask for? Natalie's life was a struggle. Her mother caused her strife, her sister caused her trouble and her best friend… she was pure drama. Everything was a struggle!

"Where the hell is he?"

Natalie closed her eyes in an attempt to relieve the burning and itching from this summer's allergy season. She sneezed and cursed the weatherman for his prediction that the pollen numbers would be off the charts this year. Time was her enemy. When she did have time to herself at home, she thought about these things. She worked herself up and unfortunately, it didn't make for a happy reunion when Anderson finally returned home. She knew she needed to make sure her attitude was in check when he came in. After all, it wasn't his fault the children were ill.

Again, Natalie pulled herself from the one place she had been the most comfortable all day, and again, she checked the time looking at the digital clock on her cherry oak wardrobe across the room. It was now a quarter to nine and she had to get herself, the house and, it seemed, a million other things ready for the next day.

As Natalie walked out of her bedroom and toward the staircase, she grabbed a pink pajama top from the floor with the toes of her bare right foot. Kayla had dropped the shirt as Natalie carried her sleepy daughter to her bedroom. Together they had sung a slow rendition of The Itsy Bitsy Spider as they made their way to the nursery. The song was still stuck in her head.

"The itsy, bitsy spider," Natalie hummed to herself. A smile spread across her lips as she thought about the precious child she carried around.

"My child must be the most beautiful on earth." Biased, Natalie was. She knew that that probably wasn't true, but she could think her children were the most attractive and the brightest. She beamed as the proud parent. She thought about how the years had flown by since the day she brought them home and realized that it wouldn't be long before her daughter wanted nothing to do with her. The smile began to fade. She thought about the pubescent years. Her brow furrowed at the thought of the fights, the arguments and the disagreements and how they were sure to come. Her head began to ache. Her father warned her that she better get in as much quality time now as she could. The years would come and go with the blink of an eye. The lovable children she had now would morph into the children of the corn, quick, fast and in a hurry. No matter how much Natalie wanted to believe that her children would be different, the probability was slim to none. She massaged her temple with her free hand.

Natalie missed the early months of her children's lives she wished away, the times when she couldn't decipher whether their cries were from hunger or from irritability. Despite what she thought then, *those* were the good old days. How soon we forget. The teenage years in her own house had been miserable. Two teenage daughters caused for unhappy days. The hormones created drama and the drama queen, her mother, was a modern day Mommie Dearest. Natalie moaned about what was to come, inevitably.

She placed the shirt in the white wicker clothesbasket she had retrieved from the hallway closet, and continued to fill it with all the other clothes and toys that were strewn in her path. She thought to herself, "I should leave it for Anderson to clean up!"

Natalie heard the deadbolt lock turn and the alarm sound at the bottom of the steps. Anderson Kelley was home. *Speak of the devil and he will appear.* He had worked over twelve hours today.

In her heart, Natalie felt sorry for him, but her compassion soon stopped as the ache in her back and the pain in her head became more prevalent. He owned the business. He had a staff of well-educated, capable people that he trusted. He didn't have to be there for so many hours. He did it to himself.

Walking down the stairs, barely maintaining her footing while attempting to avoid the fire engine on the third step from the top, Natalie saw the light from the refrigerator illuminate the dark kitchen. A muffled voice from behind the refrigerator door asked. "What's for dinner?"

She entered the kitchen, dropping the basket by the basement door and simultaneously flicking on the kitchen light. Anderson's head popped out from behind the door of the stainless steel Sub-Zero refrigerator. Removing the chicken leg lodged between his teeth, he glided over to his wife. His smile was intoxicating. Natalie felt her knees weaken. He leaned in close and the smell of hard work and cologne filled her nostrils. He licked his full lips and tried to place a wet, greasy kiss on her cheek. Natalie's round face appeared almost lifeless by this time of day. He noticed his wife's sleepy eyes, eyes that were most times bright and cheery.

"You okay, baby?" Anderson asked, sincerity laced in and throughout the three word sentence.

She smile and then brushed him away with a flick of her hand, hitting the side of his head as he turned back toward the refrigerator.

"You know I'm next in line for strep throat or whatever other debilitating disease I'll be plagued with. Right now, I am a human incubator for germs. They're festering, waiting to be set free!" Her attempt at humor was a wasted effort. No matter how hard she tried, her jokes came out sounding rehearsed and downright un-funny. She couldn't tell a joke or a story to save her life. She always prefaced her attempt with the disclaimer: *Corny!*

Anderson accused her of being the corniest person alive. Her attempt was always funnier than the actual joke.

"What do you mean? What's for dinner? Hmmf!"

Natalie rolled her eyes at her husband. She tried to feign anger, but she found it hard to maintain her stance.

Anderson giggled at his wife's stab at comedy. He had that boyish charm where his giggle seemed natural. When he would descend from the bedroom in the morning donning a suit and hard shoes, he looked as if he were a teenager playing grown-up. He looked natural in sweats. He was an athlete by nature; everything about him screamed *athlete*. He was sexiest in a pair of jogging pants, T-shirt and running shoes. He looked almost invincible— as if he could leap a building in a single bound. Natalie found herself salivating over her husband's muscular body.

"Girl, Anderson got the kind of body make you want to smack your momma," she remembered one of her girlfriends once commenting.

It was true. He was sexier than most. Natalie liked to tell him he was beautiful and then watch as he turned several shades of red with embarrassment.

"Don't act like you're embarrassed. You've been told that all your life," she would admonish him.

"Maybe handsome, but not beautiful. Give me a break." His milk chocolate-colored skin would get overcome by a bright shade of red. "Women are beautiful. You are beautiful," he would tell her and then pull her close to him. Kissing her passionately and then delivering small quick kisses around her mouth and down to her neck.

"Keep your day job!" He teased her about her corny joke. "How the kids doin'? You look tired." He looked up from his excursion through the overstuffed fridge, looked his wife deeply in the eyes, purred a sincere, "I love you!" and went back to his expedition.

It was at that moment, that very moment, that Natalie's previous questions about her feelings for her husband were answered and she knew exactly why she loved him so much. It was in his eyes!

CHAPTER FOUR

"How was your day?" Natalie asked Anderson, as she pushed him from in front of the refrigerator. She barely paid attention to his response as she rumbled through the icebox, the cold air causing her to catch a chill. She shivered, the hair on her arms rising to attention. She grabbed a Tupperware dish that contained breaded veal chops and another that contained tomato and mozzarella sauce. She took a whiff to decipher their freshness. She was surprised any of the meal she prepared two days earlier had remained. Her husband of three years seemed to devour anything edible in the house that wasn't tied down. The food was leftovers from a dinner party she organized to celebrate Leslie having met Mr. Right for the hundredth time.

Curtis Matthews, a vice president at the city's largest black-owned bank, was her new man. Leslie was proud of him and she was ready to take their relationship to the next level. It was time for Curtis to met Leslie's two best friends.

The evening began much better than it ended and Natalie hadn't quite figured out who was to blame. Leslie was not one to hold her tongue. She didn't do it when she had a gripe. And she especially didn't do it when she had been drinking. It was apparent that this man was not able to deal with such a strong and very opinionated woman. Well, stubborn was more like it! Natalie loved Leslie and could overlook the fact that her friend was inflexible and obstinate. But because of her character flaws, Leslie had very few, if any, female friends. Most males were able to overlook her negative attributes by concentrating on her hot body. It did much of the talking for her. She usually got what she wanted by using it and she wasn't ashamed of that detail.

"God gave it to me for a reason, I might as well use what I got to get what I want!" was her response when she was accused of exploiting herself. But once they got a load of the mouth that came along with the body, they were like dust in the wind. And she seriously questioned why they vanished so quickly after the tongue lashing she handed out, always querying their character, or lack there of.

Still, Natalie and Leslie complemented each other well. Natalie was the one with sense. "Girl, you'll make someone a good wife someday," was the comment she had heard often. And Leslie, well, she didn't have any sense most times, most times hearing, "Leslie, what are we going to do with you?"

Although Natalie was very understanding of Leslie's perceived shortcomings, there were times she felt that she was a much better friend to Leslie than Leslie was to her. But that was Leslie. "You have to love her in spite of herself," her grandmother would say when Natalie and Leslie would fight. Natalie knew she meant well, even if she didn't always show it.

THURSDAY EVENING

Leslie showed up for the dinner party at 25527 Windsor Gate Place with an overnight bag filled to capacity and a garment bag stuffed with at least five outfits—dresses, pants, jackets, blouses and at least four pairs of shoes. Leslie had decided to dress in Natalie's presence. She knew Natalie had impeccable taste in clothes and she would make sure that she looked her very best, even if they had to make a last-minute run to the neighborhood discount designer clothing store to do it.

Natalie's ability to coordinate not only clothing, but also furniture, food, flowers, everything, provided Leslie with the ammunition she needed to tease her good friend. And tease her she did often; however deep down she admired her talent. She often called her friend Martha Stewart's bastard love child from a seedy affair with a Black man in the late '60s. The joke was funny at times, but sometimes Natalie took offense to the chiding.

Natalie's creative ability had gotten her accepted into one of the country's most reputable design schools. However, her family insisted that that particular field would be so competitive and more than likely not allow her to earn the money necessary to repay the student loans she would acquire to attend that school. If she recalled correctly, her father's exact words were, "There's no way on God's green earth I'm paying for you to go *there*!" Those words echoed in her head often.

Monica, her stepmother, tried to play the mediator, "Dale, if this is what she wants to do with her life, isn't it up to you to support her?"

"Monica, this is *my* daughter," he retorted. "I ask that you respect my decision. She is talented, but I believe I know what's best. And if I'm paying for it, I'll have my say."

Dreama piped in, "Dale! She's my daughter as well. Stop being such as ass! If she wants to go, let her go. You're only going to have one daughter in college anyway." Her comment was a slap to Andrea. Natalie was happy she wasn't in the room.

"Then you pay for it," he quipped back. And that was the end of it.

At times, she despised her father for making her go a different educational route. But, she figured, everything happened for a reason.

In her senior year in high school, following the big family blowout, she happened across a book in the public library. It was called *Composing A Life* by Catherine Bates. The book discussed how women made plans for their future. They designed a path, and many times that path had many smaller capillaries which led off of it. The book opened her eyes and allowed her to accept what hand had been dealt to her. And, despite all the fussing, cussing, screaming and yelling, Natalie graduated from the college of her parents' choice with a degree in sociology.

Now she sat at home as a homemaker, her degree hanging on the wall and her dreams for a profession on hold until the children were ready for school. He liked having her at home, as his own mother had been while he was young. Dinner was on the table each night when his father came home from work. The house was clean and the clothes were washed. Anderson's need for that life preceded all else.

The doorbell rang and Natalie opened it to see Leslie standing on one foot leaning against the white stone column on the porch. She looked up as the door swung open. "I got a rock in my shoe." She took her left Nike running shoe off and shook it like she was trying to release the last bit of ketchup from the Heinz bottle. A cigarette dangled from her lips and her eyes were half shut in an attempt to shield them from the smoke. Leslie wasn't addicted to the high of nicotine. She only smoked when she was nervous. Natalie felt sorry for her. No man had ever, to Natalie's knowledge, made Leslie this insecure or self-conscious.

Once Leslie completed her task, she put on her shoe and made her way to the first-floor guest room, dumping her bags on the bed. She took the steps to the second floor two at a time, looking into the bedrooms and listening for the Kelly children's squeals and giggles. The house was usually filled with the clamor of rambunctious children, but tonight it was quiet. Hollering back over her shoulder, Leslie asked, "Where are my godchildren?" She stopped in the hall bathroom and stared at her reflection in the mirror. She studied her normally flawless complexion and then began to poke at the pimple she had previously attempted to burst before she made her pilgrimage to the Kelley house. She tried to remember if she had packed the cover-up she would need to disguise the scar left by her excavation.

She yelled out the bathroom door, "Natalie, do you have any concealer?"

Startled by her mysterious appearance, Leslie jumped. She looked at Natalie, who had joined her in the bathroom, "I hate this time of the month," said Leslie. "Can you believe this, me starting my period the day of my big date? Can't be nothing but nerves. I thought about canceling, but Nat, I *really* like this guy."

She was really stressed, which made Natalie even more concerned about the new man in Leslie's life. Natalie wondered what it was about this man that was different than the rest. Men to Leslie were usually disposable commodities to be used and then discarded once their shelf life had expired. She could take them or leave them, most times using them up before they had a chance to use her first. But Leslie's insistence that she "*really* liked this guy," wasn't her usual MO. Natalie was determined to get the scoop on Curtis and make sure he was the right person for her best friend.

Leslie leaned against the pedestal sink and twisted a lock of her hair around her finger. Natalie stood outside the bathroom door, inspecting the sink and toilet for their cleanliness.

"They're over at my father's," she finally answered Leslie's question about the children. "Tonight is as special for me and Andy as it is for you." Natalie spoke with a grin on her face, more so to herself than to Leslie. Leslie noticed her studying the bathroom fixtures. She knew Natalie well enough to know that she cleaned to forget. It was like her drug of choice.

"What do you mean? It's not your anniversary? Then what's going on?" Leslie raised and lowered her eyebrows, smiling while jabbing Natalie in the ribs, indicating that there might be some serious activity going on in the master bedroom that evening.

Natalie cut her off. "No, not our anniversary. We need some time alone, some time together, and this was as good a night as any. It's been so long since we've done anything without the kids. I can't remember the last movie we've seen." She tried to remember without success. "We need a date night. We used to go out to eat all the time." She smiled, remembering eating out with her husband before the children. Less noise and less screaming. "Gosh, I miss those times." She missed the courting that Anderson did to try to woo her. He even sent her love letters. No one would believe it today if she were to divulge his secret sensitive side.

"My dearest Natalie. It's hard for me to speak to you the feelings in my heart. I have never loved anyone as much as I love you. Although you are beautiful, you are so much more than your beauty. I love your laugh. It's so sincere. I love the light in your eyes when you are happy, the way your voice rises when you get excited. I look forward to spending the rest of my life with you. I will love you always, A."

Natalie saved each and every letter he wrote her. There were nights she pulled out the box she stored them in and she'd read them out loud, hoping that it would bring back some of the magic that was her earlier life. So far, it hadn't work. But she was ever the optimist.

"I'd say," Leslie responded to Natalie's comment about not getting out often. "If you'd trust someone with your children you could get out more often. I don't know what's wrong with you," Leslie added. "Where's Anderson?

Still not home from work? I swear his ass ought to be a billionaire as much as he works," Leslie said with a bit of sarcasm in her voice. She loved him like a brother; however, at times, he took the one person who would be in his corner if the chips were to fall completely for granted. "What's up, Nat? The house smells like a bottle of Pine-Sol exploded. You've been cleaning all day, I'm sure, and this could not be all for me and the man of my dreams." Leslie looked Natalie directly in the eyes as if she were putting her in some type of truth trance.

Meanwhile, Natalie vowed silently to herself to pick up a bottle of unscented cleaner. She decided that her need for discretion preceded her love for the fresh pine scent that came along with a clean house.

"Everything's cool," Natalie said as she walked away, trying to convince herself as much as she was Leslie. She and Anderson needed some alone time, some time to reconnect, that was all. She walked downstairs to the kitchen to check on her veal and sauce. It smelled great! Her stomach growled with hunger. She hadn't eaten all day in anticipation for this evening's dinner. She enjoyed her cooking as much as everyone else did.

After checking on the meat, Natalie threw the potholders on the counter and ran back upstairs to get dressed. Halfway up to the second floor, she heard the door open and Anderson walk in. She turned around, winked at him, smiled, and continued up the steps. She called back over her shoulder, "Leslie's here. She's getting dressed up here. Make us some daiquiris and she'll be done soon, then you can get dressed. And stir the sauce, please!" Surprisingly, she didn't get the negative response she expected. He held in the remarks. Was it his exhaustion that caused his silence or his hunger that drew him to the kitchen where he could do all the commands barked at him while sampling the food?

He washed his hands and picked up the spoon. Stirring the sauce, Anderson thought about his day. He couldn't wait to get home to see his wife. He loved her so much and he regretted the pain he had caused her.

"Anderson!" Natalie screamed his name. "Anderson Kelley, do you hear me!" She and Leslie stood outside the apartment that Anderson sat in. The room was dark and the red-headed female he had met at the club that night was sitting on the floor beside him.

"This is my apartment. Why am *I* on the floor?" she said, beginning to rise as if she were going to confront the enraged woman and her best friend that stood outside her apartment.

Anderson grabbed her by her arm and pulled her back down to the floor. "Bitch! What is your problem?"

"Bitch? You don't know me that well!" Her voice began to rise.

Anderson wrestled her to the ground before she could expose him any more than his car in the lot had.

"What, you scared your girlfriend is going to be mad? You should of thought about that before you came home with me."

This woman was so far from something he would have normally pursued. She was so far from Natalie. He didn't understand why he was attracted to her. He heard the car doors slam, the ignition start and the car drive away. Anderson rose to see that Natalie's car was no longer in the same spot. He waited in the apartment, arguing with the girl off and on for another two hours before he got in his car and drove away. Anderson was disappointed in himself for again making a bad decision that broke the heart of the woman he loved.

"What's up, Anderson?" Leslie hollered from the master bedroom.

Natalie walked into the bedroom, pulling her T-shirt over her head.

"Are you sure this dress isn't too tight, Nat, and the shoes match, huh? I want everything to go perfectly tonight." She twirled and primped in the mirror. Leslie threw questions at Natalie as she looked at her behind in the cherry cheval mirror in the middle of Natalie's bedroom. Natalie couldn't shake the feeling that something bad was going to happen.

Leslie was dressed and quite pleased with her clothing selection. She finally chose something from Natalie's closet. It was amazing how she made Natalie's clothes fit her. At times, all the laws of clothing physics should have been against her. Leslie was at least two inches shorter than Natalie and although they had the same curves, Natalie's were at least one size smaller. She chose a sleeveless, fitted shell and a wine-colored, silk, knee-length skirt. They both accentuated and complemented her femininity. She selected a pair of black leather sling backs. Her collection of shoes rivaled that of Imelda Marcos. Leslie had to have extra closet space built into her downtown condo to accommodate her shoe assortment. It wasn't unusual for her to shell out $500 on shoes to wear one night and never wear them again. What seemed a bit extravagant to Natalie was a way of life for Leslie. Leslie figured she grew up on shoes handed down from others, so she felt at this point in her life she had the right to spoil herself, especially if no one else would.

Anderson walked into the bedroom. He sat two frosted mugs down on the dressing table filled to the rim with strawberry daiquiris. Leslie was sitting on the right side of the bed watching the driveway for her date through the picture window. She was in the final stages of rolling a marijuana cigarette from the quarter bag she bought from her brother, Lance, earlier that day. She figured if he was going to sell illegal substances, he might as well be her supplier. If he was selling to someone he knew, maybe he wouldn't end up locked up for life like the majority of men in the West family. Her weed smoking and past experience in exotic dancing had driven a wedge between her mother, grandmother and herself. They were devout Christian women who believed in living life strictly as the Bible prescribed. "David danced!" Leslie quipped in her defense. But her family wasn't buying it. Her blasphemous remarks distanced them even more. It had been two long years since Leslie had seen or talked to either of them. She sent money to them often to make up for her absence and the pain she may have caused them when she left, but more so to relieve her guilt.

"Hey, Nat. I see a great spot down there we can plant some cannabis. The stuff practically grows itself. You wouldn't have to care for it much," she teased, winking at Anderson. She knew the comment would bother him.

"You know I don't like that shit in my house," Anderson barked. "Get out of here so I can get dressed." He sat down on the end of the bed and began taking his shoes off. He grabbed the remote control and began channel surfing. "Who is this man you got my wife cooking for tonight, anyway?"

Natalie came out of the walk-in closet dressed in a multicolored print silk halter dress and ostrich T-strap sandals. She grabbed her drink and walked into the bathroom. Out of habit or plain old consideration, she turned the shower on for Anderson and then attempted to design a hairdo for the evening's soiree. The bathroom had already started to steam up from the hot water, so for time's sake and ease, she pulled her shoulder-length hair back into a ponytail and called it a night. She wasn't trying to impress any-one, she had her man—or at least she thought she still did. That eerie thought came creeping back into her head and subsequently the same familiar pain jabbed at her mid-section. Again, she pushed the self-doubt away, trying to concentrate on the evening. Sometimes she wondered if she'd ever be able to truly feel confident again in her relationship with Anderson. Sure, they were still together after all that had happened, but did that really mean something, or was she merely playing the fool?

"Come on, Leslie Ann, let's go finish getting ready downstairs," she said with a flourish. Leslie picked up her glass of spirits, made sure she didn't spill any of her herbs, and followed closely behind her friend. "See you downstairs, Andy," Natalie called. "I picked out an outfit for you. It's inside your closet. Hurry up, please!"

Anderson grunted from the shower and continued to lather up. He could not believe that they were going through this much trouble for some man Leslie was seeing. She might not even be with him after tonight. He was aware of Leslie's history where men were involved. The story was usually short and not so sweet! Her relationships, if you could call them that, usu-ally never lasted more than a couple of months, if that long. She was so fickle with everything, especially men. Leslie had begged him more times than he cared to remember to hook her up with one of his friends, one of his clients at the gym, a man at the grocery store, anyone. He obliged her request once with Phil Murphy, and he vowed never to do it again. It ended up being way more trouble than it was worth.

Anderson finished his shower, dressed, and sat in front of the television watching the replay of *Sports Central*. Downstairs, he could hear the girls talking and giggling. He attempted to tune them out while listening to a discussion of contract negotiations between a high-paid athlete and his agent. He daydreamed about what he would have done with all that money if he would have had the chance to continue his professional career—how much more he would have. The pity he felt for himself was cut short by his mother's voice in his head, *Anderson, baby, you are truly blessed. You have a wonderful life. A beautiful wife, children, home, your health. Please don't focus on what could've been, be happy with what you have. God loves you and so do I.* He knew she was right, but all he could do was wonder what if. What if?

"Leslie, slow down on the drinks. You want to be coherent when Curtis gets here," Natalie said with her motherly wisdom showing. Leslie poured herself another glassful and lit up her third cigarette. She was now close to being smashed and as high as a kite. Leslie could taste the alcohol Anderson put in the drinks. He wasn't stingy with it this evening. She felt no pain. She thought to herself, *A little drinky-poo couldn't hurt.*

Natalie looked at her best friend and felt sorry for her. She felt sorry that she allowed a man to control her emotions the way he was, not to mention ruin her health by making her smoke like a chimney and drink like a fish. Natalie thought he probably didn't know what effect he was having, but she blamed him anyway. Natalie continued to collect the china, silverware, napkins and serving dishes. She placed them all on the dining room table. She arranged everything the way her mother had taught her. She remembered Dreama setting the table, placing the plates and silver just so. She pictured her circling the table, her heels clicking on the hardwood floor, arranging things to prepare for her dinner guests. She would snap her fingers, calling her daughters into the room showing them what she had created, informing them that they could do it, too. Her lesson was a chapter in Dreama's "Gold Digger's Guide to Snagging a Rich Man." But to appease her mother, Natalie learned the skill, figuring it couldn't hurt to know. And having entertained so many people thanks to Anderson's connections, it was a skill she used often. She had to remember to mention that to her mother the next time they spoke. That would, for sure, make her feel good.

"Natalie! Natalie!" Leslie's voice snapped her back to the task at hand. "What are you thinking about, girl?" Leslie was holding her hand under the faucet, allowing the cold running water to flow over her arm. "I burned my damn arm on the stove."

"You're not sounding as intoxicated as before. I guess it took a little heat to clear your head," Natalie joked with a smile.

Leslie scowled at Natalie. "Forget you! I was trying to taste the sauce. It smells so good. What time is it? I'm hungry. He ought to be happy I like him so much or I would start without him."

"It's a quarter to eight. What time did you tell Curtis to be here?" Natalie made the last-minute preparations to the table. Her dining room was transformed from a daycare center, with children's toys sprawled about during the day, to an elegant cream- and cranberry-colored dining haven. The lighting was accentuated by candles, on the table, the fireplace mantle, the hearth and in the two windows that overlooked the half-acre front yard. "Beautiful!" Natalie said, giving herself the compliment she was sure everyone else would agree with.

Leslie stood next to Natalie. She put her arm around her shoulder and gave her a big squeeze, "Nat, the room looks great. Thank you for making tonight happen. You're the best sister-friend a girl could ask for."

The doorbell rang, startling the girls standing in the entrance to the dining room. They looked into each other's eyes and in unison replied, "This is it!"

"Aren't you going to get the door?" Anderson asked as he extended his hand to grab the knob of the front door. He swung it open. And in walked Curtis Matthews. The men exchanged greetings and Anderson showed Curtis into the foyer. Leslie was the next face he saw. His smile brightened sixty watts. It was obvious that he was pleased by what he saw. Curtis was dressed in a gray pinstriped suit with a black silk pullover shirt underneath and black square-toed dress shoes on his feet. He had a gold link bracelet on his left arm and a diamond-bezel blue-face designer watch on his right.

He must be left-handed, Natalie thought. She caught a glimpse of his well-manicured fingernails and noticed his hair looked freshly cut. *Nice!* she thought to herself. If his personality is anything like his appearance, this man is a keeper.

"Natalie, Anderson Kelley, this is Curtis Matthews. Curtis, these are my best friends in the whole world. They are my family. I love them." Leslie held onto Curtis' arm as if they were in a crowd of people and she was afraid she would lose him.

Curtis extended his hand first to Natalie and then to Anderson.

"It's a pleasure to meet you both. I've heard so many good things about the Kelley family." He handed Natalie a bottle of wine. "This is for you. I hope you like it." Curtis pulled a cigar out of his inside right front jacket pocket. "Anderson, I hope you smoke. You haven't smoked a cigar until you've tried a Cuban."

"Wow, Leslie where'd you find him? I told you that story about finding' good men in the grocery store was a lie. You couldn't have found him there. He doesn't look like a man that does his own shopping!" Anderson joked with Leslie, giving her a wink. Neither of the women found his joke to be funny and it showed on both of their faces. Anderson laughed, motioned to Curtis to follow him to the first-floor game room, and the two men disappeared from the foyer where they left the women standing in disbelief and reeling from Anderson's tasteless comment.

Actually, Leslie had met Curtis at a karaoke bar. She had decided, after the many months of prodding from her co-workers, that she would go and see for herself what the hype was all about. Hype, of course, from the women in the office who looked nothing like herself. It was a Friday evening following a long and busy work day, hell, work week, and she figured, "What the hell!" especially after they had informed her that all drinks and appetizers were half price during happy hour. She decided to forget about the pile of paperwork that would be waiting for her on her next day of work by drowning herself in Vodka and cranberry juice tonight.

While surveying the scene, Leslie saw Curtis Matthews walk in through the double doors with two other gentlemen in tow. She decided that he would be her prey for the evening. However, her urgency to relieve herself preceded her desire to get the scoop on the fine brother in the navy blue pinstriped suit. She stood, asked for directions to the ladies room, and excused herself from the table. Even though the lavatory was in the opposite direction, she had to make a detour past Mr. Pin Striped. He smelled of a musk and citrus blend and fine cigars. *Perfect!* she thought.

Just one last test. Leslie let her baguette slide off her shoulder, down her arm and drop to the floor. Normally, any such action would be considered taboo. It was damn near sacrilegious to even consider placing such quality so close to the ground. She bent down to retrieve her bag and while down there, she took the opportunity to scope out the brother's shoes. *Hot damn! He has good taste!* He was perfect. He looked good and his shoes were the icing on the cake.

Leslie stood, straightened her skirt, and tossed back her hair. Just her luck, Mr. Pin Striped was looking in her direction. She bit her bottom lip, tucked her hair behind her ear and gave him a sexy wink. They exchanged smiles and then almost instantly she remembered her number one mission (no pun intended). As she walked toward the bathroom, she licked her lips and whispered to herself, "That man will be mine!" While thinking about her Friday night conquest, she forgot that she was in a room full of men. She had almost made it to her destination when she felt someone grab her arm from behind. As she whipped around hoping it was Mr. Pin Striped, the smile she had reserved for her dream man quickly faded to a disgusted grimace. The man that was holding her hand was a five-foot, four-inch, Jheri curl sportin', gold tooth havin', bad breath spittin' brother. Leslie snatched her hand away and sprinted to the lavatory. *He's lucky I gotta pee!* she thought.

Once her business was complete, Leslie exited the ladies room and stopped at the pay phone to check her home phone messages. There was a guy she met a couple of weeks ago she was hoping called. If this guy here didn't pan out, she'd work with him. Leslie didn't want to spend another night alone. She deposited her thirty-five cents and took a seat on the hard, flat surface that was supposed to serve as a seat. She fidgeted in an effort to get comfortable. However all attempts proved futile. Leslie assumed that this was so that no one would take up residency on the phone. She deliberately pushed her access code into the phone, entering the wrong number twice. *I know I haven't had that much to drink.* But then again, it never really took that much to get her intoxicated. She tried the access code one more time.

"Sorry, you have input the wrong access code. Please try again later." And she was disconnected.

"Damn it!" Leslie cursed the voice at the other end of the line and slammed down the receiver.

A soft, sexy, sultry baritone voice whispered in her ear, "What's a woman like you doing in a place like this?"

Leslie couldn't believe that someone in the twentieth century had the audacity to attempt a line as corny as that one, regardless of the fact that the voice melted her soul. She spun around with her serious "home girl with an attitude" look on her face and her mouth ready to give this guy some lip, as she was sure it was that homeboy she'd wriggled free from a few moments earlier, when she realized it was Mr. Pin Striped.

She rose from her seated position, smoothed out her skirt, smiled, and replied, "What's up with the corny line?" Tasting something sour in her mouth, she inconspicuously turned her head and blew into the palm of her hand. Not sure if she smelled the soap she had washed her hands with or the alcohol she had consumed, Leslie dug in her bag for some kind of mint. She retrieved a loose Certs and popped it in her mouth.

"Hey, you got another one? I'm feeling not so fresh right now myself." Mr. Pin Striped's humor lightened the moment. Still, she felt a twinge of embarrassment. She really didn't want him to see her doubt herself in that way, but she figured what's done is done. But the fact that he had the same insecurities, made the moment better, a little lighter. "By the way, I'm Curtis Matthews. What's your name, sweetheart?"

Leslie leaned in close. She spotted two other women across the room checking Curtis out. She wanted to make sure that they were put on notice that this man was hers, if only for tonight. She moved in close and whispered in his ear, "I'm Leslie, Leslie West."

Curtis extended his hands, wrapped both of them around her right hand and shook it firmly. "Nice meeting you, Leslie, do you have a table already? I'd really like to sit down and get to know Leslie West a little better." He looked around her in search of someplace to sit down.

"No, I'm here with a couple of people from work, but to be honest, I'd rather not go back to their table. Do you think we could find someplace of our own."

"Your friends won't miss you, will they?"

Leslie moved in even closer. She wanted to make sure he heard her, but also she loved the smell. She pressed her body against his, allowing him to feel the curve of her breasts. She was more intoxicated by his cologne than by the couple of drinks she had consumed earlier. "Oh, they will be alright. Let's find another table."

Leslie grabbed Curtis by his hand and began making her way through the crowd. She spied a table against the back wall. She pulled Curtis behind her, stopping every now and then when some blonde Barbie whipped her head around and slapped her with her stringy mane. Leslie sucked her teeth, frowned, shook her head, and kept moving.

Leslie and Curtis found a table in the corner of the crowded bar and they talked for what seemed like forever. Each song a karaoke contestant chose to sing from the '80s made them laugh out loud about where they were and what they were doing at that time in history. By the end of the evening, Leslie felt as if she had known Curtis forever. She had even conjured up enough nerve to perform a little karaoke herself that evening. She thought to herself, *It's too bad I don't have the singing voice to go along with these looks.* Leslie prayed as she walked to the microphone to sing Olivia Newton John's "Let's Get Physical." She hoped that when she started singing, instead of her usual flat, falsetto voice coming out, something sultry and seductive would pass her lips and dazzle the audience. But no such luck. She could see from the disbelief in the eyes of the spectators, but all she really cared about was Curtis. Although he was a bit taken aback, he smiled and supported her. Leslie had such a good time that evening that she couldn't wait to get home and dream about her newfound love.

Over the next couple of weeks, the two had several lunch and dinner dates. Curtis even invited her to escort him to an office retirement party for one of the partners. Leslie believed that this could be "it," he could be "the one"— her baby's daddy. She had decided from the beginning that she wasn't going to proceed in this relationship as she had done in the past. She wanted to know everything about him, to be his friend before they became lovers.

CHAPTER FIVE

"Can you believe him? That husband of yours…" She couldn't even finish her sentence. Leslie fumed, walking back into the kitchen. She grabbed her empty glass, opened the freezer, poured herself another drink, and lit up another cigarette.

"Leslie, calm down. Curtis didn't seem upset. Forget about it. Dinner is ready. Go get the guys." Natalie shooed Leslie out of the kitchen. She finished the last-minute preparations and removed her apron.

"I might kick Andy's ass! I am so pissed. How could he say something like that in front of Curtis? Does he not *want* me to have a man? What's that all about?" She left the room after puffing on her cigarette one more time and running it under the faucet. It fizzled out and Natalie hoped Leslie's anger would do the same.

When Leslie came to the door of the game room, the two men were at the cherrywood bar. Anderson stood behind it pouring Curtis a glass of Crown Royal. The fifty-two-inch plasma television was airing a pre-season Minnesota Vikings and Dallas Cowboys football game and the stereo had Steely Dan's "Black Cow" playing low in the background. The song took Leslie back to her childhood. She remembered vividly her mother washing dishes in the kitchenette of their small apartment while listening to the AM-only transistor radio. The disc jockey's husky voice announced the song's title and her mother would coo, "Ooooooooooh, that's my song!" She would twist her hips back and forth to the harmony of the band's cool, smooth tone. She could hear her mother's worn, dingy pink slippers swish, swish,

swish across the dull, yellow linoleum floor as she did the only dance she was able to do with her arthritic hip. The memories flooded Leslie's mind and took her back to a time she hated to think about. *I wonder where Steely Dan is now?* Leslie thought to herself.

As she snapped back to the present, she noticed the two men staring at her. She attempted to play it off and announced in her sexiest voice, "Dinner is served, gentlemen." She had left her anger and frustration in the hallway, along with her memories of her drama-filled childhood. Anderson looked over at her as if he couldn't believe that that voice came out of the Leslie Ann West he knew.

The two men left their spots and followed Leslie to the dining room. "You have a beautiful home, Anderson," Curtis proclaimed after the first sip of his drink. "And you make a helluva drink." Curtis felt the effects of his first drink and couldn't wait for the next. If he was in any pain before, it would soon be a memory. He stared at Leslie's curvaceous body as he followed her down the hallway. He grabbed her hand and held it, intermingling his fingers with hers. He imagined how she would feel next to him and look sans clothes. He could feel his excitement rise and changed his thoughts to the football game that had been playing on the television to avoid any embarrassment.

Leslie pointed out the pictures of the Kelley children that lined the wall to the dining room. She bragged, "Aren't they beautiful children?" Curtis knew what that meant. "I sure wouldn't mind having kids like that someday soon, and wouldn't you be the right man for the job." Of course, Curtis wanted children, but he was still having a good time being single and fancy free. There were so many women that tried to manipulate, connive, and trap him into a relationship that he was not ready to have. And he knew for sure that Leslie West was another one of those women. It had been one whole month since they had met and she was still holding out on sex. He knew she wanted it, wanted it as bad as he did. Her holding out wasn't going to make him want to be with her any longer than his planned, allotted amount of time. She was cutting her time down. She may be the one to suffer. She *would* be the one to suffer. She only had two and a half months, ten weeks.

By the time she decided to let loose, her time would be up. Curtis tried to tell her, tried to coerce her into letting loose, but she held out every time. *These women*, he thought. *Can't live with them, can't have sex without them.*

"I have some experience bartending," Andy interrupted Curtis' thoughts. "But we owe the home and all its beauty to my gorgeous wife. She does it all. Couldn't do it without her."

"Curtis, you sit here. Leslie, you here. And Anderson, over there," Natalie directed everyone to their seats. Everyone sat down and began to prepare for the feast. "Please serve yourselves. This may look like a formal affair, but let's keep it relaxed. Anderson, please bless the food."

"God is gracious, God is good…" Leslie lifted her head to see Curtis smiling seductively at her. His mustache curved around his lips, framing them so that they looked as exquisite as the food on the table. She couldn't wait to taste both.

Everyone began to dig in. The conversation was minimal. In between bites, the Kelleys' guest complimented the food, the décor and the ambiance. Anderson popped the cork on the wine Curtis brought and that bottle, as well as the other two bottles they'd had, were drained by the end of dessert. The partygoers were feeling quite comfortable.

"So Curtis, what is it that you do?" Anderson asked. "Nat, pass the green beans."

"I'm in banking," he answered, dabbing at the corners of his mouth with his napkin. He winked at Leslie. He pushed a fork full of veal into his mouth and chewed.

Leslie thought his chewing was even turning her on. She smiled with pride, seeing dollar signs. He was successful, good-looking and she could swear he was smitten by her charm. In her mind, she repeated Leslie Ann Matthews. Mrs. Curtis Matthews. Mr. and Mrs. Curtis Matthews. *"Oh yes, these are the Matthews twins."*

"Sounds interesting…" Anderson chewed the last bit of food in his mouth. "I own Hoop Dreams." He shoveled in another fork full of beans.

"Yeah, over on Chesapeake? I've seen it and heard good things about it. You used to play professional ball, right?"

"Yeah man… seems like a lifetime ago. But now, owning my own business seems like so much more work. Do you work out? You ought to come by sometime."

Sitting his wine glass down, Curtis said, "Sounds like a plan. I do a little. I have some weights at the house and I jog when I have time, which isn't often. But I was thinking about joining a club."

"Yeah, we can set up a workout program. Yeah, stop by, tell your partners. Do you play ball?"

"I shoot around. Nothing as competitive as you, I'm sure."

The women listened intently, happy that the two were making nice. Anderson could be so moody. It was like a crap shoot if he was going to have a good night or if the Prozac would need to be pulled out.

Once the glasses were empty and the plates were bare, Natalie began to clear the dinner dishes with Anderson's assistance. Curtis and Leslie stayed in the dining room, flirting with each other from across the table. The sparkle in Leslie's eyes and the sinister grin on her face were evidence of her intoxicated state. And if there was one thing Leslie loved to do when she was under the influence, it was have sex. She was her freakiest when she was drunk. She loved to pretend she was someone else, which made her even more uninhibited. The blond wig and dominatrix costume would emerge from her secret closet and the man was in for a wild ride. And tonight would be no different. Curtis would have the time of his life, of this Leslie was sure. If she couldn't actually have a man inside of her one way, because of her monthly visitor, Curtis would be inside of her another. It would be a night he wouldn't forget. She would be well worth the wait.

Once they were in the kitchen, Anderson complimented his wife, "You did yourself swell, babe. Everything was great." Anderson kissed Natalie on the lips and patted her on her behind. They giggled to each other, Natalie wiped the lipstick off his face and they walked back into the dining room to retrieve more dishes. Again they returned to the kitchen with another load. Together they stacked the dishes in the dishwasher and she began to wipe down the countertops. Natalie loved what she was feeling. She hadn't felt this close to her husband, not only in proximity but also emotionally, for a while. His head and body had been elsewhere. *That damned sports facility!*

She knew it was his dream and she would never deny him of that, but she needed him with her. After all, he was her soul mate. He was her man.

As Natalie was starting to let her thoughts wander to what the bedroom would hold for she and Anderson later that night, Leslie's intimate plans were starting to unravel.

Curtis, well into his fourth drink by now, returned Leslie's knowing grin. Her grin, however, was saying, "I'll be yours tonight," while his was saying, "You're not getting your hooks in me, girl." The wine had given Curtis the nerve to say what he'd been thinking all evening long.

"So, you've been picking up your men at grocery stores before me, huh?"

Leslie's grin faded from her face. She was now dumbfounded, and mentally cursing Anderson Kelley for his big-ass mouth. She could say nothing more than, "Huh?"

"Huh? You heard me." It was obvious that the liquid courage had taken affect. "Girl, you just don't know."

Leslie would have sworn she heard the man that sat across the table from her cackle.

"What are you talking about? Curtis, you are really beginning to destroy my buzz. Tonight has been wonderful. What are you trying to do?" Leslie heard herself whining.

"Yeah, tonight was nice. The last couple of weeks have been good, too. But what game are *you* trying to play? You know Sheridan Heights may appear to be big, but really, it's not. We have someone in common." Leslie felt a lump in her throat. In her mind she went over her list of lovers. There had been many and she knew she was missing someone. Phil. Carl. Andrew. Marcus.

"But…" Leslie tried to get out an explanation. But explain what? She couldn't defend herself, because she didn't know what she had done. Quiet was the best defense. She would let him finish. And then speak. But her anger began to flare. She didn't need to explain herself to him. She was a single woman. No one had placed a ring on her finger, to her dismay. And so she could do whatever to whomever she wanted.

Curtis continued, "Do you remember Greg Patterson?" He leaned back and crossed his arms. The diamonds from his watch reflected off the bright lights in the chandelier.

Leslie's head began to reel. Her stomach turned and she began to perspire. Her lips moved, but nothing came out, "Greg Patterson. Greg Patterson. Greg Patterson!" She rubbed her temple and slumped back into her chair.

"Ah ha!" She remembered. Greg Patterson was a bartender she met at The University Club. He was handsome, but a kid. His dark locks hung down onto his shoulders. Leslie was intrigued by his ethnicity. She wanted to run her fingers through them. He poured her and her friend, Valerie, drink after drink until she caved into his request to meet him after his shift which was ending in a half hour.

The two ended up at her apartment and Greg Patterson proceeded to smack it up, flip it, and rub it down. He allowed his locks to hang down on her bare breasts, moving them back and forth as she bubbled over with excitement. It had been a long marathon evening of lovemaking. Leslie was wrong about the young boy by underestimating his skills. She deemed him her project for the next couple of months, thinking that she would use him for her pleasure, knowing that he wanted nothing more from her than the same.

He made her beg for mercy and she craved his excitement. Leslie found herself fiending for his talents. They spent nights together until one night Greg's overly jealous, twenty-something girlfriend confronted them in the parking lot of her condo. Shanequa was her name and she donned a switch-blade and threatened Leslie with bodily harm if she ever caught them together again.

"Bitch, I know where you live!" she screamed at the top of her voice as Greg Patterson carried her back to her car, got in with her, and drove away. Half of Leslie's neighbors were awake by then—their lights on, curtains pulled back, watching the drama unfold and her pride getting damaged. Suffice it to say, they never saw each other again after that.

"How do you know Greg Patterson?" she asked, now sitting up in her seat, intrigued by this new revelation. She figured he was a colleague's son, maybe a cousin, nephew at best.

"You're not the only one captivated by his talents." He smiled and sat back. Curtis ran his hand over his head and then brushed the food that had fallen on his lap during dinner off and onto the floor. The smile never left his face. He was smug and overconfident.

Disgusted, Leslie pulled away from the table. She wanted to wrap her fingers around his neck and squeeze until his air supply was depleted. Her eyes widened and her nostrils flared. She couldn't believe what she had heard.

By then Natalie and Anderson had returned to the dining room. Not quite sure what happened in the short amount of time she'd been loading dinner dishes into the dishwasher, Natalie noticed a distinct difference in the demeanor of her guests.

"Oh. My. God. Curtis! I can't believe you said that to me."

Leslie turned to Natalie. Not knowing what to expect, Natalie grabbed the back of the chair closest to her to steady herself for what she was about to hear.

"You will never believe this." Nervously Leslie laughed and then sat back in her chair. She rose quickly and began to speak to Natalie, who was disturbed by her erratic behavior.

"Natalie. Don't know if you've ever met one in real life, but now you have. Meet Mr. Curtis Matthews, a real 'down low brother.' I can't believe I thought about being intimate with your gay ass!" Her eyes surveyed the table.

Natalie knew Leslie was looking for alcohol. She needed a drink herself. Anderson looked a little green around the gills. Natalie knew for sure he wished he could rescind his offer to Curtis to join his club and he really didn't want him to bring any of his "partners."

Leslie continued, "So what if you make a lotta money! Money most definitely ain't worth this bullshit."

"Gay? I am not gay." Curtis was defensive. It was obvious he wasn't used to having to defend his lifestyle choice. It must be a newfound hobby.

"What do you call it?" Leslie screamed across the table. "You're sleeping with other men. Oh, I think that's the definition of gay. Can't get much gayer than that." She threw her hands up in the air and paced back and forth in front of her chair.

"I don't have to defend my choices to you. You were all for it before you found out. And if I would have laid on you what I laid on Greg Patterson, you would have hung around despite it. He probably was putting on you some of the tricks I taught him."

Leslie thought she might be sick. She held her stomach and then covered her mouth with her hand.

He continued, "I know the statistics. There are more of you women falling all over men who are down with it simply because the alternative isn't as appealing."

Anderson backed away as if he were distancing himself from the accusation. He wanted to scream it at the top of his lungs that he didn't swing that way. That was one thing his wife could be sure of, that he wasn't attracted to men nor intrigued by the idea of having sex with them. "But thou dost protest too much."

Ugggg!" All Leslie could do was scream. She gripped the table and shook it. The dishes that remained on the table rattled. Everyone stared at her, unsure of what she was going to do next. Leslie kicked off her heels and she screamed, "Break yourself, fool!" She was pissed she had been deceived by this man and now fearful that she could have gotten caught up in some of the same drama with some other man.

"Greg Patterson had a girlfriend!" She threw that fact out there.

"And, I had a wife." He looked at Anderson.

Natalie placed her hand in front of her husband. If she knew one thing, it was that he was on the verge of opening up a can of whoop ass. He didn't want to be included in the charge that was being handed down by this brother. "But thou dost protest too much."

And then Leslie thought about she and Greg Patterson together. Their sexcapades had been so wild and uninhibited. She could have been exposed to anything. Her heart sank and she couldn't catch her breath. She grabbed her head, closed her eyes and then opened them.

Leslie wanted to destroy any remnants of the man that contaminated the room with his bad news. She stared at Curtis Matthews trying to burn a hole through him with her glare.

Curtis continued talking, "What? And you're supposed to be so classy!

Bitch, please! Get the hell out of here. All you women are looking for is someone to be your baby's daddy! I don't get all that drama with men. They aren't so high maintenance! We can hang out, and not feel obligated to talk about feelings. We can drink, smoke cigars, watch a game. You and all those other women are too much work. Your time was almost up anyway! I'm out!"

The word "bitch" hung in the air. Curtis was the bitch. How could he throw the word around like that? Leslie heard nothing after that. That was one word that triggered her to lose her mind. Natalie nudged Anderson as if to say, "Aren't you going to do something?" His frozen state served as his answer of an adamant, "No!"

"Bitch? Motherfucker! I will cut you!" Her words were slurred, but were quite comprehensible. "You call me a bitch. I'm going to show you a bitch." Leslie tried as hard as she could to get on the same side of the table as Curtis Matthews.

"Leslie!" Natalie called out.

Stopping in her tracks, Leslie turned and ran to the guest bedroom, slamming the bedroom door behind her.

"See, all women are alike," Curtis mumbled to himself.

Anderson and Natalie stood looking in disbelief. Not sure how to proceed, Anderson left the room as well. His inability to find the perfect words in an imperfect situation resulted in his turn and run behavior. But always the gracious hostess, Natalie remained to see Curtis to the door.

Curtis grabbed his jacket from off the back of his chair. He managed a half-hearted smile. "Well, the evening was, I guess I can say, interesting!"

"To say the least," Natalie retorted. "Uh, thank you for the bottle of wine," she added, unable to identify the appropriate farewell. She was curious about the whole down-low brother movement. She wanted to ask him what was it that made him abandon his wife, neglecting her feelings for another man. But not wanting to keep him any longer and wanting to look in on Leslie, she escorted him to the door.

They smiled at each other. He wished her a good evening and he left.

T he telephone rang while Natalie sat in the kitchen watching her husband spoon his dinner onto his plate. For some reason she wasn't hungry tonight, but she enjoyed the time they spent together.

Natalie grabbed the cordless phone, "Hello?"

"Darling? Natalie? It's me, Dreama." Her voice was like nails on a chalkboard. Natalie loved her mother, but she was like her menstrual period, she was happy that she had one but didn't want it around all the time.

"Hi, Dreama. What's up?"

Natalie had been calling her mother by her first name since she could remember.

"Natalie, have you talked to your sister lately?"

"No, I've tried to get in touch with her but she hasn't returned any of my phone calls."

"Well, she left a message with Juanita to have me call her and when I did, she wouldn't answer the phone. Can you go over there tomorrow after church? You are coming to church, aren't you? I would do it, but Mitchell and I are leaving to go on vacation tomorrow. I'll leave you all the travel information so that you can contact me with your findings. I really appreciate this Natalie. Natalie, are you listening to me?" Dreama is such an elitist. Her tone uppity and somewhat obnoxious.

Natalie was only half paying attention to Dreama. She despised the fact that everything that had to do with her sister was dumped on her. It seemed to Natalie that her mother had no use for Andrea. Andrea wasn't able to maintain Dreama's unusually high standards. Andrea was a lost soul. She had always marched to the beat of a different drummer, however, now she had sunk to an all-time low. Drugs, prostitution, you name it, and she had at least tried it.

"Yes, Dreama, I'll look in on her."

Dreama sensed the annoyance in Natalie's voice, but that didn't bother her. She had gotten what she wanted. "Thanks darling. See you and the children tomorrow at church. Is everything alright? You sound a bit down." Natalie knew that her mother was probably preoccupied with other things on her end. She wouldn't have the time to hear all the details of what it was that bothered her. She swore her mother had ADD.

"I'm fine." Natalie blew into the phone. "The kids are sick, Dreama. Monica's coming to get them in the morning. They won't be at church." Natalie welcomed the opportunity to enjoy a church service without having to worry about two toddlers and their short attention spans. Too bad it had to be at the expense of their health.

Dreama had disappointment in her voice. "I'll miss them, but let them know Dreama loves them and I'll bring them something back from Cannes. Love you. Give everyone kisses and hugs. Ciao!" And she was gone.

Dreama realized the bullet she dodged as she stared at her reflection in her bathroom mirror. She had never had any health challenges until her good friend, Joan Weiss, who happened to also be her gynecologist, informed her that she had a lump in her right breast.

"Dreama, feel this right here." Dr. Weiss guided her patient's hand to where she noticed the mass.

Dreama's heart dropped and she stopped breathing. Her lungs began to ache until she was forced to exhale. Never before had she had to deal with her own health challenges. Dreama had always been the strong one and, right this moment, she wanted to break down and cry her eyes out. She wasn't sure if she knew the exact reason for her melt down. Would it be because she could potentially die from this illness or was it the fact that she might live but be permanently disfigured? No longer perfect. Dreama was torn.

"Dreama? Are you okay?" Dr. Weiss asked as she pushed herself away from the examining table. She discarded her plastic gloves in the receptacle and then stood up.

"Hmmm?" Dreama asked, not sure of the question posed to her.

"I think we should have it biopsied. I think we should take care of this as soon as possible. Once we find out what we're working with, we can handle it." Dr. Weiss stood at the end of the examining table waiting for a response. She turned her back, grabbed Dreama's file, and began making notes, saying, "Dreama, I think cutting back on the alcohol may help. You're not as young as you once were. None of us are. It's time we start taking care of ourselves. An occasional drink isn't going to harm you, but let's cut back a little."

Dreama enjoyed drinking. She drank with her meals, in between her meals and whenever the mood hit her. But she wasn't a careless drinker. She remained intact and under control.

"Hmmm?" The whole thing was so incomprehensible. When she walked into the office she was a perfectly healthy woman with two perfectly healthy breasts. But now she was someone who might be living with and then ultimately dying from cancer. Although she had started to receive her AARP subscription, Dreama never thought about her mortality. She knew that death was inevitable, but her death was not one she thought about. And now, here it was staring her in the face, closer than she'd like. A tear fell from her eye.

"Dreama, *please* think positively. Not only am I your doctor, but I'm your friend." Dr. Weiss touched Dreama's hand. She held it and wouldn't let it go. "I would want nothing more than to have not found the lump, but what's done is done. It's better to know than to not. Let's take care of it and deal with it."

"Positively? Positively? How can I think positively? What are the statistics?" Dreama searched the room for her clothes. She wanted to run, run away, far away.

Dr. Weiss released her hand and moved closer to the door. She pushed it, ensuring that it was closed and secure. "Damn it, Dreama! What *is* this? We are friends because you have that spunk, that drive! It makes you exciting and fun. I know you're not about to change on me now? Snap out of it!" Dr. Weiss snapped her fingers at Dreama. "If you have a defeatist attitude, you will be defeated. I believe in being realistic about this, but before we know if it's something to be concerned about, don't fall apart."

Her approach was so undoctorlike. Dreama was caught off guard by her surroundings. If they were having this conversation at Rex's, over dinner and drinks, it would have been easier to accept, but staring at the stirrups at the end of the table and the cold sterile instruments around her, she expected more of a theoretical philosophy. Here, it was so life or death.

She broke down. Never before had she shown so much emotion. Dr. Weiss moved closer to Dreama and allowed her patient and good friend to cry on her shoulder. She was at a loss as well. Dreama was the strong one. She had helped her through the death of her own husband two years ago when he succumbed to liver cancer.

Dr. Weiss pushed Dreama's shoulders back and looked her in her face. "I'll be in touch so that we can make the arrangements. The procedure is simple," she said.

Dreama cried out, "Okay." Her body shook and she wailed, years of drama escaping from the depths of her soul. She knew that the procedure needed to be preformed and she would trust her friend to take good care of her.

It had been two months since Dr. Weiss found the lump. And the results of the biopsy were benign. But she couldn't help but believe that God was trying to tell her something. Despite her many efforts to stave off the aging process, she was growing older. And her body was changing. The event was a wake-up call. Dreama made several life changes. She cut back on her drinking drastically and changed her diet. Her prayers each night ended with a sincere thank you to God for sparing her life and a genuine promise to continue to live life to its fullest.

She continued to admire her voluptuous body in the mirror. Her black negligee skimmed her in the right spots. She saw her curves and mountains.

They dipped, swooped and turned. Dreama wondered if she had had cancer how much about her life would have changed. Would it have made her husband love her any less? If she would have had to have her breast removed, would he have been supportive or would he have gone for a newer version? Insecure, Dreama was not. She pushed the thoughts out of her mind and continued to admire what she saw in the mirror. She was thankful that she didn't have to learn the answer to those questions.

CHAPTER SEVEN

D reama and Monica were two totally different women. Still, Natalie could see how her father was attracted to and had love for them both. Dreama was comfortable around all types of people. She could hold a conversation with anybody. But it was obvious to all that she fit better with her second husband, Mitchell Ellis. Mitchell was the owner of his own consulting company. He had a huge client base, which included top city and state officials. He and Dreama hosted numerous parties and receptions for these bigwigs and they traveled all over the world. She was much happier now than she was with Natalie's father, Dale Richards.

Monica, on the other hand, loved to stay at home. Going out and attending parties was not what she enjoyed doing. She was happy renting a movie, eating instant popcorn and curling up with her husband in front of the television. She loved to cook, clean, and shop. The shopping was how the relationship between she and Natalie blossomed. It was the glue that bonded them together. *And* the fact she loved Kayla and Kendall. She would do anything for them. And Natalie believed that anyone that loved her children as much as she did was aces with her.

SATURDAY EVENING

Monica Richards lay on the floor at the foot of her bed. The television lit up the room, but the sound was on mute. She pulled her knees up to her chest and manipulated and contorted her body until she felt the burn of the stretch. Her husband, Dale, lay sleeping in their bed. He dozed off while watching his favorite television program. His soft purrs were the music to her evening meditation. He sneezed, she mouthed a silent "bless you," and then smiled.

She loved everything about her man. He was sensitive, kind, giving, honest (sometimes to a fault) and loving. He kissed her every morning when he awoke and he, again, kissed her before he closed his eyes each night. Monica would do anything for him and she knew that he would do anything for her.

Rising from the floor, she bent over one last time to stretch before she put another load of clothes in the washing machine and let the dog out for the night. Monica grabbed her robe from off the bed, careful not to wake her husband.

"Where are you going, beautiful?" His voice rough. He smiled at her without opening his eyes.

"Hey, babe! I thought you were asleep," she said, wrapping the pink terry cloth belt around her waist.

"You know I can't sleep without you next to me. Come here." He raised his hand from under the comforter and reached for her.

"Dale! No, Dale! I've got some things to finish up before coming to bed." She laughed, her voice filling up the room. She had a tone that was "deep sexy," Dale called it. "And I'm all sweaty."

"It can all wait until tomorrow. Come here," he whined. "I need you right here with me." He grabbed her hand and pulled her down onto the bed.

She smelled his cologne. He slid his hand into the opening of her robe and rubbed on her warm, moist breasts. She moaned. He moaned.

Rolling over, Monica ran her fingers through her husband's salt and pepper hair. He was distinguished looking and his years made Monica feel safe, protected. Her father passed away before she was born. He had been killed in an automobile accident and so she grew up never having the guiding hand of a man. She planted kisses on his forehead, his neck and then his lips. And again she thought that there wasn't anything she wouldn't do for her husband.

He rose to attention. Monica eased out of her robe and pressed her hot body against his. They moved together. Back and forth. Up and down. He was gentle. His years were evident in the delicateness of his touch. Dale caressed and stroked. He nibbled and kissed. He held her hand, intertwining her fingers with his. She felt the connection. A connection like no other. She had had younger men. Men her age, but there were none who had made her feel as important and as special as he had.

She called his name, "Dale."

He moaned back, "Monica."

"Oh my God!" she screamed with pleasure.

"Monica!"

"Dale!"

Worn out, they both collapsed. He pulled her close to him and she feel asleep in his arms. The evening slipped to early morning and now no work had been completed. Monica figured if Tabitha, their Cocker Spaniel, was that desperate to relieve herself, she'd wake her.

Monica had heard the warning words of women her mother's age. They warned her against marrying such an older man. They warned that he would die on her, leaving her to mourn his death. They warned her that he wouldn't be able to satisfy her in bed. They warned her that he would treat her as if she were his daughter instead of his wife. And so far they were wrong on all accounts.

But her mother, while lying in her hospital bed gave her the real dirt, "Girl, those old biddies are upset 'cause you done hooked a man that is close to their own age. They feeling the years and they lonely. Girl, don't you pay them no mind. If you love that man and you know he loves you, too. You do what you feel is best."

Monica was the happiest she had ever been the day she said, "I do," to Mr. Dale Richards in front of family and friends.

CHAPTER EIGHT

The great thing about all four of Natalie's parents was that they all seemed to get along. They all believed that their grandchildren were the best grandchildren ever conceived, that their son-in-law was the greatest thing for their daughter, and that Andrea was the child they were most concerned for, the black sheep of the family. They all loved each other. And now, after some rough years following the divorce, Dreama and Dale knew that they were much better off with their present mates.

But even where the grandchildren were concerned, Dreama attempted to hold onto her youth, insisting that Natalie's children call her by her first name instead of Grandma.

While lying with her children in her arms following giving birth, Natalie lamented to Dreama, "Well, what about Nana?"

"No, Natalie. What's wrong with Dreama? You've called me that all your life."

She tried again, "Well, what about Mimi?"

"Natalie, they can call me Dreama." The decision had been made. Dreama had put her stilettoed foot down and there was to be no more discussion. Natalie knew when she was tired of talking. She wouldn't hear any more debate and to continue would be futile.

Dreama believed that if you acted old, you would inevitably become old and whatever she had to do to hold off the aging process, she most definitely would do it. Anti-aging creams, hair dyes, face-lifts, reconstructive surgery, whatever it took, she would attempt it. But at this point in her life she didn't have to go under the knife for any cosmetic procedures and bragged of that fact. "Girl, I'm 50ish and still got it!" Dreama would boast with a snap of her fingers and a flip of her hair.

Whoever found out that Dreama was in her fifties, found it hard to believe. "Natalie, is *that* your mother?" The question would be asked from someone who had never had the pleasure of making her acquaintance. "Dag, your momma sure does look good."

She wore her age well. That was another thing Natalie thanked her mother for: great genes. If it was true that a person could forecast how they would look as they aged by how their mother aged, Natalie knew for sure losing her looks was one less thing she'd have to worry about. It was a curse and a blessing.

Dreama had a coffee with cream complexion, color and texture. Her hair was cut in a short, dark brown bob that moved with every dramatic gesture she made. Even in her 50s, there wasn't a sign of gray and Natalie couldn't figure out if it was because Dark 'n' Lovely made a hair color in Dreama's shade or if it was genetics. She was healthy looking, not too skinny, which made her name-brand haberdashery—she wouldn't be caught dead in anything else—fit her perfectly.

One of Dreama's favorite activities was her weekly visit to the hair salon. She sat in Salon Royale with the other pampered women and dished dirt about a sundry of things going on in their community and in their lives. Who got what, who's going where, who's divorcing whom. They would talk nonstop as the salon employees moved quickly from room to room washing, styling, filing and painting. Dreama would have one technician styling her hair, another manicuring her fingernails and then another finishing up her pedicure. She smiled as this was her time to be fawned over by others who adored her.

"Can I get you something to drink, Ms. Dreama?" The Laotian manicurist asked Dreama.

"Yes, darling. I'll have a latte." She paused her conversation with Mrs. McGinnis. Della McGinnis was the first lady of Sheridan Heights. Dreama and Della were good friends because of their husbands hard worked to improve the situation of economic development in Sheridan Heights.

The door swung open and an unfamiliar face entered the salon. The women stopped their gossip and stared at the young girl struggling to pull in the large green plastic trash bag. She dropped the bag at the entrance of the door and flashed a wide smile. Her look contrasted with the royal appearance of the room; the hardwood floors and the majestic purple color of the walls. It was obvious that she was nervous to be in the room with the women who had designer bags on the floor next to their chairs and who drove luxury cars that were parked in the lot.

"Ladies! Good morning. Do *I* have something for you." She began to walk toward the chairs. Her tennis shoes squeaked on the floor and she laughed, her nerves getting the best of her. "My name is Tina. I see you ladies like your designer bags." The salesperson in her came out.

Mrs. McGinnis allowed her eyeglasses to slide down to the tip of her nose. She and Dreama stared at the products Tina pulled from her bag. Not sure if she was getting a good look at what she thought she saw, Dreama dismissed her technicians with a wave of her hand and rose from her seat.

"Child, let me see what you have in that bag?" Her request was smug and full of superiority.

Tina reached her hand in and pulled out a designer bag. She handed it to Dreama. Dreama fondled it, she violated it, inspecting the inside, the outside and then passed it to Mrs. McGinnis, who did the same.

"Let me see another one?" she requested, snapping her fingers to get her to move faster.

Again, Tina pulled one of her handbags out and gave it to the demanding woman.

"Where did you get this bag?" Mrs. McGinnis asked Tina.

"I have a distributor," she responded shyly.

"Is that real?" The question came from somewhere else in the salon.

"It's real leather," Tina responded.

"That's not the question," Mrs. McGinnis called out.

"Well..." Tina began, "It is the best quality designer bag you can get. Genuine leather..."

Dreama barked out a hearty laugh. "Dear, do we look like the kind of women that need to purchase bags that aren't the real thing?"

The whole salon erupted in laughter, sending Tina scampering out of the building with her tail between her legs.

As Dreama grew older, she became more and more spoiled. And Mitchell was to blame for it. He lavished her with gifts, bought her little trinkets, diamond baubles and chic furs. Dreama requested help around her 5,000-square-foot home, a penthouse condominium she never occupied longer than a couple of weeks a month, and so Mitchell hired a live-in maid, Juanita. Natalie knew that Mitchell loved her mother, but he was not helping anyone else in the family by turning her 50-year-old mother into a spoiled rotten brat.

Natalie could deal with the fact that Dreama was so vain. She had been that way since she could remember. But what bothered her most about her mother was her lack of attentiveness when it came to her sister. Andrea needed her mother now more than ever. Natalie knew that the motherly instinct was not something that all women possessed. And Dreama definitely did not have it. It was not something she could run to the department store and pick up like she picked up so many other things. But what got Natalie was that Dreama tried to fake it. She would substitute money for love. She dropped checks in the mail for Andrea several times a month. Checks that were cashed at local liquor stores. The cash went toward Andrea's drug of the moment instead of necessities, like food and clothing. Dreama couldn't understand that fact regardless of the number of times Natalie attempted to explain it to her. Dreama wanted Andrea to snap out of it. To pull herself up by her bootstraps.

Natalie wanted to help her sister. She wanted Andrea to be the same girl she was when they were younger. The same girl Natalie rushed home to from school to tell her secrets to. It seemed like her youth was so long ago.

A knock at the door came while Natalie and Anderson were seated eating at the dinner table. Annoyed, Anderson rose from his seated position, threw his napkin onto the table, and made his way to the front door. He had dreamed about his dinner all day, looking forward to the leftovers that waited for him at home, and this disruption was putting more time between his dream and reality.

"Who could be at the door at this time of night?" he fussed. The rumble in his stomach and the pain in his head were causing his attitude to sour.

He swung open the door to find Andrea. She was teetering back and forth. She fidgeted with the buttons on her denim jacket. Was she nervous, or was she high? Her checks were bright red as the cold night air whipped around her and rustled the leaves in the yard. Her clothes reeked of the pungent odor of the crack house on 81st and Gates, her usual hang out. The smell wafted into the doorway and revealed the answer to Anderson's question. He had the urge to slam the door in her face. He wanted to keep this deviance away from his family. Anderson hated the fact that his wife was so torn over her relationship with her sister.

"Hey brother-in-law!" Andrea smiled, exposing a missing tooth that hadn't been missing the last time he saw her. She looked around him, searching for her sister and feeling the warm air from the house on her face. Pulling the jacket around her, she asked, "Is Natalie home?" Continuing to teeter back and forth, she looked back at the loud Toyota in the driveway that had been her ride. Switch's "There'll Never Be" played on the radio. Anderson was surprised that the car still had a working system. He couldn't tell whether the driver of the car was male or female. He wondered what their relationship was. The whole scene was disgusting and Anderson turned his nose up at his sister-in-law. He wondered how she was Dreama's daughter, they contrasted each other so distinctly.

Angered, he refused to answer her. Anderson knew his wife had a weak spot for her sister. He had tried over and over again to explain the concept of tough love, but the idea was beyond her understanding.

"Natalie, what is her motivation to end this way of life? If you continue to bail her out, she's never going to stop." Anderson paced back and forth, trying to convince his wife to leave her sister down at the 19th precinct. She had been picked up by an undercover police officer when she tried to solicit sex in order to get money for drugs.

"Anderson, I'll never be able to explain to you why I have to go." It wasn't the money Anderson was concerned about. He had always told his wife, "What's mine is yours," but he wanted her to have a backbone. "She is my sister, Anderson. We're the same family. Just because you can forget some-one just like that," she snapped her fingers, "doesn't mean I'm able to distance myself from someone who is my blood. She is *sick*. She needs me." Natalie grabbed her purse and left the house, leaving Anderson standing there alone. She was right, he would never be able to understand.

Coming to find out what was keeping her husband, Natalie pulled the door all the way open. Andrea rushed in and wrapped her arms around her. She whispered in her ear, "Hey, baby sister." The smell of smoke and funk filled Natalie's nostrils and caused her stomach to turn.

"Hey, Andrea, Dreama was looking for you." Natalie watched Anderson walk away, shaking his head on his way back to the kitchen. He sucked his teeth before leaving. Andrea held on a few seconds longer and then stepped away. She continued to teeter back and forth, dancing her way around the foyer.

"Yeah, I know." She rubbed her nose and then tried to straighten her hair after getting a glimpse of herself in the hall mirror.

"Well, didn't you call her?" Natalie followed her around the room.

"I guess I did."

Andrea's short answers were beginning to annoy Natalie. Andrea had never merely dropped by. It confused Natalie.

"It's late. What's up?"

"Nothing. Can't I come over and see my sister and my niece and nephew? Why do I have to want something?" Andrea's mood shifted with the evening wind. The air had cooled down considerably and Natalie felt uncomfortable standing in the doorway with only a T-shirt on. "Where are the kids?" She began to dig in her pockets.

Natalie was unnerved by her actions. She had hoped that the promise her sister made when they were younger still existed, that she would never hurt her. In her defense, Natalie began, "I didn't say you wanted something, I..."

"Forget it!" Andrea shouted. The car's horn honked, startling the sisters. Andrea spun around and stumbled off the porch. She struggled to open the car door that creaked as if it hadn't been opened in years and fell into the passenger's seat. Natalie heard the driver holler out, "Well, did you get it?"

But before Andrea could answer and before she could close the door, the driver peeled out of the driveway. Natalie watched the car race down the street, exhaust smoke contaminating the clear, brisk night air. Her heart ached for her sister, not knowing how long it would be before she saw her again.

Once before she hadn't heard from or seen Andrea for three months. During that time Natalie attempted to find her sister by visiting the neighborhoods she knew were frequented by the kind of people Andrea associated with. Many nights, Natalie enlisted Leslie to ride with her through these areas of town. Anderson was left in the dark about her trips and if he knew, he'd be upset that she put herself in such danger. It was quite obvious that the navy blue luxury SUV was out of place weaving through the narrow streets that were infested with that "unwanted element," as Dreama would call it. It was definitely true that "the freaks come out at night." Every time Natalie rolled down the passenger-side window to ask a 200-pound, bleach-blonde woman (or was it a man?) in a red spandex mini-dress if they had seen her sister, Leslie would warn, "Girl, have you lost your mind?"

CHAPTER TEN

Anderson Kelley was an only child with parents who doted on him. They attended all his sporting events and academic ceremonies. His birth had been their first after many failed attempts. Anderson's mother and father were up in age and were exhausted by the time of his birth.

He had a modest upbringing and he never really caused his parents much trouble while in school. However there was the one time while his parents were on vacation that he had a number of boys from his basketball team and some girls over to his house for a small party.

"Yes, officer?" Anderson asked when he swung the door open. "Can I help you?" He swatted at the guys who sat on the couch behind him, motioning to them to turn the music down and to put away the beer bottles. He flashed his million-dollar smile, in an effort to prove that he was coherent and in charge of the situation.

"Son, are your parents home?" the officer asked, looking behind him to see the neighbors standing on their porches watching the situation unfold. Anderson knew that he could have answered his own question.

"No, sir, they're out of town. What can I do for you? Is there a problem?" He even surprised himself. He had consumed at least five beers so far and his head was swimming. Anderson burped, covered his mouth with his hand, and wondered if the police officer doubted his sobriety.

"We received a complaint about the noise. Can you fellas keep it down?" The officer attempted to peek around Anderson. Anderson knew if he really wanted in, he could make a case for his need to enter, but he wouldn't make it easy for the officer.

One of the girls invited to the party screamed and giggled in the background and it was obvious that she was quite inebriated. Anderson lowered his eyes, not sure what was going to happen next.

"Son, my suggestion to you is that you get those girls out of here. I've seen situations like this get really bad. I know who you are and I know you've got a bright future in front of you. And I can tell that you have neighbors that make it their business to be in yours." He tipped his hat, turned and walked away.

Anderson's parents were notified of the Friday night party. He was grounded for two months as a result and to make matters worse, Natalie found out about it. She found out he had been with another girl and to punish him, she gave him the cold shoulder, ground him for an additional three months.

Mr. and Mrs. Kelley were part of the working class, and tried to give Anderson anything and everything he desired. But what they couldn't give him was the NBA career he so longed for. Unable to pursue his lifelong dream of playing professional basketball, he became the proprietor of a basketball training and workout facility called Hoop Dreams. His inability to play pro basketball was hindered only by his lack of height, not his lack of skill in handling the ball or his ambition. While in college, Andy had broken the school record for free-throw attempts and three-point shots, all the while managing to maintain the high academic status of an all-American student-athlete. He was even drafted ninth in the 1990 NBA draft, but was unable to carry over his college basketball success into the pros.

Natalie was attracted to his skin that was the color of milk chocolate and his six-foot athletic frame. But what really drew her to him was his ability to make her laugh, feel special above all others, and make her feel better, especially when she knew for sure her world was coming to an end.

Natalie Richards first saw Anderson Kelley during her junior year at Sheridan Heights High School. She knew he was a senior at her school's biggest rival, Providence Glen, and that he was on his way to Penn State on a basketball scholarship. Everyone in the city knew that. Even though Natalie was one of the most popular girls at her school, she never thought that such an intelligent, handsome, athletic guy would be interested in her.

Natalie had a short, smart haircut, coupled with caramel-colored skin and a curvaceous dancer's body which helped her win a spot on the high school varsity cheerleading team during her freshman year. She was definitely easy on the eyes! Her looks and her dazzling personality made it easy for many of the males in the city to fall head over heels for her. She was given this news often, but despite that, she still found it hard to believe that she had eventually won the heart of Anderson Kelley.

Natalie traveled to all the games and that's where she saw him, Andy Kelley, always surrounded by males and females alike. She thought she never had a chance. At each game, their eyes would meet but they never talked. Andy left for Happy Valley, Pennsylvania at the end of the 1986 school year and Natalie never gave him another thought. She had her own future to prepare for and Anderson was not a part of it. Or so she thought.

"Is this seat taken?" Natalie had been reading a book she bought at the bookstore in the mall. She was waiting on Andrea to return to take her home. She had disappeared with a group of girls Natalie knew were no good.

Not looking up to see who it was that asked the question, she answered, "Yes."

"What's your book about?"

Natalie was annoyed. Couldn't he see that she was busy? She knew she looked out of place, reading in a mall that was buzzing with the laughter of teenagers. And she felt out of place. She would have been more comfortable at home in the quiet of her bedroom, but Dreama told Andrea if she wanted to leave, she had to take Natalie with her. It was a punishment for both of them.

"I've never had to try so hard to get a girl's attention," Anderson later admitted.

A voice called from across the mall, "Hey Anderson!"

And he called back, throwing up a two finger peace sign. "What's up?"

She was suddenly nervous. Natalie lifted her head out of her book and all she saw was his megawatt smile. From that point on, she was hooked and she knew that she was in love.

Their dating was intense. They spent all their free time together. She went to his games when she was able and listened to girls call out his name when he scored. She would be embarrassed by Leslie calling back to them, "Hey, girl, back off my friend's boyfriend. He don't want you!"

And on her prom night, he was charming and debonair in his tuxedo. They rode to the prom in a limousine, sharing the ride with Leslie and her date. Leslie was ready to bypass all the prom festivities and head to a hotel, but Natalie convinced her that they had to at least make an appearance. She tried to explain to Leslie that she would appear loose if she were to move too quickly. But Leslie didn't care. She thought her date was hot and she was instantly attracted to him.

Naturally, Natalie won prom queen and she danced with Anderson to the song of the night "Make It Last Forever." She whispered in his ear, "I love you, Anderson."

"I love you, too," he whispered back. He hummed the words to the song in her ear and she closed her eyes. It was the best night of her life. They danced close together, their bodies pressed tightly as one. She felt his excitement and she knew that he was as eager as she.

"Are you going to do it?" she heard Leslie's voice say in her head. From the time she met Anderson, Leslie had chided her about whether or not they were going to have sex; if he was going to be her first. For two years, Natalie was able to put her off. Leslie pressured her more than Anderson had ever. But on prom night Natalie promised Leslie that it would happen. They had planned it to the very last detail. She had started birth control pills months ago, telling Dreama that she needed them to ease the pain of her cycle. She had condoms with her as well and she even had a small flask of liquor in her purse to ease her nerves.

"Anderson?" Natalie was nervous about what she was about to say.

"Yeah, babe."

"I love you," she said again. Natalie loved when he said it back and she found every opportunity to have him voice his feelings for her.

"I know. I love you, too." He kissed her on the neck.

"I want tonight to be special." She stopped dancing and looked at him.

"It is. I'm having a good time." He smiled at her.

"I mean, *really* special."

He appeared stunned by her words. A smile spread across his face. He patted his jacket as if he were looking for his car keys. Remembering that he didn't drive, he grabbed her hand and pulled her toward the door. He found his roommate, George, and Leslie at their table, gave them a "it's time to go" look, and rushed toward the exit. He dragged Natalie through the room, her dress flying behind her. She said her good-byes to her friends, bidding a fond adieu to them as well as to her virginity.

CHAPTER ELEVEN
SATURDAY EVENING

Annoyed by the disruption, Anderson stormed back into the kitchen. He moved around the room, anger in all he did. He slammed down a glass. He slammed the refrigerator door closed. He haphazardly poured himself a glass of juice and spilt some on the counter. Entering the kitchen, unbeknownst to Anderson, Natalie grabbed a dishrag and cleaned up his accident. He couldn't help his behavior. He was a typical only child and he knew he was somewhat selfish, but he wanted what he wanted when he wanted it and tonight he wanted his wife's undivided attention. It wasn't often that he had her all to himself and the disruption from her sister cut into his quality time.

What a baby, Natalie thought. She smiled to herself. She knew what the problem was and she knew how to fix it. It had been some time since they'd been together, and the other night she promised herself that she would show him some attention, but after the unfortunate discovery that Leslie's Mr. Right wasn't particularly looking for a Mrs. Right—that he would have settled for his very own Mr. Right—the mood had been destroyed.

Anderson and Natalie sat down at the island to eat. He tried to be the bigger person and he began to give her the details of his workday. While in the midst of his description of his difficult day and the new, overweight athlete charged to him to whip into shape for the upcoming season, he lifted Natalie's hand and kissed it. The feeling was reminiscent of the day she whispered to him, "I do," through tears of joy. There was no more Natalie. And that was okay with her. Natalie tried to listen to Andy.

"I tried to tell him what he needed to do..."

His voice was drowned out by her own thoughts.

She watched his lips move, entranced by their shape, and remembering how they felt when they kissed.

"Hmm-hmm." She tried to feign paying attention. She smiled and nodded her head. She thought about the autumn four years ago, one short year before their storybook wedding. Natalie felt her smile fade and she tried to check herself.

Anderson was eating the last bit of food on his plate, "I don't get paid enough to deal with this craziness." He started laughing. He had no idea that Natalie had slipped back into time, remembering how she felt when she found out that he had cheated on her, yet again.

"Anderson! Anderson Kelley! Do you hear me?"

Natalie stood at the door of the locker room after the game Anderson and his team had won. His teammates passed her, snickering at her behavior. He hadn't come home the night before. And as far as she was concerned, her behavior was warranted. His side of the bed was cold and remained untouched. He didn't even bother to call her before he had to report to the arena for today's game against the Minnesota Timberwolves.

She pounded on the door, her anger meeting new heights. Leslie sat back and watched. She continued to ogle the sweaty jocks that entered and then left the locker room, winking and whispering to one of them a sultry, "Hey, baby."

Natalie thought back to the woman's voice that had phoned her earlier that morning.

"Sweety," she said, her voice waking Natalie out of a medication-induced sleep. "In case you're wondering where Anderson's been all night, he's here with me," she purred, her voice Southern and saccharine sweet. Natalie felt sick to her stomach and her head pounded to the beat of her heart.

The woman held the phone next to his mouth. His breathing reverberated in Natalie's ears and tears filled her eyes. She had been with Anderson Kelley long enough to know the sounds he made while he slept. Natalie heard her giggles in the background. And then she heard Anderson regain consciousness.

"What the…?"

Natalie could hear them wrestle for the phone and then the call was disconnected. She jumped out of the bed and paced the room, planning her next move. She ran to the closet and grabbed her clothes, pulled the suitcase out from under the bed, and packed all she had in the apartment. She woke Leslie, who was sleeping on the couch, and explained to her the last few minutes, tears and sobs sometimes causing her to be incoherent.

Together they moved quickly, not sure when Anderson would return. Her intent was to leave the apartment empty of all that would remind Anderson that Natalie had ever been there.

Anderson finally exited the locker room. He stared Natalie in the eyes. Words escaped him.

Then he managed, "I'm sorry."

She looked down, focusing on the engagement ring on her left hand. The diamond sparkled under the bright lights in the hallway. She looked up at him. And before she could contain herself, she lifted her hand and slapped him across his face. She snatched off the ring that was to symbolize their intent to marry and become one and she threw it at him, striking him on the corner of his right eye.

Moving his hand from the original point of contact and covering the blood that oozed from the new wound, he watched Natalie run down the corridor and out the door marked "Exit."

Leslie turned to follow, delivering a "sorry-ass bastard," before leaving.

As a result of his indiscretion, Natalie began to doubt her belief in God. How could He let this happen to her? How could the man that she loved so much betray her? She believed in God's ability to give her anything she asked for. She had prayed for God to give her her soulmate. And she had faith that Anderson was it. Why else had God put him in her life? But then why would God allow him to cause her so much pain? Her heart ached, literally ached for weeks following his latest indiscretion. She walked around in a daze unable to find meaning in her heartache.

Anderson and Natalie finished their late night dinner. It took all she had in her to push away the evil thoughts that crept into her head while they dined. Once he was able to track her down, Anderson pleaded for her forgiveness. They participated in counseling and he was home every night, begging off the invitations from friends to hang out. Finally, believing that his actions were sincere and that he would never, ever, ever cheat on her again, Natalie gave into his request for her hand in marriage, provided he propose to her all over again.

And now it had been three years since their nuptials, and although she sometimes had doubts about his commitment, they were now together as husband and wife. So far, there hadn't been any concrete evidence that he had been unfaithful, but he was distant at times and so that in itself brought back her insecurities.

But tonight Natalie felt excited by her husband's desire to be so close to her. The children were now deep into their sleep and she wanted him as badly as he wanted her. She smiled at Anderson and grabbed him by his hand. She ran her fingers down the center of the palm of his right hand and they both smiled.

Leading his wife through the kitchen and up to the second floor, Anderson was excited at the idea of being intimate with his wife. He sat her down on the bed and pulled her T-shirt over her head. He kissed her on the neck, on her left shoulder and down her arm to her fingertips. The gesture was a mixture of innocence and eroticism.

Natalie scooted back onto the bed. He unbuttoned her jeans and slid them off over her feet. Anderson grabbed her foot in his hand and began kissing each of her toes, sliding one after the other in and out of his mouth. She smiled and moaned.

Standing back and watching his wife squirm and whimper on the bed,

Anderson began to undress. He unbuttoned his shirt and dropped his jeans. The white wife-beater T-shirt and athletic shorts accentuated the muscles, his pecs, his lats and his quads. She smiled at her man and motioned to him to join her on the bed.

She whispered, "I love you."

He smiled and repeated her gesture. "I love you, too."

Anderson raised one finger, telling Natalie to wait a second. He lit strategically placed candles all around the room. The glow from the flames were much more romantic than the light from the television. He then switched on the small CD radio combo in the corner and smooth jazz music piped into their bedroom. The mood was sensual and Natalie couldn't wait for her husband. She felt a sense of urgency and almost couldn't contain herself. She moved seductively, reaching him at the end of the bed, and Anderson's excitement almost got the best of him as well.

He took her face in his hands and kissed her. Their lips met and touched gently, passionately. It had been the first time in a long time that they kissed more than quick pecks before departing from each other in the morning. Natalie ran her fingers up and down his arm. Anderson shivered and wrapped his arms around her, hugging her tightly. He removed her bra and panties and his hands followed the curves of her body. Caressing each and every hill and stroking all her valleys. Once all of his clothes were removed, he lifted his body and placed it on top of hers. Their bodies melted into one. The room heated, causing him to sweat and her to glisten.

They held hands, their arms twisting, their legs intertwining. It became difficult to tell where her body began and his ended. The seconds turned to minutes and the minutes turned into an hour. They moved around the bed, Anderson taking the time to cater to her needs. He took every opportunity to stare into her eyes. She looked back and then she closed them, tight. She lost control and couldn't last any longer. She exploded.

"Anderson!" Natalie called out.

He lifted her leg, taking her lead and then detonated.

"Natalie. Natalie. Natalie!"

They lay together, his arms wrapped around her. She studied the hair on his arms until she couldn't keep her eyes open. Away she drifted, her husband's heavy breathing the last thing she heard before sleep.

Natalie could never leave her kitchen in disarray. Dirty dishes, grimy floors, trash in the garbage can; it all had to be taken care of before she could sleep peacefully. She rose from the warmth of her bed after a few minutes of her eyes closing. She kissed her husband on his shoulder and grabbed his sweats from off the floor. She dressed, the smell of his cologne relaxing her and then she blew out the candles that remained lit. Opening the door to the nursery, Natalie saw that her children continued to sleep. She smiled and descended the stairs, making her way to the first floor. Natalie quickly cleaned her kitchen, attempting to be as quiet as possible. She hummed to herself, smiling in the glow of her time with her husband, and once the kitchen was finished to her liking, she found the cordless phone in the den. She dialed Leslie's number. It was past midnight but Natalie couldn't get to sleep. She wanted, needed to talk to Leslie. There were some things she had to get off her chest. Leslie's answering machine came on. "I'm not here. Leave me a message if you want me to call you back!"

Instead of leaving a message, Natalie disconnected the call, placed the receiver back in its place, and made her way back to her bedroom. Anderson remained asleep; he hadn't moved from his original position. He was exhausted, his snoring louder than normal and echoing off the walls of their room. Again, she kissed him on his shoulder, removed her clothes, and crawled back into bed. She stared at the ceiling, her thoughts entertaining her, disturbing her, prohibiting her from drifting off to sleep.

Hours passed and once sleep came, she began to dream. It wasn't a dream so much, though, as memories of a past experience that tempered her sleep that night.

They were in Atlanta and Natalie and Anderson had been invited to dinner by Earl Walters and his wife, Amanda. Angelina's Restaurant had become Natalie's favorite place for dining. It was the only reason she accepted their invite. Natalie didn't much care for Earl. He played on the Atlanta Hawks basketball team with Anderson and he was becoming a constant in Anderson's life. He wasn't the role model Natalie would choose for her man, but there was an attraction between the two that she couldn't break.

The Walters had lived in Atlanta for about two years and Amanda and Natalie were quickly becoming friends. Natalie spent time with Amanda and her three children—two boys and one girl. Two were from Earl's first two marriages and one child was with Amanda. He had gotten the eldest boy and the girl in each of his divorce settlements.

Earl Walters was 32 years old. He had been employed by the National Basketball Association for 10 years earning a six-figure salary. He was reaching the end of his career, his game showing his age, and he had a difficult time keeping up with the younger men that were currently being drafted. Natalie thought he looked a lot older than his 32 years. He was graying, and not gracefully. His salt and pepper hair was more salt than pepper and his hairline moved back toward his neck. Natalie had a hard time understanding why Amanda was so drawn to him. She decided in order to maintain their friendship not to question her motives.

"Right this way, Mr. Walters," the maitre d' said, escorting the party to their table. Earl slipped $20 into the maitre d's pocket, and the man lowered his head to show his appreciation. The meal had been a quiet one. The conversation had been monopolized by the men, discussing the upcoming games scheduled, who was having a good season and who wasn't, and the possibility that their coach may be let go at the end of the year. Every now and then Natalie would slip in a question to Amanda about her children. However, as she attempted to answer, she was cut off by her husband. He was a rude man, apparently unhappy with his life and the choices he had made, and he took his despondency out on his wife.

Earl raised his hand to the waiter. "Can I get another drink? Anderson, do you want anything else?"

Anderson looked over at Natalie. She cut her eyes at him and he shook his head in the negative to Earl's request. Anderson had had many disagreements with Natalie about the amount of alcohol he consumed and he decided against rehashing the conversation tonight.

Once the dinner was consumed and the empty dishes were removed from the table, Natalie and Amanda excused themselves and headed to the ladies room. Earl looked up at Amanda as she pushed herself away from the table and grabbed her arm. Her arm slipped out of his grasp and in his attempt to grab at her again, he pulled at her lilac cashmere sweater, stretching it out of shape. He yanked her toward him and whispered something into her ear. The smile faded from her face as she listened. "I won't be gone long, Earl," she reassured him as she attempted another smile. Looking toward Natalie and Anderson, she explained, "He hates for me to be away from him." It was obvious Amanda didn't believe what she said. Natalie smiled in an attempt at affirmation; however, tension flooded the air.

In the ladies room, Natalie outlined her lips and applied lipstick. Her actions were meticulous. She waited for Amanda to return from the only available stall. Once she came out, Natalie went in to take care of her business.

She hollered over the stall door, "Amanda, was it just me or did you notice eyes on us during dinner?"

"Oh girl, you'll get used to it. People always ask for autographs. It comes with the territory," Amanda answered rather nonchalantly.

"No. No," Natalie said deliberately. "This was not people wanting autographs. There was a table of three females and they were staring at us and talking about us practically all night. You didn't see those girls at the table behind us?" Natalie's question hung in the air while Amanda attempted to find the right way to divulge her deepest secrets. She needed to talk to someone, anyone, at this point. She hadn't been in the company of another adult woman in what seemed like months. Earl tried to keep her away from other people, particularly women. It was his way of making sure she didn't find out about his dirt.

Amanda plopped down on the pink velvet couch in the corner of the ladies room. She placed her head in her hands and began to cry. Her body shook as she tried to hold back the tears. Her straight, jet-black hair fell forward, framing her covered face. The floodgates were open and the tears rolled uncontrollably down her cheeks. Natalie wasn't sure what to do. Should she hug her and try to comfort her? She didn't really know Amanda that well, their friendship being relatively new. She nervously looked around the ladies room for tissues, hoping no one would come into the bathroom. Not that she didn't want anyone to see Amanda crying, she didn't want the news to get back to Earl before she could find out what the story was. Finding a box on the vanity, she handed it to Amanda.

Amanda grabbed a tissue, blew her nose, and attempted to pull herself together. With an occasional sigh and sniffle, she confided in Natalie and began to tell her the whole uncensored story.

"I don't know what it is about him that has me so addicted." She dabbed at her eyes again. "He isn't all that handsome, he isn't charming and he's disrespectful."

Natalie looked at her, silently agreeing with every word she said. He *is* a hot mess.

"Girl, it's been so bad." She shook her head from side to side, seeming as if she was finding it hard herself to figure out why she stayed with him. "I can't tell you how many times I've caught him with other women." She looked down and stared at her feet. She was embarrassed by her lack of pride. "Please don't think I'm crazy. But he's the father of my child. I was brought up to believe that the mother and father should stay together for the sake of the children." She looked up, talking directly to Natalie, "His other children have been through so much. I couldn't bring myself to subject them to any more dysfunction. I try so hard." She looked down at the floor again and wiped at the tears that fell.

How could Natalie judge her? She, too, had endured the philandering ways of a man even though there were no children involved. She realized that she, too, had been duped by Cupid, his arrow piercing her soul and blinding her to any concept of self-respect. She loved Anderson, despite the many times she had caught him with other women. She couldn't explain it either. But it felt good to know that she wasn't the only one. Misery certainly loves company.

"Girl, and get this. Earl and I were at dinner one night. One of the many women he had been with followed us and brought her newborn child. She sat down at the table and told him she was leaving the child with him. I guess even though she had proven paternity, he refused to provide financial support."

Natalie sat dumbfounded by what she was hearing.

"The girl just looked at me. She had the nerve to turn her nose up at me. Like I was the one in the wrong. Can you believe that? To make a long story short, the girl left this child at the table with us. Earl said nothing. Natalie, he said absolutely nothing. He didn't try to explain. He didn't try to refute what she was saying. He sat there and said nothing." Amanda had anger in her voice. Her words were callous and forceful, but Natalie doubted she spoke to Earl Walters in that same manner.

"What did you say?" Natalie asked, leaning forward, obviously interested in the conversation.

"What could I say? She set the papers in front of us proving that Earl was the father. But I was in shock. I knew that he was having sex with other women, but I figured he'd be smart enough to use protection." Speaking to herself, she added, "But why would I think he'd be smart about it?"

Amanda walked to the sink and ran the cold water, wet a paper towel, and wiped at her eyes. They had become swollen and red.

"And so where is the baby now?" Natalie asked, her question a whisper. There were other patrons in the room by now.

Amanda waited for the women to leave and then she continued, "With us. Yeah, you ask how could I? But how could I not? I couldn't send away a child that was a part of my husband. A child that was the same blood as my very own child. There are so many kids out there today that don't know that they have brothers and sisters. So many kids probably dating their very own brothers and sisters." They both snickered, the mood being lifted momentarily.

"Don't be upset with me," Natalie began, "but what is it about him that attracted you?"

Amanda smiled. Natalie could tell that she was remembering the good old days. "There was a time when he was charming and charismatic. He showered me with gifts and attention. He wined and dined me. Girl, he was the perfect gentleman. I knew there wasn't anything he wouldn't do for me." The smile continued. "He ignored the other women and he spent all his time with me. And then there was the sex." She laughed. "He laid it on me, big time."

"Girl, that's how they get us, huh?" Natalie asked laughing.

"Girl, and then he had me. He knew it and I was caught. We didn't go out anymore and his time was spent elsewhere. The only thing that he doesn't do is hit me. He has never hit me." Sitting back down, she continued, "And there are still gifts. He tries to continue to buy my love. But he really knows that I won't break up the family. He knows that I have a soft spot in my heart for family, it's so important to me. I'm a product of divorce, so I know how devastating it can be." Her eyes began to tear up again. "He's a dog. I know he's a dirty dog. But I can't leave him." She put her head down in shame.

Natalie stared at Amanda, now with a better understanding of her new friend. It was a predicament many had been in and a dilemma that most didn't know how to escape from. They both pulled themselves together and decided that it was time to return.

"Amanda, if you need *anything* or someone to talk to, call me. I'm here. I know what you're going through." Natalie grabbed her hand and squeezed it. Amanda smiled and pulled Natalie to her. She hugged her, showing her gratitude for nothing more than being there to hear her troubles.

Upon their return to the table, they found their seats occupied by two of the three females Natalie had questioned Amanda about earlier. Natalie looked at Anderson as if to ask, "What the hell is going on?" His ability to look her in the eyes proved that his conscious remained intact; however, his inability to make good decisions was still evident. The two women slithered away from the table looking over their shoulders to see who, if anyone, was watching their departure. Giggles followed them.

"What took you two so long?" Earl slurred. His uncouthness was exaggerated by his intoxication. He barked an obnoxious laugh that not only startled the guests sitting at his table, but also annoyed the patrons occupying adjacent tables in the restaurant.

"I saw someone I knew. We stopped at their table to talk." Natalie lied, knowing that it would save Amanda from the callousness that was her insolent husband.

"How much did you two have to drink? We weren't gone that long." Natalie inquired, directing her questions to Anderson. Natalie's face was distorted with a look that expressed her total inability to understand the situation at hand. She surveyed the condition of the table and the two men. Her glare remained on Anderson. She hoped he wasn't as intoxicated as Earl looked. She recognized on the table the two carafes that were, before they left, full of wine. Amanda sat down next to her husband as if the situation were acceptable. But Natalie knew things between her and her mate were far from copasetic.

"You were gone long enough. What were you two doing in there? We had a couple of drinks and Earl knew those girls." He motioned behind them. "They came over to say hi. Do you want something to drink?" He was nervous.

"No, I don't want anything to drink. I'm ready to go." She looked over at Amanda. "Amanda, are you ready to go home?"

Earl piped in, "Amanda ain't driving! Anderson, check your woman! She ain't running this show!"

Anderson placed his hand on Natalie's knee under the table. The anger that was boiling up in her chest waiting to spew from her lips fizzled out and settled back down into her stomach. "That's okay, Earl-man. Me and Natalie, we'll take a cab home. I'll holler at you tomorrow."

Anderson pushed himself away from the table, helped Natalie up, and assisted her with her jacket. She shot Earl a look that would have burned a hole straight through him, scalding him from the inside out. She glanced over at Amanda, who appeared worn. Natalie wanted to grab her, hug her, and assure her that everything would be all right. But would it be?

"Call me tomorrow, Amanda." Natalie scribbled down the number to the hotel they had been staying in on a napkin and handed it to her. "Maybe we can go shopping or get some lunch."

Earl grunted and sucked his teeth at their future plans.

The two walked away from the table with the sound of Earl's inebriated voice disrupting the calm of the restaurant to their backs. As the couple continued their departure, Natalie looked back over her shoulder to take one last look at Amanda. Her thin, pale face appeared frustrated and haggard. It was evident that she was tired—tired of fighting, tired of listening, tired of Earl Walters. Natalie became overcome with sympathy and stopped in her tracks. Anderson grabbed her by the hand to pull her toward the outside door. She snatched her hand away, still upset with his performance tonight. And to add insult to injury, she heard, "Bye, Andy!" The girl from the table behind them purred a seductive adieu. She spun around on her heels to get a good look at the woman speaking to her future husband, but only got a glimpse of her Clairol-dyed black hair sliding into the backseat of a yellow cab. Natalie and Anderson sat in silence on the ride back to the hotel. Natalie and Amanda became good friends. Was it because they had many things in common or was it because the only thing they had in common was that they continued to love men who were constantly cheating on them?

CHAPTER TWELVE
SUNDAY MORNING

The doorbell rang at eight o'clock in the morning. "Who the hell?" Anderson grumbled. The sun shone brightly through the window, causing the room to be abnormally hot for this time of the year. Anderson pushed the comforter off of his sweaty body as he rolled over, rubbing the sleep from his eyes. He strained to see the clock.

The doorbell rang again. He reached behind him in an attempt to awaken his wife so that she could answer the door. Anderson wondered if it was Andrea again. Natalie wasn't there. He should have known. She hardly ever slept in anymore. Seven o'clock and she was up, doing whatever she thought needed to be done around the house. "Something always needs to be done," she would tell Anderson. If something always needed to be done, why didn't he ever see it? Sometimes it seemed to him that she made things up to do, so she could complain how tired she was and that he wasn't doing enough around the house.

In Anderson's groggy attempt to make sense of the scene, or the lack of characters in it, he heard tiny footsteps running down the hall and squeals of joy Natalie was trying to keep her hold on them so that she could get them dressed.

"I am not playing with you two. Get back here this instant!" Natalie's threats were so prim and proper. How could she expect anyone to take her seriously?

The doorbell rang again. He laid his aching head back down on the goose feather pillow. He still wasn't acclimated to the early rising that accompanied having small children. It had been two years, but his attempts to adjust to their schedules frustrated him. Old habits died hard. But he wouldn't trade what he had now for the world. Once his head hit the pillow and he had located a comfortable position under the blankets, he was instantaneously rushed by two re-energized toddlers.

"Damn it! Anderson, can't you get the door?"

"Damn it! Damn it! Damn it!" Kayla repeated the expletive over and over. She heard Anderson giggle and attempt to hush his daughter. "Shhhhh-hhhhhhhhhhh!"

"Don't laugh, correct her. Tell her what she said was bad. And answer the door! It's Monica, here to pick up the twins. Are you going to church with me? You need to start getting ready!"

"Uuuuggggg!" was Anderson's answer to all the questions spewed at him.

Natalie heard the three wrestling around on her California king-size bed. She knew would have to answer the door. She ran down the stairs, punched in the alarm code, unhooked the chain lock, turned the deadbolt, and opened the door. The house was as secure as Fort Knox.

"I didn't think anyone was home. Good mornin', darlin'!" Monica was such an old soul, but it fit her. Her smile warmed Natalie from the early morning chill. Even though it was sunny outside, the air was as brisk as if it were an early winter morning.

Monica's Virginian drawl comforted Natalie's overworked nerves. She was the epitome of a southern belle, from her well-coifed hair, which was immaculately done every Tuesday of every week of every month of every year, to her perfectly put together attire. She looked as if she were the one dressed to attend Sunday morning service, instead of baby-sitting two semi-well toddlers. Natalie felt better by seeing Monica's face.

Monica made her way through the archway of the front door and turned to hug Natalie. Recognizing that Natalie was experiencing a family over-load early this morning, she gave her a little extra squeeze. She could feel Natalie's body relax and Natalie could feel the tension ooze from her body right through the soles of her feet. She backed away from the edge she had been so close to and it wasn't even nine o'clock in the morning. You would think she would be used to the whole experience. But every day brought new things, new events, new occurrences, new episodes she never in her wildest dreams thought she would be able to handle. She wished Dreama had told her that with marriage and children came experiences so different than what she was accustomed to. But what did she expect? Dreama wasn't a typical mother. Natalie doubted seriously Dreama had changed much after she had had her children. Things came so easy to her. At times Natalie wished she had a mother who was more motherly, more sympathetic, more of what Dreama was not. She hadn't a clue what to expect when she woke up each morning and no history to resort back to for help. She was basically out here on her own.

"Well, is everyone ready?" Monica asked calling out to the children whose footsteps she heard running from one upstairs bedroom to the other.

Natalie sat down on the bottom step and blew at the loose hairs that dangled in her face. Her two children bound down the steps and landed in the arms of their grandmother.

"Let's go!" Monica encouraged the two toddlers. "Is this everything?" she asked Natalie as she bent to retrieve the bags at the door. "Give Momma a kiss goodbye and let's go!" Monica's voice was cheerful.

The two smothered Natalie with wet kisses. They all laughed and away they went.

Once at church Natalie stood in the first row of the choir box. She hummed to herself, swaying back and forth to the instrumental music being piped into the sanctuary. She was oblivious to anyone else standing beside her. Her attention remained on the front door of the chapel as she returned greetings of "good morning" or 'blessings unto you" to those who squeezed by her trying to get to their seats in the choir box. She nervously ran her hands up and down the sides of her lightweight jersey gray dress. The softness of the material helped to ease the tension remaining from the early morning's activities. She studied how all the couples filed into the sanctuary together—

the men and women in their Sunday best. How the men helped their women remove their coats. How the mothers settled their children down for the service. She missed her own children. Her heart ached at their absence. You would think that they had been apart longer than a couple of hours, but she had been obsessed with them since they were born. Any time away from them seemed an eternity to her, and upon their return, up like newly struck matches.

"Excuse me, baby!" It was more of a command than an apology for her violation. Sister Hill bumped Natalie in an attempt to squeeze her size forty-four hips through the narrow pathway and on to her seat in the choir box. Natalie barely maintained her footing from her jolt back to the present. She smiled at the good Sister to hide her annoyance. Her gaze remained on the front door. She was waiting to see Leslie, who promised that she would be at church this morning.

Natalie glared down at Sister Hill who was slumped over digging in her gray, faux leather bag. Her worn, jet-black stockings bagged at her ankles and slid down into her Shop-n-Save black patent leather shoes. Her legs were spread open and her right knee laid heavy against Natalie's thigh, who was now seated. She wanted so desperately to push the heavy log off, but she knew that she would be unable to move it and it would fall back into its original position anyway. She hoped the good Sister found what she was looking for quick, fast and in a hurry. Natalie was thankful that there was a two and a half foot wall in front of the choir. She knew the men and women in the front row would be thankful for that wall as well. They would have gotten an eyeful of something that they may not have been ready for this early in the morning.

Sister Hill's perfume stung Natalie's eyes and irritated her nose. She wondered why the pungent stench didn't bother the good Sister, or anyone else in the choir. The bag revealed the good sister's true age. It was truly reminiscent of the '70s. Her hunt caused the bag's contents to spill over onto the floor. "Got it!" She found the golden prize. Her hymnal was lying among the wrinkled papers, tubes of lipstick, pens, used checkbook carbons, Camel filter cigarettes and a black hair pick. She smiled a toothy grin, exposing her tobacco- and lipstick-stained teeth. It was the same thing every week. Sister Hill was always late. She disrupted the choir with her search, week in and week out, for the same hymn book.

Sister Hill had been warned that if her behavior wasn't corrected she would be relieved of her duties as a choir member. But no one had the nerve, nor the heart, to let her go. They felt sorry for her. She was alone. Her husband had passed away, rather had been murdered when someone broke into their home. And from what Dreama could remember, Sister Hill was sexually assaulted during the robbery. It all happened about two years ago and something snapped in her. Dreama told Natalie that at one point in time she was so together. "Not as together as myself of course, but who is?" Dreama would add to the story. Natalie had a difficult time trying to place her, before the incident. The Sister Hill of today was the only one Natalie was able to remember.

Sister Jones, the choir director, threatened the good Sister with dismissal from the choir, but her threats went unheeded. She always said she tried to get to church on time, but she confessed that no matter how early she left her home she was still late. The rumor was that she went back to her house five times to make sure no one had entered the house and that it was secure. She had an obsessive-compulsive disorder. Sister Hill had one of the most beautiful and melodic voices that Natalie had ever heard. If it wasn't for that voice, she would have been history a long time ago.

Natalie couldn't complain much about the good Sister's tardiness. After all, Leslie was always late, too. And all of sudden, there she was, Leslie Ann West. Natalie could see the plumage of her burgundy-colored hat over all the other people that waited in line to get into the sanctuary. The hat and the matching outfit. She was so much more like Dreama than Natalie could ever dream to be. It was like the sea parted and Leslie made her entrance. And on her arm…Anderson Kelley. He came. He actually came! Whenever Natalie felt he wasn't in her corner, he surprised her with an act of selflessness. The usher escorted Leslie and Anderson to their seats next to Dreama. Every week Dreama sat in the same spot. She could see everything. She had a bird's eye view of the pastor and his wife, and whatever else was happening in the congregation. She could see the husband and wife having the disagreement. She could see the teenagers flirting with each other. She could see it all. But what kept her attention was the beautiful voice of her beautiful daughter who led the choir. Dreama was so proud of Natalie. But that was something that Natalie would never know.

With the nod from the choir director, Natalie stood and made her way to the microphone in the middle of the stage. She positioned herself and the microphone just so. She turned her head to clear her voice, covering her mouth with her right hand, and then winked at the other choir members behind her, putting them on notice that it was time to give thanks. Natalie closed her eyes and opened her mouth and the words floated out as smoothly as water flowing down a rock-free stream. She heard the good Sister behind her providing her the harmony and she felt free, safe. The words of the song wrapped around her like a cashmere blanket and engulfed her with every note. With every word she thanked God for all His blessings. She expressed her gratitude to Him for who He was, not for what He gave her. She prayed that He heard her pleas. She sang! Every now and then, she would open her eyes to see the congregation taking part in her praise. Her praise became theirs. It brought tears to her eyes to see others rejoicing in her tribute. As the tears flowed down her face and stained her maroon choir gown, she broke it down. She lost herself in the moment and at that point it was only her and her Master. She was standing at the foot of the altar asking for forgiveness for all she had done in the past. It seemed as if an eternity had passed and finally the music began to crescendo, which was her cue to reel it all back in. She opened her eyes and glanced around the sanctuary. She wondered if she looked as spent as she felt. Most Sundays she was only able to sing one solo with the choir backing her up. She would then have to take a spot with the rest of the group and sing with them. She would put so much of herself into that one song that she would have to leave the choir box and go to another room to regroup. Even though she was close to exhaustion, she let out one more note that caused the hairs on her arms to stand up and take notice. The pain and doubt she felt in her personal life flowed from the depths of her soul and escaped through her mouth, filling the air. She prayed that God would take her troubles and banish them to wherever old problems were deposited.

The plumage from Leslie's hat caught Natalie's eye. Everyone else around her was on their feet taking part in the praise session. The congregation was on its feet jumping up and down, shouting, clapping and singing. The song ended, but the music continued to provide the background noise for the Reverend.

"I feeeeeeeela spirit in the room this morning!" Pastor Jackson shouted from the pulpit. His excitement was contagious and spread to the members of the congregation. The shouting went to another level. Natalie had to sit down. She felt lightheaded and thought back to the morning when everyone else ate the breakfast she prepared, but she passed due to lack of time. She was disappointed in her time management skills. And thus many times when she needed the energy a good meal would give her, she had to do without. This morning was one of those times. She was happy when the good Sister tapped her on the shoulder. She bent down and proceeded to rummage through her briefcase a second time. She sat back up and produced a strawberry breakfast bar, handing it to Natalie knowingly. "The Lord is good!"

"All the time!" the congregation agreed in unison. Natalie concurred, especially now that she had something to put in her empty belly. And it was especially great that the breakfast bar was wrapped in its original packaging. She wasn't sure she trusted anything that would come out of the good Sister's bag if it wasn't wrapped up. Natalie nodded a sincere thank you to the good Sister and sat back to enjoy her belated breakfast.

The pastor continued to preach, "God said that He would, 'never leave us nor forsake us' and that He would be with us 'always even unto the end.' How can we feel as though God has abandoned us, when He has made that declaration to us? How can we doubt His word? When we are feeling discouraged and depressed, I know we think, we believe that God has forsaken us, Elijah thought it, but God proved him wrong! Can I get an Amen?"

"Amen!"

"I didn't hear you! Can I get an Amen? Say it like God has brought you out of your trouble!"

"Amen!"

"Hallelujah!"

"God is good!"

The church rumbled with the spirit. The band played and the choir praised His name. No one ever doubted Pastor Jackson's dedication and belief in what he preached. The words flowed from his lips and blessed the congregation. He was an attractive man, and that made it even easier for the parishoners to follow him. Many would follow him anywhere.

At the conclusion of the service, Natalie filed into the choir room with the rest of the chorus. She sat next to Angela, an acquaintance from high school, whom she had grown closer to after they had graduated. To be honest, Natalie hadn't a clue who Angela was when had she told her that she remembered her from Sheridan Heights High. Yet Angela told her that they spoke often and, in fact, that they had hung out together at one of the many high school house parties she attended. Natalie attributed the lack of memory to aging and lack of sleep due to her overactive children. That breakfast bar helped only momentarily. She needed real sustenance, something with some meat in it.

"Natalie, are you able to sing with us tomorrow?" Sister Jones' inquiry caught her off guard. Her thick, New York accent took Natalie back to her college days.

CHAPTER THIRTEEN

"Nat, girl, you are wearing that suit!" Natalie heard Kya Sanchez's East Coast accent bellow at her from across Jamison Avenue, the main drag at the university. Kya was a sophomore from Brooklyn, New York, and one of Natalie's suite mates in Madison Hall, also affectionately known as The Zoo. The dorm housed the freshman girls. And that's how they acted, like they were animals that needed to be caged. It was a self-fulfilling prophecy. It wasn't unusual to see males leaving the quarters at all hours of the night. Girls hung from the windows overlooking the quad, howling at the good looking guys walking to and from the gymnasium adjacent to the dorm. The whole scene proved the myth to be true, that girls go buck wild when they get away from home for the first time. Natalie was proud that she didn't fall into that category. Her heart belonged to Anderson and she wasn't doing anything to ruin it, despite his many slip-ups. The memories of Natalie and Kya's first meeting rushed back to her as if it were yesterday.

The doors opened to the third floor of Madison Hall and Natalie saw one of the most beautiful females she had ever laid eyes. The girl's caramel-colored skin was so clear and so smooth. Her jet-black hair cascaded down her back and stopped right below her shoulder blades. The front was flipped a la Farrah Fawcett. With each gesture she made, her hair moved seductively, as if it had a mind of its own. Her black backless leotard stretched evenly and smoothly over her taut, perky breasts. Her jeans were bleached and torn in the exactly the right spots, giving her that rugged hip-hop look that was so fashionable at the time. The matching belt and biker boots made her look raw *and* sexy. Kya Sanchez was standing at the pay phone spewing curse words at the individual on the other end as if they owed her money.

"You know what? Forget it! I'm tired of your bullshit!"

While she listened, she propped her hand on her hip and poked out her lips.

"Oh, you think I need you? Kiss my ass!"

She listened again, attitude all over her face. Staring at her fingernails, she gasped in astonishment and then slammed the receiver down. The loud noise caused Natalie to jump and drop her suitcase. But not before she found room 316.

Natalie had listened, infatuated by the feminine looking brut who had the spirit to use such strong words and the gumption to give someone what they deserved. The gestures Kya made with her head, her hands, her arms and her hips illustrated her point even more. Too bad the person on the receiving end couldn't see it.

Natalie's thoughts rushed forward to the news report almost four years ago that flowed so effortlessly from Cathy Haskell, the Channel 3 news anchor's lips. Tears formed in her eyes and trickled down her cheeks, staining her white cotton shirt with black mascara. It was obvious that Cathy rehearsed reporting with no feeling and her poker face was emblazoned in Natalie's memory. She cursed the reporter and hoped for that split second that she was fired from her job. It was common knowledge around the city, based on accounts from Dreama, that she was sleeping with one of the assistant football coaches. A man who was supposed to be happily married to his wife of twenty-two years.

"That bitch!" Natalie knew it wasn't Cathy's fault for what happened to Kya, but this time the messenger was shot with wishes of despair and gloom.

Natalie remembered the events of that day as if they had recently happened. She was standing in the kitchen over the sink peeling potatoes for the evening's dinner when she heard, "Dancer found dead in the suburban mansion she shared with football star."

Normally Natalie paid little attention to news reports. The news was so depressing. It was a blast of reality, when reality was something that Natalie so desperately wanted to retreat from. But she recognized the name, something St. James. *Roger St. James. Who is he? Why do I remember that name?* And like a bolt of lightening, Kya's face flashed in front of her eyes. She heard herself scream, "Kya!" She wasn't sure if it was as a result of the pain from the deep gash she had just slipped and cut into her left hand or from the news that her best friend from college had been brutally murdered by a man who claimed he loved her. Slowly she backed away from the sink, holding her hand as the blood squirted on the wall, the curtains, everywhere. She grabbed the first towel she saw from off the counter and wrapped it around her injured appendage. She continued walking until her back slammed against the refrigerator. She slid to the floor, sobbing so uncontrollably that every muscle in her body ached. She scanned the wall where the cordless phone rested usually, but it wasn't there, of course not. She knew this all had to be a mistake. She had to remember Kya's phone number so that she could clear this all up and prove that it was all a mistake. But for some reason the number wouldn't come to her. Any other time, she dialed Kya so effortlessly. The 10 digits would come to her as if she called them daily. But there were times when weeks, months even would pass before they talked to each other. And then, just like that, the phone would ring and it was Kya, and they would pick up right where they left off.

Natalie discarded the saturated towel, throwing it down on the floor beside her. Feeling weak and a bit dizzy, she let her hand fall to her side in a pool of blood. She was oblivious to the pain or to the wetness of the liquid that soaked her shirt and then her shorts. The kitchen was no longer shades of tan and gray, but was splashed with accents of bright red.

"What did you say, Natalie?" Anderson asked, entering the kitchen.

Behind him was Dreama. Both entered the room startled by the sight of the blood-streaked kitchen. They stared down at Natalie, who was now on her hands and knees. "Natalie, what's wrong with you girl? Oh my, child, you're bleeding! Get up! Anderson, get her up!" Dreama demanded.

Natalie saw her mother's lips moving, but the words were on mute. Her ability to comprehend the scene was inhibited due to her search for the telephone and, of course, her loss of blood. She had to call someone to get more information about what she had heard. All Natalie could think about was choking the life out of *that* Cathy Haskell. How dare that wench send out a message that absurd about her friend? Natalie knew she would have Darcy, Kya's ghetto fabulous sister, to back her up when she heard this story. Darcy had mopped the floor with plenty of girls in her day and even though she was pushing thirty-five, she wouldn't hesitate to set a bitch straight.

"I can call Darcy. She'll know what the hell is going on here. Damn, what's her number? Why can't I remember anyone's number? Anderson, get my phone book!" Natalie muttered, startled by the sound of her own voice. It seemed as if it had been years since she had heard it herself. She felt as if she were living in a dream, floating through everything she did, everything she said.

As Natalie continued to search the room hunting for the phone, it came to her why Dreama was in her home, why she was in costume. Natalie had extended an invitation to Dreama and Mitchell for dinner before the annual Memorial Day Costume Ball at the country club. Even though Natalie and Anderson weren't attending this year due to previously scheduled plans, or at least that's what she told her mother, in order to see what costume Dreama had come up with this year, they had invited her to a pre-ball meal. Dreama had chosen to be Marilyn Monroe. She thought of herself as one of the sexiest older women she knew, even of women she didn't know. And she was vain enough to pull it off.

Natalie continued her search and crawled around on the floor desperately looking for the phone, leaving steaks of blood in her wake.

"Nat, get up, baby!" Anderson's lips were moving, but his words still needed subtitles, the mute button was on again. Anderson reached out his hand to help her up but Natalie slapped it away leaving his hand wet with the blood from her wound. The only help she needed from him was his assistance in finding the telephone. How hard could it be to see that she wanted to make a phone call? She cried, "I gotta find the phone." She knew it had to have been a sick joke played on her by some anonymous group. She knew for sure was that Kya had to be alive. Anderson looked at his wife with horror in his eyes. He was frozen, unable to move. He knew she needed medical attention, but he always went into shock mode at the sight of blood. He was always so in control. He attempted to control every situation in the Kelley house, and this one was so far out of his realm of understanding that controlling it was impossible. He wasn't handling the situation well and that hurt Natalie. But she wasn't in control either. They both were at the mercy of Roger St. James.

Dreama came back into the kitchen with the cordless phone in her hand. But instead of handing it to Natalie, she placed it back into its cradle on the wall. She knew what her daughter needed and it wasn't the use of a telecommunications device—it was an ambulance. Ever since Natalie was a child, she was a bleeder. She had been close to death once before due to a cut on her leg from a bicycle riding accident and Dreama wasn't going to let anything like that happen again. Almost instantly, the siren from an ambulance filled the silent air of Natalie's world. She could finally hear again. The mute button was deactivated. The lack of blood flowing through her veins caused her to become lethargic and listless. She convinced herself that a brief break from her excursion was acceptable and she rested her head on the kitchen floor. The cool ceramic tile soothed her already chilled body. A blue blur moved toward her and stopped. The toes of the blue shoes rested at her freshly manicured fingernails. She began drumming her nails on the floor in front of her. The movement made a splash in the puddle of blood. Was it a nervous reaction to the entire scene or was she really bored by her languid state? She couldn't decipher her moods and continued to move her fingernails around in the puddle of blood.

"How long has she been like this? What happened to her?" the unfamiliar male voice questioned whoever was in the room with her. He placed a large black bag down on the floor to the right of his big shoes. Natalie read the name on the tag: Jones.

He hollered behind him in the direction of the front door. "Joe, bring in the gurney!" He turned back. "Is she allergic to any medications?" He bent down to begin his examination. Why was she only hearing his voice? Where was the response? In her inability to provide the answers, she needed someone to be her voice. She had neither the strength nor the inclination to talk to anyone at this point, anyone other than Kya. Normally she would be the one depended on in an emergency situation. She would be the one responding to the barrage of questions. How come no one else was ever up to the job? She felt slighted. The stranger's hands moved toward her.

"Ma'am, can you get up?" The paramedic slid his hand underneath Natalie's arm in an attempt to lift her up off the floor. As she was rising to her feet, she immediately felt the effects of all the blood loss causing her to feel faint. The room went black.

Natalie awoke to the suffocating aroma of flowers. The air in the room remained stagnant and the heavy aroma from the flowers created a fog in the small space. Luckily she wasn't allergic to the blossoming buds, as they were everywhere. The sun shone through the vertical blinds, throwing the shadow of the large rose, tulip and African violet arrangement onto the opposite wall. It was a beautiful sight, however, the large collection of flora made her wonder if she was alive. She needed affirmation of still being among the living. She looked around to see Anderson sleeping in the only lounge chair on the opposite side of the room. "Anderson! Anderson!" She was hooked up to so many wires and contraptions that she was confined to limited movement.

Anderson jumped at his wife's voice. His smile was so sincere. It was obvious he was happy to see her. She was now alert and responding to outside stimuli. Much different from a couple of hours ago, or was it days? But she now had her confirmation that she was still alive.

"I'm sorry. I didn't mean to startle you. Where am I? What happened?"

"You don't remember anything?"

"Not really. Why do I remember seeing Marilyn Monroe standing over me? And I remember our kitchen being red. But mostly everything is a blur. I feel so weak."

"Nat, babe. You scared us. You cut your hand real bad and you were bleeding so badly that the doctors were having trouble stopping it. We all had to give blood. It's a good thing you aren't a hard blood type to match. Babe, I'm glad you're okay though. I've got some good news." Natalie looked down at the bandage that covered her left hand. She wiggled her fingers, only to receive a throbbing pain that shot from her hand straight to the front of her forehead.

The brightest smile spread across Anderson's face. He sat there, frozen in the same spot, for what seemed like twenty minutes with that same silly grin on his face. The smile went from endearing to goofy.

"Well, what is it, Anderson? Spit it out."

"We're going to have a baby…well, two babies."

"What?"

"You're pregnant! With twins!"

She sat in silence.

"Nat, aren't you happy? What's wrong? This is a good thing!"

It seemed that another 20 minutes elapsed before Natalie could speak. She sat in shock. Should she be hearing this news now—in her condition?

"Anderson, are we ready to have children? We just moved into the house. Our finances aren't where they should be. You're trying to start your business. I don't have a job. I can think of so many reasons why we shouldn't have a baby right now. *And* quite frankly, I'm not sure that you can be faithful."

There it was. That was the number one reason. Everything else was secondary. But his inability to prove his fidelity was what would destroy any thoughts of a great future together.

Anderson sat still. His smiled wilted.

Natalie continued, oblivious to his change, "And it won't just be one—two, *two* babies. Anderson, come on, what are we going to do?" Natalie looked over at her new husband in disbelief. She couldn't believe that they were in this situation. She tried to be so careful when it came to not getting pregnant.

"Natalie, we've been through all of the counseling. We'll be fine. Everything will be fine, I promise."

She believed him before. Why was she having such a difficult time believing him this time? Because this time it wasn't just the two of them. She looked at him and allowed him to continue with his dialogue.

"Why can't you be happy? Instead of letting things simply happen, you always overanalyze, over think everything. Just go with the flow. Things will work themselves out." He reached out for her hand and held it. "We both have so much family that would help if we needed them. Let me be the man and take care of my wife and my children. I promise everything will be fine. Trust me."

They looked at each other. Neither of them knew how to continue the conversation. Anderson had a point, but Natalie had one as well.

The door to Natalie's room swung open, allowing the clamor from the hallway into the quiet room. They both turned toward the door, the looks on their faces remaining the same.

"If someone delivers another flower arrangement, I'm going to scream!" Natalie complained.

Trisha, the nurse who was assigned to Natalie, popped her head into the room, blurting out, "Oh, I'm sorry sweetie, I'll come back later. No, no more flower deliveries." She smiled, winked, and closed the door behind her.

It had been two long days since Natalie was admitted into the hospital. She was once again scolded by Dr. Richardson about the seriousness of her illness. She had a blood platelet defect. He told her she had better take better care of herself, congratulated her on her great news, and insisted she needed a couple of more days in the hospital.

Everything was happening way too fast. She couldn't deal with it all. She wanted to sleep. She was tired of all the nurses coming into her room congratulating her on the news of her pregnancy. She felt guilty for carrying life around in her when her friend's life was cut short. She wanted to forget about everything. Nothing anyone said comforted her. And she turned away visits from Dreama, Monica, her daddy, Leslie, even her husband.

Anderson's inability to understand caused him to turn to Dr. Samuels, the hospital psychologist. She tried to explain his wife's dilemma, her battle with depression and what it was that he could do to deal with her while she was going through it.

One day while Natalie was sleeping, Anderson met the doctor after wandering into the hospital cafeteria to grab something to drink. He found it difficult to eat in hospitals, his stomach always got so queasy. He sat at a table overlooking the hospital gardens, cradled his head with his hands and rubbed his freshly shaven head.

"Good afternoon. It's *so* beautiful out there, isn't it? Sometimes I like to come here to think."

The voice was calming, but made Anderson feel uneasy. He lifted his head, smiled at the stranger, and took a sip of his soda.

"Oh, I'm sorry, I'm Doctor Samuels. I'm the resident psychologist. Seems we have a celebrity among us. You play basketball?"

"Yeah, I play for now." Anderson's voice trailed off. "Look doc, my wife is here in the hospital and I am sure she wouldn't appreciate this…"

"Oh, I apologize. Maybe I started the conversation off wrong. I was in the E.R. when your wife was admitted. I know the whole story. Congratulations! I hear you're going to be a father. It's going to be a great time. Cherish every minute."

"My fault, doc. Just trying to prevent any problems. Do you have children? Excuse my rudeness. Please have a seat." He pushed the chair out from under the table with his foot.

"I have one, a boy. He's great! Sometimes a little too active for his ol' mom, but I couldn't imagine life without him."

"Thanks, doc. I wish my wife, Natalie, would be as excited about this whole thing. She doesn't seem like she wants the babies. I don't understand. She pushes me away when I try to explain to her that everything will be fine. She criticizes me when I don't do anything," he said, sighing. "You don't know how hard it is for me to come here every day…" He lowered his head. "I don't know what to expect from one day to the next."

"Please, call me Patsy. If you think it's bad now, wait for a couple of months into her pregnancy. My husband thought I was possessed with the spawn of Satan." She laughed at her own joke.

Anderson's mood wouldn't allow laughter to cross his lips. "I bet there were times when he wished he could have that one night back."

This time they both laughed.

"You know, a lot of what is going on with Natalie, her so-called 'instability' is her dealing with the loss of her good friend, but then there is the hormonal imbalance associated with her pregnancy. It's something men throughout time have had to deal with. You won't be the first and you certainly won't be the last. You can handle it. I bet there was at least one time in your relationship that you told Natalie that you would do anything for her. Am I right?"

Anderson rolled his eyes up in his head searching for the answer. "Yeah, I guess I have."

"Well, you're being called on it now, buddy."

Doctor Samuels rose from her chair. She searched the pockets of her royal blue suit jacket and produced a business card. "Anderson, if you or Natalie ever need someone to talk to, please do not hesitate to call me. Sometimes it helps knowing that someone else has gone through what you are trying to cope with." She patted Anderson on the shoulder and whispered to him, "Be patient with her. You have someone who loves you. I can tell."

She walked away and Anderson felt a little better about the whole situation. The doctor's scent lingered in the air after she left. The fragrance was warm and it relaxed him. It made it a little easier to accept the information he had received. He said a little prayer to God for strength, "Thank you, God, for Natalie and now for our babies. I guess like my mom used to say, 'God doesn't give you more than you can handle,' so if You didn't think we could do this, we wouldn't have this. Please God, get Nat through this. It hurts me to see her down. I do love her no matter what has happened in the past. She's my heart and I would do anything for her. Give me strength, Lord. Oh, and could You work this basketball thing out for me. A brother could use a little money right about now. Amen!"

"Okay, troll! Open these blinds and let some light in. You can't stay in the dark forever." Leslie burst into Natalie's hospital room and started making changes. She carried with her a vase full of tulips and a pizza from Natalie's favorite restaurant. It was a pepperoni, extra cheese, green pepper and mushroom pizza that made everything all right for Natalie when she was a teenager, but now her problems where so much bigger than whether or not Joey Christensen was going to ask her to go with him to the DeBarge concert. It was now issues that impacted more lives than hers.

"Where are you on your way to?" Natalie asked Leslie as she grabbed a slice of the New York style pizza from the box. The cheese stuck to the box and Natalie pulled it away, wrapping the end around her index finger.

"Girl, big date! Huge date! Lawyer from Denver." Leslie was so animated. She checked her teeth for lipstick in the paper towel dispenser. "I can't believe I hadn't met him before a couple of weeks ago. He lives in my building. Girl, two floors up."

"Bad idea, Leslie Ann." The emotion wasn't present. Normally when discussing Leslie's love life, the conversation was so lively and heated. Natalie would present an argument to Leslie so convincing on why she shouldn't date a particular guy that she would at least consider what Natalie had to say. But this time Natalie didn't have it in her. She swallowed the pizza in her mouth and continued, "If things don't work out and he still lives there in your building and you see some other babe going to his apartment… hmmm, what do you think you'll do? Hey, thanks for the pizza, but you could have saved the flowers…," pointing around the room, "it already looks like a freaking' funeral home in here." As soon as she said it, both women knew she regretted it. Today was Kya's funeral.

Dr. Richardson warned Natalie against attending. She was still too weak to leave the hospital and so she mourned in her own way. That morning she had asked the phone operator to hold all her calls and she begged the nurses to hold their conversations with her to only what needed to be said. The television was on, but the sound was on mute and she kept the blinds closed tight. The sun shone bright that day and she was not up to the cheer that came with a bright and sunny afternoon. Many times during the day she pulled the blankets from her bed over her head and cried. She apologized to her unborn children for shaking them up.

"Look, Nat, Kya wouldn't appreciate all this…" She pointed to Natalie and her whole pitiful look. "I know you knew her much better than I did, but I knew her, too. She would tell you, 'Girl, get your ass up and take care of yourself!'" Leslie had the accent down pat. She sat in the chair beside the bed and began going through her new designer bag. "Let me show you this new lipstick. Girl, hot! " She was speaking more to herself than Natalie as she perfectly applied the new lipstick using her compact mirror. She kicked her burgundy stilettos up on the side of the bed and continued, "I may sound unsympathetic, but what good is sitting in this bed moping going to do anybody? You need to concentrate on your health at this point and I am sure Kya would agree. She loved you, Natalie, and she sure as hell would love those kids and would not appreciate you jeopardizing their health for this…"

Natalie's gaze was locked on the emergency helicopter leaving the heliport on the building across from hers. "Leslie, I don't expect you to understand…"

Leslie interrupted, "Oh, I understand all right. You're being selfish. You're only thinking about yourself. Maybe you're not ready to be a mother. You can get mad at me if you want, but you're getting awfully close to being like another mother, whom shall remain nameless." Leslie gave Natalie a knowing look and a slick wink.

"Oh, I can't believe you said that," she said. "Look, maybe if I could have gone to the funeral to say goodbye…"

"Why? Kya ain't there. That is only her body, a shell. You can say goodbye to that girl anywhere. Believe me, if she's out there she *will* hear you. If it will make you feel any better, I will bring one of her pictures tomorrow and you can talk to it. Anyway, when can your ass go home? I'm tired of coming up in this hospital."

"You know, if I didn't know that all the stuff you are saying was true I would…"

"What? So now you're making threats. At least it sounds like you have your heart back. I'm tired of the wimpy Natalie. Show me my best friend." Leslie slugged Natalie in the arm. Natalie hugged her like she hadn't hugged anyone in a long time.

As Leslie was pulling away from Natalie's death grip, the door swung open. "Natalie, turn me loose. When was the last time you bathed?"

"What's going on in here?" Anderson walked in the room with a newspaper under his arm. He pulled the empty chair over beside the bed, sat down, opened the paper, and began to read. "Continue, ladies. What are we talking about?" He flipped through each section and closed the paper after removing the only part that really interested him, the sports page. The expression on his face changed as he perused the articles.

"What, what is it, Andy?" Natalie questioned with concern in her voice, sitting the piece of pizza she couldn't finish back in the box. He wished she wasn't so observant, at least not at this moment.

"Oh, it's nothing. Keep talking," he said, looking at Leslie.

Although she didn't know what was troubling him exactly, she read his queue to change the subject. "Natalie, did I tell you I saw Andrea..."

"Bullshit! What's going on?"

Her tone of voice was his indication that she was serious. "It's an article about Kya and St. James."

"Read it!" she demanded. She closed the pizza box and listened intently as Anderson began reading the story.

Anderson looked over the top of the paper. "You know, Natalie, you may not be up to hearing about this right now. Let's wait until later, okay? Let's talk about something else. So, Leslie, you said you saw Andrea? What's that girl doing now? She's so crazy!" Anderson began folding up the newspaper.

"Anderson, just read the damn newspaper! You know what? Never mind, I'll read." She grabbed for the paper, only to retrieve air.

"I'll read it!" he said, straightening out the crumpled newspaper. He started to read the article. It outlined the gruesome details of how St. James came home following an away football game and strangled the life out of Kya, subsequently cutting off the air supply to their unborn child. As Anderson read the article to his wife, tears flowed down her cheeks, staining the white sheets.

"Nat, you need your rest. We can finish this later."

"No, go on, Andy," she pleaded.

Hesitantly, Anderson continued to read. "Kya Sanchez, 33, was three months' pregnant when she was found strangled to death. Accused of murder is her common-law husband, Roger St. James, a linebacker recently released from the New Orleans Saints." Anderson watched Natalie as he read. He noticed as the article got more and more detailed, she got more and more restless. He rushed through the particulars of Kya's death and slowed down when it came to, "Prosecutors are seeking the death penalty for St. James." It was like he could see the look of revenge wash over his wife's face. It was like she took solace in knowing that this man might die for Kya's murder.

Anderson knew that the women were close, but this was certainly unnatural for Natalie. She had to have been the most forgiving person Anderson knew. He was proof of that.

"See, brothers like him give men a bad name." Leslie talked to the slice of pizza in her hand more so than to Anderson. "I knew he was a sick bastard when I went out with him in a…" Leslie looked up searching for the year, "in a, uh, '94. Girl, he wanted me to do some sick shit. I told his ass he would have to pay me first. And he was *psycho*. He would call me all the time, but I would screen my calls. If I wouldn't answer, he would come over anyway. You remember that pediatrician I was dating? Well girl, he was over one night and St. James came over, girl, trying to show out. I had to call the police to get him to leave. Girl, psych-o! Do you hear me?"

"You mean you were going out with him while Kya was seeing him?" Natalie dabbed at the tears in her eyes and then she blew her nose.

Startled by the question, Leslie jumped to answer, "Natalie, like I said, Kya was *your* friend, not mine. She was cool and all…but girl, all's fair in love and war."

Two months later, it was reported that St. James was convicted of two counts of voluntary manslaughter and was sentenced to twenty-five years to life in the state penitentiary in Texas. He was placed with the general population in the prison. St. James was found murdered in his cell with a sharpened number two pencil lodged in the base of his skull a short time later.

Natalie prayed for the St. James family. She felt sorry that they had to mourn the death of such a foul and perverse man. As far as Natalie was concerned, he got what he deserved. For years he had tortured her good friend, and then when he was disturbed over being released by the team, he killed her. She also said a little prayer for herself, "Please God, forgive my wicked thoughts." Natalie reveled in the fact that it was proven, yet again, that God punishes those who cause harm to His children. He may not have done it directly in Kya's case, but He worked it out anyway.

CHAPTER FOURTEEN
SUNDAY MORNING

Normally Natalie didn't sing with the choir when they visited other churches. She was needed more at home by her husband and children, and besides Angela or the good Sister Hill was up to filling in when she wasn't around.

"Director, sorry I won't be able to sing this time, I have a previous appointment." Natalie thought back to the night before and the phone call from Leslie requesting her presence at Hoop Dreams on Monday evening. It was a waste of time to attempt to figure out why she was needed there, so she conceded to the request. What could be the harm, right?

The choir meeting ended and the members headed toward the door. Natalie pulled the knob, opening the door and pushing her way through, only to be greeted face to face by Pastor Jackson. His hot breath filled her nose. There was something about the pastor she found attractive but she couldn't put her finger on it. He wasn't a very masculine man, which made many believe that he swung the other way. And having a wife and three children was no longer a factor that could be used to prove his sexuality. Natalie found that out the other night with Leslie's "Mr. Right," Curtis Matthews.

She was more apt to believe Leslie's theory as to why she was so attracted to him. She told Natalie that it was the fact that he was supposed to be so powerful. He, after all, was a man of God and he was the head of a fairly large church. For some reason she had always placed men of the cloth on a higher plain, judged them by different standards, when she knew good and well that they were human. That they put their pants on one leg at a time, like everyone else. How many times had she read in the newspaper that some priest had molested a choirboy, or how a certain minister embezzled money from the church? But it was the responsibility that went along with having accepted God into one's life that she revered. How could someone take that vow and misuse the power, the authority that came along with it?

The pastor wrapped his arm around Natalie's waist, cooing, "Beautiful solo, Sister Kelley. Your voice is so angelic. We are blessed to have you as part of our choir."

Natalie squirmed to loosen the grip he had on her. He felt her struggling and tried to distance himself from her. His compliment teetered on being lecherous. Natalie heard rumors about the pastor, that he had a difficult time keeping his hands off some of the woman in the church. Another reason why she questioned the rumors of his sexuality. The stories were so contradictory, that she had a difficult time deciding which was the truth, if any of it. But she chose to ignore the rumors. Oddly enough, Natalie hadn't seen those same woman in a while. She wrote it off as coincidence. "Not Pastor. He couldn't. He wouldn't. Or would he?"

"Thank you, Pastor Jackson. It's easy to sing when you believe in the powers of the Lord as much as I do. Excellent sermon!"

"Brother Smith, have you ever seen such a lovely woman?" He winked at Natalie and continued speaking, moving his eyes from the Brother back to Natalie. "Are you going to sing with the choir this Monday? I like to show off the talents of our church and you sure are one of the most talented." He flashed a wide smile and grabbed her hand. He began to swing it back and forth.

"Sorry, Pastor, previous engagement. Maybe next time." She smiled back. Natalie glanced around the church, searching for Anderson. Her husband's radar kicked in and she saw him across the sanctuary in front of the baptismal. He was watching her. He had to have seen the hug, the wink and his holding her hand. He had warned her about Pastor Jackson. Anderson had told her to stop being so naïve when it came to men, but that man in particular. Just because she was married, it didn't stop men from being attracted to her. Her ring was simply that—a ring, not a shield, not a barrier, just a ring. It wouldn't protect her from anything. It was many a Sunday that he watched Pastor Jackson stare at his wife while she sang. He knew what lust on a man looked like and it was certainly the possibility that this man was lusting after Natalie. In the old days, Anderson would have rectified the situation with a littler persuasive dialogue, but he was taught to respect the church and those who represented it. Still, Pastor Jackson was making it hard for Anderson to keep his cool.

Natalie watched Anderson saunter over to where she and the Pastor were standing. She removed her hand from the pastor's grip. His sweaty hand caused hers to do the same and she wiped her hand on a tissue she found in her pocket.

Reaching out to Anderson, she grabbed his hand when he got to her. "Hey, baby. Are we ready to go? I'm starving. Pastor Jackson, you remember my husband, Anderson Kelley?"

"Oh, yeah, Brother Kelley, how ya' doing? I remember last year you were a strong force on the church basketball team. Can we count on you again this year? We need another trophy to add to the case out there. Can you bring it back for us?"

"Yeah, well, I'll have to check my schedule. Natalie, are you ready, baby?" Anderson leaned over and kissed his wife on her cheek. He glanced up at the Pastor while his lips were still attached to her face.

"Yeah, babe, I have everything. Is Leslie going with us to get something to eat? I'm starved. Have a nice day, Pastor, Brother Smith." Natalie nodded her head at the men.

Anderson grabbed Natalie's bag from off the floor as she grabbed her purse. The Pastor cooed, "You take care, darling. See you next week."

"Come on, babe," she whispered. Natalie smiled politely at the gentlemen and grabbed her husband by the hand. Natalie laughed to herself about Anderson and his paranoia about Pastor Jackson.

She wondered if Anderson's jealousy was any indication of the love he felt for her. Natalie wasn't above playing a little game with her husband to find out where his head and heart were. She knew that it wouldn't be with that man. He had enough scandal associated with his name. And she didn't want to be a part of his drama. She would have to plan her next move carefully.

After a quick drive across town, they entered the restaurant. The crowd spilt out onto the sidewalk. "It'll be about a 25-minute wait," Andre, the maitre d' informed Leslie when she gave him her name. It was obvious that Andre was too busy today to shoot the breeze. He and Leslie were tight, hanging out in the clubs drinking to all hours of the night. He blew her a kiss and continued with his phone conversation. He was taking a reservation.

"Leslie, why didn't you call ahead?" Anderson fussed.

Kimberly's was known for their fried catfish and pork chops. The aroma from the restaurant wafted out onto the street, drawing in people from far and wide. It was intoxicating.

Kimberly Parks was an old friend of Anderson's from way back. They went to junior high together and they were boyfriend and girlfriend until Kimberly decided that she was more attracted to women. She explained to Anderson and Natalie that a woman was more attentive to her needs emotionally, spiritually and, most certainly, physically.

"Come on, kids!" Andre beckoned to Leslie and her party. "We've got a table ready for you. You are looking fabulous, Ms. Leslie." He stared at her hat. "And I'm loving the hat. You are wearing it, Ms. Thing! You'll have to let me sport that. What's up this evening?"

"We'll talk," Leslie said. "I'm feeling a bit antsy." She smiled at Andre, giving him a wink and an air kiss.

"Hi, I'll be your waitress today. My name is Mandy. Can I get you something to drink?"

"Yeah, give me a Martini and can I have three olives? Three black olives, please?" Leslie studied the menu.

"Leslie, you just got out of church and you're drinking already?"

"Shoot, Natalie you're the only one who believes any of that shit that man says. He can recite the scripture, but he sure don't live by it."

"What? Who?" Anderson asked.

"Let's just say he ain't as holy as you all think." She snickered and hid her face behind the menu.

"Leslie Ann, what have you done?" Natalie asked.

She began humming, rolled her eyes up in her head and avoided Natalie's question.

"Does that answer your question?" Anderson asked.

"He's so full of himself. And such a hypocrite. Andy, order a drink, I know you want something to drink. I saw your little confrontation with the Pastor Hypocrite, oops, I mean Pastor Jackson. He's a trip! Girl, if it weren't for Dreama and her theatrics, I would go someplace else. But she makes going to church an event. I thought I was going to scream this morning. Charlotte King is back. She had her baby. Did *you* see it?" Leslie made a face, indicating that the baby wasn't cute.

"Leslie, you are so bad! You haven't had your children yet. You know what can happen!" It was a warning that what goes around comes around.

"Oh, yeah, and I couldn't miss the choir. Girl, you sang your butt off this morning!" She waved at the drink menu. "Go ahead, Andy, order something so I'm not the only one your wife believes is a heathen."

The waitress smiled impatiently while she waited for the rest of the order. She transferred her weight from one foot to the other and blew into the air.

"Oh yeah, can I get an order of cheese sticks, too?"

Anderson looked at Natalie, "Yeah, I'll have a strawberry lemonade."

"You punk!"

"Damn you, Leslie." Anderson retorted. "Don't sentence me to your hell. What are you drinking to forget, anyway?"

"And for you, ma'am?" Mandy rushed Natalie with her order. She blew the hair out of her eyes and nervously hit her order pad with the end of her pencil.

"Make that two lemonades. Thanks. Yeah, Leslie what's wrong with you today?"

"*Today*?" Anderson piped in over his menu.

"Shut the hell up!" Leslie shot back.

The three looked at their menus in silence.

The waitress came back with the drinks. The service at Kimberly's was fast and usually pretty friendly and the view was great. The building overlooked the river. It was especially nice at sunset. The lights shimmered off the water which made for a romantic mood.

Leslie grabbed her glass and took a big gulp. "I've decided to be artificially inseminated. I'm getting older and I'm tired of waiting around for the right man. I figured, I can pay for it and not have to be bothered with some crazy man trying to tell me how to raise it. You know, the kid. I know you have something to say, so go ahead." She spit out all the words, took another long sip and waited for a rebuttal.

"No, I'm not going to say anything. No matter how much of a bad idea I think this is, I'll support you on this one."

"*But*?"

"But what? I said I'll support you. Anderson, what are you having to eat?" She looked down at the menu again.

They both looked astonished. Natalie had never let anything go that quickly, especially anything that had to do with Leslie and her life.

"Well, hell, I'll say it." Anderson piped in. "I think it's a bad idea. I don't think you're ready to become a mother. You are still too self-centered."

"Look who's talking?" Leslie shot back.

"What do you mean?" Anderson questioned.

"*You* don't think about anyone but *yourself*."

He cut his eyes at her and turned his head to look out the window.

"Are you sure, Leslie?" Natalie asked. "Have you thought about this?"

"All I've done is think about *this*. All I've wanted is a husband and babies."

Natalie shook her head. She'd known for a long time about Leslie's urge to have a family. Her efforts were so…misdirected.

"I'm tired of jumping from one relationship to another wondering if the man is the right man and then finding out that he is the absolutely wrong man. There may be no good way to find a husband, but I can have a child alone. There are many women who raise children alone. My clock is ticking so loud, sometimes it wakes me up at night."

Leslie had never looked more sure of herself. Natalie didn't want to break her spirit. She reached across the table and held her hand. Trying to be supportive and encouraging, "If this is what you want. Whatever I can do to help, let me know."

Anderson turned back and sucked his teeth.

"Go to hell, Anderson," Leslie fumed.

"I'll see you there," he threw back.

Natalie wished Leslie's relationship with Phil Hatcher would have worked out better. He would have been the perfect husband and father. He was such a kind and caring man; however, Leslie's personality proved too much for him. Phil owned the company Anderson purchased all of his workout equipment from. When Phil saw Leslie he asked Anderson to introduce him. Anderson was hesitant at first, not sure Leslie was right for him. Eventually he conceded, warning Phil to proceed at his own risk. Anderson hoped that if things between the two ended on a wrong note, that that wouldn't destroy the friendship he and Phil shared.

"Leslie, this is Phil Hatcher." Anderson cautiously made the introduction. He watched Phil's eyes light up when he shook her hand. He was obviously smitten by her beauty. But who wouldn't be?

Leslie flashed her smile and held on tightly while shaking his hand. His hands were soft and warm. They were large and she was impressed by their size. She wondered if they were any indication of the size of other things.

"Hello, it's my pleasure," she purred at Phil.

"Oh, the pleasure is all mine." They were both oblivious to Natalie and Anderson standing there.

It was Leslie who struggled with the difference in color. Her paranoia got the best of her when they were in public, convinced that dirty looks and nasty judgments were coming from everywhere. She had a hard time deciphering his agenda and she didn't know how to read his kindness. He would lavish her with expensive gifts and compliment her when he saw her. But she always felt he wanted something more from her, something more than she had to give. Most times she was defensive, always on guard. But Phil wanted nothing more from her than companionship and a good time.

Although they disagreed often and argued endlessly, there was a distinct connection in the bedroom. He was willing to perform in ways most men of color objected to. It was Phil who taught her tricks she still used to this very day.

Leslie would fight off his advances at first. In her mind, she repeated over and over, "No, Phil! No Phil!," but her body was a willing participant.

They would start in the entryway to her apartment, barely closing the door behind them before the action started. He would pull her skirt down with his teeth, torturing her with his slow and deliberate movements. He made use of her whole space. Her body was like a canvas he would paint on. He found places on her she never would have deemed "her spot."

Her skirt would drop to the floor and he would kiss her knees while making his way up her body using his lips, his tongue. His hands followed her surfaces, dipping and diving. Her sounds drove him to explore more. When her breathing slowed, it was nothing for him to find another spot to rev her back up.

"Leslie," he would whisper in her ear, his hot breath smelling of peppermint. "Leslie," he would say as he kissed down the back of her neck, running his tongue down the center of her spine, kissing the curve of her back. She twisted and turned, trying to release herself from the firm grip he had on her arms. Her inability to move was even more of a turn on for her. She laughed—seductively, sensuously, wickedly—and he placed both of his hands on either side of her face. He positioned his lips over hers and kissed her, long and hot. She felt her knees weaken and her heart rate quicken.

He would unbutton her blouse and let it slide down her arms, adding it to the pile of clothes he was creating on the floor. She used her hands to explore his body. It was her turn next. She led him to her couch, pushing him down while standing in front of him, her chest heaving, trapped in the white lace bra she wore. He reached up, turning her around and releasing what was trapped. Leslie stroked, fondled and rubbed. He groaned, becoming louder and louder the more excited he became. She turned him loose and it was all too much for her. She let go. Uninhibited, they moved around her apartment and took advantage of the entire space. He begged her to give in to him; his movements forceful and erotic. She'd smile, denying him what he wanted more than anything, treasuring the fact that she held the key to his desires.

They were animals. On top of furniture. Down on the floor. On counters. Under tables. And exhausted, they'd finally collapse. It was what kept her coming back. It caused her to fear him. She felt herself wanting to give into his request to be his only. But she was scared of their differences.

And so she created ways to make him dislike her. Leslie thought that if he left her it would be so much easier than she leaving him. They always left, and that's what she expected. She was cruel to him. She disrespected him. Natalie thought he must be a glutton for punishment. That's exactly what he got from Leslie outside of the bedroom—cruel, brutal and malicious punishment. Natalie thought back to one instant in particular.

Leslie's voice was loud and obnoxious, "Phil, I don't give a damn." She had had one too many drinks.

"Let's go, Leslie," he said, grabbing her jacket and her bag, trying to lift her drunken body up from the table. His eyes showed embarrassment, frustration and irritation.

"Get your hands off of me," Leslie mumbled under her breath, her eyes cutting at Phil, death rays boring a hole through him.

Anderson and Natalie sat still. Natalie was disappointed in her best friend. She knew Leslie allowed her fear to cloud her judgment when it came to Phil. And Anderson, he was annoyed. The foursome was out that evening to celebrate the new client Anderson received. The client had recently been drafted and it was up to Anderson to whip him into shape for the upcoming season. Thanks to Leslie, the mood had been destroyed.

Leslie rose from her seat, grabbed her belongings from Phil, and stumbled toward the door of the restaurant. Hastily, she pushed herself through the crowd, knocking a tray of drinks out of the hand of the waitress.

Phil, always the gentleman, knelt to assist with cleaning up the mess. Leslie spun around and accused him of flirting with the wait staff.

"Oh! I see," she said, barely keeping her footing. "I'm not enough for you.

If you wanted someone else, you should have just said so," Leslie's words were slurred. "What does that bitch have that I don't?"

"Leslie, that *is* enough!" Natalie intervened, grabbing her by the arm.

Leslie snatched away. "You are *not* my mother! You get your hands off of me, too!" She began to sway back and forth.

The manager of the restaurant came over to intervene. "Ma'am," she began, "I'm going to have to ask you to leave."

"What?"

Natalie spoke to the manager. "We're leaving. Anderson!" she called over her shoulder. She pushed Leslie out the door and guided her to the car.

Once the night air hit them, Leslie perked up. "Oooh, it's cold out here." She tried, without success, to wrap her jacket around her shoulders. She bellowed, "Hey, Phil, baby, I'm feeling a little frisky. Momma is in the mood." She spun around looking for him, dancing from side to side to the music in her head.

"I am ashamed of you," Natalie said sternly to Leslie.

The smile that was on Leslie's face turned quickly into a frown. Tears formed in her eyes. "I am so sorry." She leaned against the car. "I am so sorry."

"You don't need to apologize to me." Natalie had no mercy.

Leslie looked around for Phil. Still somewhat inebriated, she stumbled toward him. She grabbed his hand, held it to her heart, and blurted out, "I am so sorry." She lifted his head up so that their eyes met, "I am so sorry. There is so much I wish I could tell you, but I don't know how to." She didn't know how to tell him that she was afraid of him. He was such a good person, but she felt that she didn't deserve to be with a good man, even though that's exactly what she wanted. Even though she faked self-confidence, it was something she lacked. And her low self-esteem manifested itself as abuse of those she loved.

"What about Phil?" Natalie asked hesitantly, envisioning her idea of the perfect "sperm donor" for Leslie. She knew he was a sore issue with her.

"Look, Natalie, Phil and I are not compatible."

Anderson dropped in the conversation. "And like you've been compatible with any of the other two hundred men you've been with."

"You know what…?" Leslie started.

"What?" he retorted.

The waitress showed up at the table in the nick of time. "Are you ready to order now?" she asked, pen and pad in hand.

"I'll have the meatloaf," Anderson ordered.

"That sounds good," Natalie chimed in. "Me, too."

"I'll have a salad," Leslie said. "Ranch dressing on the side."

"Very good," Mandy said. She jotted down the orders, smiled, and walked away.

"I'm about sick of you, Anderson!" Leslie said, returning to the subject at hand. "I'd appreciate it if you *and* your wife stopped talking about Phil Hatcher. He's not interested in being my husband or the father of my children, and, quite frankly, I'm not sure I want him to be."

"Whatever!" Anderson threw in the towel.

Leslie finished the rest of her martini and waived for the waitress to bring her another one. The waitress returned to the table with a second round of drinks.

"If you'll excuse me, I'll be back." Natalie took a sip of her lemonade and pushed herself back from the table. She left Anderson and Leslie sitting there in silence. She hoped in her absence they wouldn't kill each other or destroy the restaurant.

Making her way to the ladies room, Natalie thought about Leslie. If her best friend was insistent on having the procedure she spoke of, who was she to tell her not to?

She entered the bathroom and waited in line for an empty stall. Once she had completed her business, she stood at the sink washing her hands. Natalie glanced in the mirror. She recognized a face that seemed so familiar, but she couldn't place it. The woman smiled and exited the room, leaving Natalie alone with her thoughts.

Returning to the table, the restaurant had cleared some. Andre flew by

Natalie, his animated words following him as he berated a young male who was clearing tables. She looked around the room. Kimberly had come a long way, beginning her career as a restaurateur at a much smaller and less attractive site. Taking advantage of her friendship with Kimberly, Natalie used the space often for numerous events. It just so happened to have been the site for the small party she had with her bridesmaids before her wedding.

Rushing to get to Kimberly's to have dinner with the other women in her wedding, Kya and Amanda, Natalie maneuvered her car in and out of traffic with Leslie in the passenger's seat. Her stomach growled as she dug in her bag, searching for something to erase the pain that throbbed in her head. Headaches were more and more frequent as the day of her nuptials grew closer and closer. In her head, she went down the checklist her wedding planner, Charlotte, had created for her.

"You got the flowers, Leslie, right?" Natalie asked as she swerved, barely missing the green Toyota that moved into her lane.

"For the last time, I told you I have them," Leslie shot back. "I hope this is the only time you get married. You are going to drive me crazy. I promise I will not be like this when my time comes." She gripped the side of her seat, nervous by the erratic driving of her friend.

"Okay, flowers. And you have your dress?"

"If you ask me one more question, I'm going to scream and then I'm going to kill you. My list is done."

"You certainly aren't supportive of the bride," Natalie chastised.

"Well, if she wasn't acting like a crazed woman! Everything is fine. Let it marinate." Leslie smiled, leaning back in the seat, taking in the sights.

Natalie turned into the lot and parked. As usual, Kimberly's was packed. Natalie had made reservations ensuring that they would have a table. Kya was already seated at their table. She was the prompt one of the bunch. As Natalie and Leslie took their seats, Kya hung up from the conversation on her cell phone.

"What's up, girl? Just checking in. He's still tripping, ain't nothing changed. What's up, Les?" The accent was so reminiscent of her past. Natalie smiled and waited for Kya to stand up. She wrapped her arms around her and squeezed her tight.

"I have missed you so much." Natalie's eyes welled up. The last month had been filled with so much emotion. And she knew that her wedding day was going to be an emotional rollercoaster. But she couldn't wait.

"Girl, same here. You know I wouldn't have missed this for the world. It's about time that man came around to his senses," she said teasingly. "I am so happy for you both. But this is the exact reason I haven't gotten married. Roger and his entire family would get on my *last* nerve. They are so ghetto fabulous." She laughed a hearty laugh.

"Hey, Kya, cute outfit. I'm going to have to come to New York and go shopping with you. You always have the fliest gear. How was your flight? How's the hotel?" Leslie rushed her with questions. She sat down, found a pack of cigarettes in her bag and lit up.

"Everything's cool! What's up, Leslie? You're looking good?"

Peeking down at Kya's shoes, "I'm good, I like those shoes?" Talking to Natalie, she quipped, "See I've got to get to New York. Excuse me, miss," Leslie flagged down the waitress, "could I get a martini with three black olives? The first round's on me, ladies. Order up!"

"I'll have a Long Island iced tea. What are you drinking, Kya? Still Heinekens?"

"Yeah, bring me a Heineken in a glass and a shot of Crown Royal."

"Are we eating or drinking this evening, ladies? I'm starving. Should we wait for Amanda before we order food…?" Before Leslie could finish her question, the maitre d' floated around the corner with Amanda in tow. Her face lit up when she saw Natalie.

"Nat, it's been too long, you don't know how much I've missed you."

They both hugged each other hard. It was obvious that the stress of Amanda's life was beginning to take a toll on her. Four children and an asshole for a husband can run even the best woman down. Her face was starting to wrinkle, no matter how much she was trying to hold off the process.

There was only so much those expensive facials could do. And her hair was graying—a fight she chose not to pursue. But she was as sharp as ever—designer shoes, purse and suit. And even though she was gray, her coif was immaculate. If clothes really made the woman, this woman was put together and it seemed as if nothing could tear her down. But all four women knew better.

"Ma'am, can I get you something to drink?" The waitress directed her question to Amanda.

"Yeah, I'll have a vodka on the rocks. Make it a double and I'd like top shelf, please." Amanda never looked at the waitress while dictating her order. She rummaged through her bag and finally removed a pack of cigarettes. She lit her first of many, crossed her legs seductively, and proceeded to listen to the rest of the conversation.

"Of course, ma'am, I'll be right back with your drinks. Will you ladies be having dinner this evening?"

The group answered in unison, "Yes!"

"Okay, who is going first with the news? I want to hear about everything. What's going on with all of you? Amanda, how are the kids?" Natalie's enthusiasm bothered Leslie. She could understand why she was so happy; after all, she was getting married. But why did she have to be so happy all the time? Natalie's blissful demeanor only made Leslie realize how empty her life was. Yes, yes, she was jealous of Natalie Yes, she wanted her life. Yes, she wanted her friends. She wanted her family. She wanted a man, but not her man. Anderson would really drive Leslie up a wall and back down again. She knew that union would never work, but she would take someone similar in most departments. "Please God, forgive me for coveting Natalie's life! But I can't help it!" she said silently to her Maker.

"Nat, let's save all this for another time. Let's talk about the dresses, the spa day, the wedding. We'll catch up later. Is that alright with you ladies?" Leslie tried to spare the other women of having to reveal the details of their lives she was sure they'd rather not divulge. If they were anything like her, this weekend was a diversion from their realities—realities that were taking their toll. Leslie was trying to spare herself from having to hear about the lives of three women who had men she would kill for, regardless of all their indiscretions. They were men and that was what men do—cheat. Leslie's daddy did it, her granddaddy did it, his daddy's daddy did it and so on. She could handle that. It was being alone that she couldn't handle. But what saved these assholes was that they had enough money that would allow for a little character flaw. She could live with that. As long as they were sending home the checks and not bringing anything back that couldn't be cured with a shot of penicillin, she could deal with it. What was all the bellyaching about? Deal with it or try living her life. If they think their lives are all that bad, why don't they try sleeping alone night after night, week after week. The trade-off isn't that bad.

"Yeah, Nat, this time is all about you. We'll give you all the details another time. What's for dinner?" Amanda called out.

"Okay. I guess it can wait. Let's order and I'll tell you about the dresses. I got the ones I sent you guys the pictures of. I know you'll be pleased. They are really cute! You guys are going to look great! You know I can spot a bargain! I found three designer dresses that were similar and had them altered to the measurements you gave me…"

Natalie noticed the disgusted look on Leslie's face. For a second, she questioned herself as if it were something she may have said. But then she noticed the tall lean man standing next to the table. She followed the line of the navy trousers right up to see Marcus Bailey, Leslie's ex-fiancé. He was still as attractive as ever and if Natalie knew Leslie like she knew Leslie, that pissed her off even more. If he had gained weight, lost his hair or, even better, lost a leg, Leslie would have been happier. But Marcus was still the same handsome guy Natalie remembered from high school, only now he had that distinguished look that comes with age.

"Hey, Marcus, how are you?" She pushed back her chair and stood up. She grabbed the hand he had extended to shake and wrapped her arms around his shoulders.

"Don't act like we don't go way back!" Natalie didn't have a problem with him, the problem was Leslie's. She brought a lot of her misery on herself and that relationship was right in line with her MO.

"I'm doing well, thanks. Business is taking off. Basically, life is great! I hear you and Anderson are finally tying the knot. I'm not surprised. You guys were the perfect couple. You had a lot of people jealous in high school. The athlete and the beauty queen. It was inevitable that you two would get married. The question was, 'What took you guys so long?'" It was obvious who his remarks were aimed at. And they hit her square in the stomach. Natalie could almost see Leslie double over in pain.

Natalie blushed. "You know, we had to wait for the right time…"

"Marcus, who is this?" A tall, tanned, blonde, curvaceous model-like woman sauntered over to Marcus and looped her arm through his.

A groan escaped from the bellies of the women seated in the green-room section of Kimberly's restaurant. It was almost deafening. No he didn't! He really did it. Marcus Bailey bought into the whole cliché of once a man finally makes a little money, he grabs the lightest thing he can find and attaches her to his arm. In this case, he attached himself to a tanned, blond Barbie doll.

Still standing, Natalie offered her right hand in greeting to the Barbie. "Hi, I'm Natalie. I went to high school with Marcus. You've got a great guy here!"

Bullshit, Leslie thought and it showed on her face. Kya giggled and kicked at Leslie under the table. Leslie sucked her teeth and lit up another cigarette.

"Yes, I know he's a sweetheart. I love my man! Look at my ring. We're getting married next month." She offered Natalie her hand to show off her ring. It was a nice sized diamond, about two and a half carats, pear shaped. "Wow, did the sun just come out or did that rock light up the room?"

Leslie sucked some more air out of the atmosphere. She blew smoke over her shoulder and deposited her cigarette ash into the ashtray. She took another drag, again blowing smoke into the air.

Kya and Amanda watched the theatrics. They laughed to themselves as Leslie pouted.

Natalie had a way of making people feel more comfortable and it was obvious with her joking that the Barbie doll lightened up a bit.

"Let me check out that rock!" It was almost expected that Kya was going to pull out a jeweler's eyeglass to inspect the diamond for clarity and color. "Oh girl, you got a man with some class and taste. Hi, I'm Kya. Marcus and I didn't go to school together, but it's a pleasure meeting you both!" Kya was being generous with her compliment. St. James had given her a ring that would have most certainly put the rock Barbie was flaunting to shame. But Kya did it more so to piss Leslie off. She saw how annoyed she had become with the presence of Marcus and his girl, and couldn't contain herself. Leslie exhaled and slumped down into her chair. She was a true picture of disinterest and disgust.

"It was nice meeting you all," Barbie said, then spoke to Marcus, "Come on, darling, our table is ready." And she sauntered away just as she had come.

"Ladies." He looked at Leslie; his expression blank and emotionless. "Natalie, it was great seeing you. Good luck with everything."

"Thanks, Marcus. Right back at ya!" And he was gone.

"I know, I know, Leslie. Save the drama, he's gone."

"You know, Nat. I don't even have to say anything. You know exactly what I'm thinking! Where's that damned waitress?"

"Leslie, you didn't want him anyway. I don't know what the big deal is. It's been years. Let it all go. You have moved on and are doing great." Natalie tried to appease Leslie, but her demeanor hadn't changed; she still sat moping.

Marcus Bailey didn't leave Leslie standing at the altar. At least he had that much decency. He had finally decided that he was fed up and it took him all the way up until the night before the wedding to get up enough courage to call the whole thing off. Natalie couldn't blame it all on Marcus. It was just as much Leslie's fault.

Leslie and Marcus planned to marry when he returned home from technical college. The two had dated on and off during high school and their senior year they really got serious. They went to the prom together and let's say that grad night at Six Flags, for them, consisted merely of a hotel room and room service. "Don't come a knockin' if you hear the bedroom a rockin'!'" Leslie had declared.

Marcus Bailey aspired to be a video game developer. Although, at the time he was starting out, there weren't many games available, but he had vision.

There were those who thought he was crazy, not realizing that video was the wave of the future. And Leslie was one of those people. As far as she was concerned, there was no money to be made in that industry and Marcus was wasting his time. She criticized his choice in careers, she badmouthed his family and she harped on his momentary weakness in dating Misty Grossman. He cheated on Leslie with Misty, claiming that he had heard that Leslie was cheating on him with Antonio Harris. The rumors floated around school, wreaking havoc on all involved. It was the one time that Leslie was faithful and she had a difficult time accepting his indiscretion. She decided that her pride was greater than her love for him and resolved that she would make him pay for his imprudence. If he survived her wrath, she would reward him on the night of their wedding. Well, unfortunately for Leslie, Marcus didn't make it all the way to his payoff. He decided the night before that he had had enough and called her to tell her that he was going to California to pursue his dream. He left that night, leaving her the responsibility of informing everyone that the wedding was off. Natalie believes that it was that very incident that distorted Leslie's idea of what men should do and exaggerated her knowledge of what they were and are capable of doing. She was damaged goods. And it showed.

The waitress brought the meals. Everything looked great and the women proceeded with their ritual. Each woman was required to cut a portion of her meal and place it on the other's bread plates. This way everyone had the opportunity to taste everything. It was a tradition the four practiced whenever they ate out together.

Once all the food was removed from the table, the bartender brought over one drink and sat it down. "The gentleman at the bar would like to buy you a drink," he said, placing the drink in the center of the table, not directly in front of any of the women in particular, and then left. His negligence in identifying for whom the drink was intended placed speculation in the minds of all four of the woman. Each was flattered and naturally assumed that the gentleman in the black and blue jersey, ball cap and diamond stud earring was interested in her, despite the visible age difference.

"Excuse me, ladies, let me go teach this young boy a thing or two," Leslie proceeded to push herself away from the table.

"Whoa, Nelly! What makes you think that drink is intended for you? You are not the only attractive female at this table!" Kya didn't hold her tongue and the accent was thick. Her head bobbed and her finger waved. It was quite evident that she was upset. Upset that Leslie assumed that she was the targeted female and didn't even consider anyone else to be the chosen one.

"Oh, and you think it's for you. What are you so worried about? You got a man, save some for someone else."

"See, Leslie, you are so worried about a man that you would sacrifice yourself and run your happy ass on over to the bar looking like a desperate-ass woman."

Natalie and Amanda acted as if they weren't even in the same room. They continued to look around the table in search of any leftover food, anything that would occupy their minds so that they wouldn't have to comment on what was being said.

"Natalie, aren't you going to say something, anything? You don't have my back? Do you think I'm acting desperate?" Despite her attempts to hold her own, Leslie let her feelings slip through this time. It was obvious that her feelings were a little injured. She questioned herself and then questioned the other two women at the table, "So I guess you two think he wants you, too?"

"Look," Natalie started in her defense, "I don't care who he wants. Why doesn't someone go over there and ask him? Why do any of us care? What, he's all of twenty-one. The only thing he could do for me is wash and wax my car." Natalie exaggerated his age. He was most definitely older than that, but she was hoping that the point she was making was that he wasn't right for any of them.

The girls giggled, all but Leslie. "See, you guys don't have to care. You've got who you want. So, I'm at an age where selectivity is out the window. When was the last time you, you or you were out there trying to find a man!" She pointed in the face of each woman. It was quite evident that her drinks had caught up with her.

"Oh, Leslie, stop acting like you are this old woman who has to take any man she can find. You're attractive and if you would stop giving it away...," Amanda finally chimed in.

The look on Leslie's face transformed from hurt to amazement. "What?" She turned her whole body to face Amanda. "What the hell did you say to me? You sit around and take the abuse of a man that looks like the bottom of my shoe and you want to give me advice about relationships? Earl sleeps with all kinds of woman, in your bed and you know it and you stay with him." Every word out of Leslie's mouth cut through Amanda like a knife. "And you know what? Why should Earl leave your ass? He's got everything he could want. Yeah, you are pretty, but hell, a pretty face comes a dime a dozen. But your ass takes care of his kids, cleans his house, cooks his food, and sucks his dick whenever he wants it. Girl, but I understand why you stay." She turned back to face the rest of the table and grabbed for the pack cigarettes in front of her, lit one, crossed her legs, and continued, "He's a pretty good fuck!" She blew the smoke in the air and stared at Amanda, waiting for her response.

Amanda was caught off guard and her face reflected it. Leslie spewed at Amanda all the hate and animosity she had held in during Marcus' time at the table. Amanda didn't deserve it; she was an innocent bystander. But there it was. All over her face, in her lap and hanging in the air—Leslie's venomous attack. All the times she had been confronted by the women from Earl's past and present, Amanda never had the feeling she was experiencing at this moment. Her stomach was packed tight with the dinner she had enjoyed. However, the disdain thrown at her from Leslie worked like bile making its way from her stomach through her intestines, up her esophagus and it sat there, burning her throat and causing her eyes to water. What should she say? What could she say? Everything Leslie threw at her was correct. Her husband was infamous for his wandering eye and promiscuous ways. But she rationalized that what hurt her the most was the fact that someone she knew, someone she actually broke bread with today and many times in her past, had the audacity to sleep with—no, actually fuck—her husband. She expected it from women who didn't know her personally, but not from someone she actually knew. But what should she expect from Leslie West? She may be attractive, she may be intelligent, but she is still a whorish woman and it was obvious that she had no heart.

"You know what, Leslie? It's too bad that you feel that you have to reduce yourself to fucking another woman's husband. It's too bad you don't have enough class and self-respect to know that any prideful woman would know that that type of behavior is an insult to Black women everywhere." Her voice was calm and clear and her words were slow and direct.

"Honey, please, if your man was satisfied with you and what's happening at home, he wouldn't look elsewhere. Amanda, you are weak. Face it. What is he going to have to do to you before you grow a little backbone and let him go? Shit, at this time there is nothing he could do! He's already done it all and your ass keeps him around."

"Look, don't you question me, question yourself. You open your legs for any man with a little cash and a nice pair of shoes…" Leslie glared at Natalie, who was looking down at the floor. "…And you wonder why you can't hold onto a man for longer than, what six months. Don't think I'm the problem, it's you. Yeah, I may be a little naïve, because I love my husband. Yeah, my marriage may not be perfect, but I *am* married. When you get one of these…," she flashed her five-carat platinum princess-cut wedding ring and band in Leslie's face, "you give me advice on my marriage. But until then, fuck off!"

The patrons in the restaurant were past annoyed at this point by the confrontation. "You know, Leslie, you shouldn't be so flattered by Earl's choosing you to fuck. Earl has gone after any and every kind of woman. You are one of many; something to do for that evening. You could have been his first choice or his last…," Amanda added, drinking the last drop of her drink. "You know, I stay with him because I truly love him. You fucked him because he promised you something. That may make me naïve or even a little stupid, but what that certainly makes you is a whore!"

Once that was said, it was over. Each woman sat in her corner, eying the other and the drink—the infamous drink that started it all and remained in the middle of the table. And to top it all off, the b-boy was gone. No one saw him leave, so it must have been during the battle of wits over Earl Walters. And nobody won. Amanda had to return home to a man who had little respect for her and Leslie had one night with a man who probably didn't even remember her name. They both tied, and neither one got the prize.

But what killed Natalie was why it always had to resort to men. Why did four very attractive women have to spend their entire afternoon discussing and debating men? Weren't they intelligent enough to converse about issues dealing with world affairs, the country's budget, presidential issues, anything other than men? Or was the issue of men the only thing that was interesting enough to occupy their discussion? Now that was truly a sad state of affairs.

The food was at the table when Natalie returned. The table was quiet except for the clank of silverware against the plates and the occasional request for the salt and the pepper. Natalie decided not to disrupt the silence, choosing to enjoy her food without the bickering of the two grown children at her table.

Once Leslie had finished her meal, she studied the patrons in the restaurant. She quickly skipped over the women and took long, hard looks at the men. She hoped to see a familiar face, always wondering if her baby's daddy was in the room. Everywhere she went, she secretly prayed that she would find her soul mate, someone to live happily ever after with. And this time was no different. It could happen. So many times she had sat and listened to story after story from her co-workers who bragged about their love-at-first-sight encounters with men who later became their husbands. And these weren't ordinary, working, run-of-the-mill men. These men had long dough, big cheddar, nice jobs and they were handsome. She felt that if it could happen to them, why couldn't the love gods smile down on her and bless her with the perfect man? She was jealous of her work associates. But, she would ever begrudge them any of their happiness. Nevertheless, she couldn't help but wonder, "What's wrong with me?" Maybe that was something that only happened to other people. Maybe she shouldn't have ruled out Phil. Naaaah! She couldn't go there. She wasn't that desperate. Not yet at least. Or was her decision to be artificially inseminated her last resort?

Each night before turning in, before laying herself down to sleep, Leslie would ask God, "What's wrong with me?" She couldn't see it. She had a great job, made good money, was attractive, had a bumpin' body, but why had she not found the man of her dreams? As far as she was concerned, she deserved it. Didn't she? But why hadn't it happened yet?

Leslie stopped scoping when her eyes rested on two men seated at the bar. She felt for her purse in the seat next to her. She searched for her glasses, being sure not to remove her eyes from the men. She didn't want to lose sight of them. She was certain that she had seen at least one of them before and she wanted to be sure. This town was pretty big; but, the movers and shakers of color generally congregated in the same spots. It was difficult not to run into someone you knew.

Leslie made her way to the bar, leaving Anderson and Natalie sitting at the table. She made sure she had her sexy sashay in check and inspected her grill in the window she passed for flaws. No telling who she would see while she crossed the room. Almost to her destination, she dropped her napkin on the floor. She had mistakenly brought it along with her on the journey. She knelt down to retrieve it and as she rose to continue her stride, she came face to face with a woman from her past. The familiar face was not a pleasant one nor did she seem happy to see Leslie. In true Leslie spirit, she returned the nasty look and then continued her task at hand.

Once at the bar, she climbed seductively up onto a stool and motioned for the bartender.

"Yeah, what can I get you this afternoon?"

"I'll take a martini and can you send the gentleman in the orange sweater another one of whatever it is he's drinking."

Once the bartender served the drink, the sexy man lifted his glass and gave a wink in appreciation. He waved Leslie over and she, of course, was eager to oblige.

"Hey, hi. How are you this afternoon, young lady?"

"I'm great now. What's your name?"

"Stephen. Stephen Walker. And you are?"

"I'm Leslie West. I've seen you somewhere before. Where could that have been? Do you work at Morrison Communications?" It was the company

Leslie worked for. They had more than 2000 employees, there was no way she knew them all.

"No, no, I don't work for Morrison. Is that where you work?"

"Yes. Going on five years now." She smiled and took a sip of her drink.

"Hmm. Well, I'm not sure where we would have seen each other before, Leslie West. But I'm sure glad we met today."

"Me, too." She smiled and blushed.

"Hey, thanks for the drink."

"You're very welcome. Are you from Sheridan Heights?"

"No, I'm from Baltimore, Maryland."

They continued to talk. Leslie was excited by Stephen's witty personality. He told her that he was a professor of mathematics at the university and had been divorced for about three years. He had a six-year-old son. He loved the outdoors, particularly water sports. He owned a boat and invited her out to go waterskiing.

Natalie noticed that Leslie was having a good time at the bar. Her laughter floated across the room and it made Natalie smile. She grabbed her cell phone, recognizing that it was Dreama's number and moaned before she answered, "Hello?"

"Natalie, where are you?"

"I'm at Kimberly's, Dreama. Aren't you on your way out of town? What'd you forget?" Annoyance showed on her face and it rang out in her voice. Natalie wasn't sure why she was always so irritated by her mother.

"Nothing, darling. Beautiful solo this morning, dear. Well, I did forget that someone is coming over to the house tomorrow to look at my roses." Natalie could hear the flight arrivals and departures being announced in the background as she listened to her mother.

"Okay?" Natalie yawned and continued to listen. Clearly, she was uninterested. She and Anderson's late-night escapades were catching up with her. She smiled at Anderson and rubbed on his leg with her shoeless foot. She motioned to Anderson that she liked the taste of the bread. He nodded that he agreed. "Go ahead, Dreama. And what do you want me to do?"

"I have a new gardener. He doesn't have a key to the backyard gate. You know, since I put that new wrought iron fence up. I need you to let him in... Is that our plane, darling?" Natalie heard Mitchell respond to the question. Dreama continued, "Anyway, Natalie, I need you to let him in. Can you do that for me? His name is James Martin. I'm coming, dear! Natalie, did you hear me?"

"Yes, Dreama, I heard you. Yes, I'll go. What time?"

"He'll be there tomorrow at 9:30 in the morning. Is that too early?"

"Can I change the time?"

"No, Natalie, you cannot change the time. I hear Andrea coming out in you. Speaking of your sister, are you going over there today as I asked? I want to make sure she's alright, I haven't heard from her and I wanted to talk to her before I left town. She knew I was going. I don't know why she didn't call. I left the phone number to where we'll be on the counter at home, so call with the news. Juanita is out of town visiting her family, that's why she can't let the gardener in. Please take care of that for me, please? I love you! Kiss the children for me! Ciao!"

And she was gone. She didn't have time to tell her mother she planned on finding some time tomorrow to see Andrea, or about her sister's short late-night visit the night before.

"Ugggh! Dreama is going to be the death of me."

"What does she want you to do? Where is that waitress with the check?" Anderson asked, searching the restaurant for their waitress.

Natalie's cell phone rang again. "Hello?"

"Hey, dear," Monica said. She sounded so far away.

"Hey, Monica! How are the children? Are they feeling better? They're not giving you any problems, are they?"

"The children are beautiful," she answered. Her voice was filled with happiness. She put Natalie in a totally different mood than her own mother. "My mother is in the hospital again. We are on our way to Kentucky. We'd like to take the children with us. Is that alright with you?"

"Are you sure you and Daddy are up for that?"

"Natalie, they are no problem. And you know I have tons of nieces and nephews that will help."

Natalie heard her children in the background. She missed them sorely and wondered if she was doing the right thing. She knew if she could trust anyone, it was her stepmother.

"Well, okay, that *would* be a nice break. Do I need to bring the kids any clothes? When are you coming back?"

"I have everything we'll need. We'll be back tomorrow evening. It's a short trip. Is that alright with you? Your dad says hi and the kids send their love."

"That's fine. Again, are you sure, Monica?"

"It'll be fine, Natalie. Take this time to pamper yourself, honey. You deserve it. I love you." Natalie could picture Monica, a bright smile illuminating her face.

"Well, okay then. Kiss the kids and Daddy for me and have a safe trip. I guess we'll see you Monday night then." And she hung up.

"What, what's going on?" Anderson questioned.

"Monica's mother is in the hospital again in Kentucky, so she and Daddy are driving down there today and she wants to take the kids."

"And you're going to let her? What about them being sick?" he asked, drinking the last of his lemonade.

"They're doing better. And I'll be fine." She half smiled, not sure if that was the truth.

Leslie joined them back at the table.

"Natalie, Anderson, this is Stephen." Her smile was wide.

Natalie knew what Leslie was thinking. Maybe with the entrance of Stephen Walker, she'd put her plans of being artificially inseminated on hold.

"Well, Leslie, we're about to get out of here. Are you ready to go?"

"I'll take her home," Stephen offered.

"Sounds like a plan to me. Nice meeting you," Anderson said quickly, standing as he retrieved his credit card from the waitress and shook Stephen's hand in one smooth motion. "Let's go, babe."

Natalie was hesitant. She didn't know this man and worried about her friend getting into his car. Her face registered worry. "But..." Her words were interrupted by the movements of the three patrons.

Leslie brushed past her, grasping Stephen's hand, leading him to the parking lot. Anderson pushed her toward the door. The plumage from Leslie's hat getting into the new luxury car was the last of her Natalie saw.

CHAPTER SIXTEEN
SUNDAY EVENING

Evening had crept up on her. She visited the mall and took in a movie, bored by both. Time to herself was something she always claimed she never had enough of, but when she got it, she had no clue what to do with it. Deciding to allow Calgon to take her away. Natalie sat in the bathtub. The bubbles tickled her nose, causing her to sneeze.

Anderson rushed into the bathroom. "I'm heading to the gym. You need anything before I leave?"

"Huh? What? Why?" She slipped down into the water, trying to pull herself up.

"I'm going to work."

"But why? It's Sunday night. Is there really something you have to do tonight that can't wait until the morning?"

"Natalie, you know with having your own business you don't have the luxury of working only forty hours a week." Anderson pulled on his sweats and running shoes and began brushing his teeth.

"But, Anderson, I thought we could spend the night together. Maybe have a repeat of last night." She smiled, raising her eyebrows up and down, hinting to her mood.

"Gotta go, Nat." He bent down and kissed her on the top of her head. "I'll be home soon," he called to her as he descended the staircase.

Natalie heard him grab his car keys and head out the door. She heard his car start and his tires kick up rocks as he exited the driveway. She slid back into the water, allowing it to soak her entire body, even her hair. She felt free floating in the water.

Natalie wondered if Anderson was telling her the truth. Was he really going to the gym? She was somewhat inclined to follow him. Natalie thought about Leslie's friend Curtis. She literally shook her head in the negative, attempting to banish that thought to the land of the ridiculous.

The telephone rang. She twisted herself up from the water, rising back to the surface, barely catching herself from sliding back under. She searched the ledge of the tub for the cordless phone. Her eyes remained closed.

"Hello?" She coughed into the phone. Wiping the water from her face with her towel, she questioned again, "Hello?"

There was no answer. She threw the phone out of the bathroom door. It landed on the floor, shattering. Paranoia caught up with her, again.

Tiring of the bathtub, Natalie rose from the water and wrapped a towel around her wet body. She padded through the house, strolling from one empty room to the next. She picked up knick-knacks, inspecting them, and placing them back down. Deciding that she was in the mood to rearrange the living room furniture, she ran back to her room and threw on sweat clothes.

Pushing and moving the couch to the opposite side of the room, she sat back, out of breath, glancing around the space. Unable to tell if she liked the couch's new placement, she moved the chair, the table and the book-case. She removed all the pictures from the walls and placed them in the center of the room. Natalie huffed and puffed, her frustration level rising, causing her head to pound. She lifted the settee over her head and dropped it in front of the French doors. If she had paint, she would have changed the color of the room. Nothing she tried satisfied her. The room began to spin, the furniture moving on its own. She closed her eyes and tears ran down her cheeks. Leaving everything where it was, she ran up the stairs and threw herself on the bed. She cried herself to sleep.

Waking, the darkness of the room surrounding her, Natalie noticed that the numbers on the digital clock were blinking. She deduced that the electricity had gone off during the time she slept. Noticing that her husband wasn't lying next to her, she sat up and proceeded to look for him, opening and closing doors on the upper level. Natalie heard the television in the game room. A chill ran through her. She checked the temperature on the thermostat and raised it two notches. *Put on a sweater, my behind,* she thought. Anderson had admonished her for keeping the temperature too high. He told her that all she needed to do was add clothing.

She saw her husband, sprawled out on the sectional, two beer bottles on the coffee table. The television was blaring, competing with the snores escaping from his open mouth. She grabbed the fur throw that was draped across the arm of the chair, placed it on him and turned down the sound on the television. His cell phone message alert signaled that he had a call waiting. It took all she had in her to ignore the sound and return to her bedroom. She stood frozen for a few seconds, wondering if Anderson would even notice her breach of trust. Resolving to disregard her suspicions, she left the room and went back to bed.

A couple of hours later, the telephone startled her out of her sleep. Fearful of what she would hear on the other end, only bad news coming in the wee hours of the morning, she whispered into the phone, "Hello."

"Hello? Natbo?" The voice on the other end of the phone was familiar. No one called her Natbo but Andrea. Natalie sat straight up in the bed and threw her legs around to the edge, dangling her feet off the side.

"Andrea? Is that you?" she whispered.

"Yeah. Natalie?" Natalie heard car horns blow and people laughing in the background. But she didn't hear Andrea anymore.

"Andrea! Andrea! Are you okay?" Her voice rose, ignoring the fact it was the middle of the night.

"Yeah, I'm fine. How are you and the kids and Anderson? Where's Dreama? I called the house, but no one answered the phone, not even Juanita." Andrea's diction was perfect. If Natalie thought people strung out on drugs spoke in broken English, used slang and spurted out an expletive for every other word, Andrea was far from what "street people" should be. She was beautiful, despite her rough around the edges exterior, and she was educated. So then how come she didn't know what drugs were capable of doing to her body? She continued using drugs, ignoring what harmful effects they were having on her and dismissing the fact that they caused her to distance herself from her family and lose the only person she ever felt loved and cared about her—her sister.

"Natbo?"

"Yes!"

"I'm tired. I can't do this anymore. Help me, please?"

"What do you want me to do?"

"Meet me tomorrow. In our spot. Do you remember our spot?"

"Yes. When, what time?"

"Tomorrow at eleven-thirty. Is that okay? Can you be there?"

"I'll be there, Andrea. Are you sure you're alright? Will you be alright until tomorrow?"

"Yeah, I'll see you tomorrow. Natbo? I love you, never forget that!"

"I won't. I love you, too, okay?" Natalie didn't hear her sister anymore, nor did she hear the background noise. Did Andrea hear her response?

Natalie didn't move from her position on the bed and she continued holding onto the telephone receiver. She sat and thought about her sister. *Why did things have to change?* But Andrea said she was tired. Was she really tired? Was she really ready to go back to before or as close to before as she could get? Or was this merely another excuse to get off the streets for a couple of days until it was safe again? She tried that mess once before. She had pissed off some woman and even though Andrea had been on the streets for a while then, she hadn't quite mastered the art of street self-defense. The woman, who it was rumored was really a man named Paul, threatened to hurt Andrea if she didn't leave her man alone. Andrea said the story wasn't true, but who was going to mediate that problem? As a result, Andrea decided that she wanted to leave the mean and dirty streets and come back home. So everyone worked together to help her get off the streets. Well, that lasted all of two weeks. She was back at her old game and coincidentally, she and Paul became friends. Maybe she did learn the art of self-defense, or her version of it, anyway.

Andrea weighed heavy on Natalie's heart and mind. That, coupled with Leslie and her circumstances, were enough to keep Natalie up all night. But then she thought about all the errands she had the next day—Dreama and her gardener, Andrea at their spot, and then she had to meet Leslie at the gym for her little mystery.

"Natalie…Natalie…," Anderson interrupted Natalie's train of thought. The telephone must have awakened him. He dragged himself and the blanket that Natalie placed on him into the bedroom and fell onto the bed. He wrapped himself up and drifted back to sleep. "Natalie, hang up the phone."

Natalie snapped out of her daze and placed the phone in its cradle. She stared at her sleeping husband and smiled. She placed a kiss on his cheek, curled up next to him, and tried to sleep herself.

Natalie cuddled next to Anderson. She loved spooning with him. She could hear his soft snores and smelled the alcohol he had consumed as he lay watching television downstairs. She finally began to relax, now that she had her man home and next to her.

"Hey?" His words surprised her.

"Huh?" she answered, not sure what she was about to hear.

"What's with the mess downstairs?"

She laughed, embarrassed by the disorder she created and left in the living room. "I'll fix it tomorrow."

And his snores began again.

Her muscles loosened and she leaned into Anderson. Inhaling deeply, she sniffed the faint hint of cologne—or was it perfume? She pushed the thoughts out of her mind. She felt safe and secure as if nothing could her hurt. Natalie closed her eyes and thought back to when they were younger and had no children. They were together, maybe not as husband and wife, but as man and woman a while before the twins. And the sex was great. They had sex everywhere and it had gotten to the point all Natalie had to do was think about it and Anderson was right there to pleasure her. He could read her mind.

But now, as their relationship had matured and grown, they both thought differently about being intimate. Luckily, they both had grown together. Now they were at the point where lying together reminiscing about the past was as sexy and intimate as the act. They could be totally undressed in the comfort of their bedroom and have no thoughts whatsoever of intercourse. Anderson's whispering in her ear of how beautiful she looked the first time he saw her on their wedding day was enough to make her hot. She melted at his description of her. Moistness formed between her legs at his explanation of how his heart raced as she walked toward him to the sound of Babyface singing, "You Are So Beautiful."

Natalie and Anderson's wedding day had all the drama and spectacle of a musical production. She remembered it as if it were yesterday down to the very last detail. She loved to, often, in her mind go over the whole day's events. Tears of joy, most times interlaced with tears of frustration and disheartenment, often came with such thoughts.

One of many confrontations took place in front of the wedding planner at Events Just Right. Natalie had warned Charlotte about her mother and her inability to go along with the program.

"Don't worry, Natalie." Charlotte's Jamaican enunciation was light and lively. "Natalie, I've dealt with all kinds, my child, don't you worry your head none. Whatever you want is what you'll get." Charlotte made the comments in front of Dreama, which didn't make her or her ideas any better received. But Charlotte's thick skin sealed the deal as far as Natalie was concerned.

"Dreama, please stop with all the fussing. Everything is going to be alright." Dreama was still running the show. Natalie caved into Dreama's insistence about what food was being served, what flowers were being ordered, and what type of champagne would be consumed at the reception. But Natalie had to put her foot down on what song she walked down the aisle to. Dreama, of course, wanted the traditional wedding song, but Natalie was adamant about her song of choice, despite the fact that Dreama accused her of needing to have the right amount of ghetto fabulousness in the wedding to make her look ridiculous in front of her country club friends.

"You know what, Dreama?" Natalie finally confronted her. "I don't know which is more relevant right now, that I could care less about how you look in front of your friends or what you think in terms of what is ghetto fabulous and what isn't." Natalie never wanted to be disrespectful to her mother, but she had had enough of her incessant need to be in charge.

"Look, I know this is your wedding, but can we show a little class? You know, like I raised you right." Dreama tossed her hair and left the room.

Natalie followed her mother. "Dreama, don't walk away from me! We need to discuss this." Natalie hiked up the train to her dress and followed her mother out of the dressing room. "How can you do this on the day of my wedding? What makes you think you can change the music five minutes before it's about to start." Her eyes began to well up. "I have let you choose just about everything for my wedding, but this is something that I want to do, and if you don't like it..." The look on Dreama's face, everyone's face for that matter, froze in anticipation of what was coming out of Natalie's mouth next. She didn't want to dismiss her mother from her wedding, but she had had enough of her officious behavior.

Leslie had to jump in and separate the two the way she did when she and Natalie were teenagers and the two would get into it. Kya and Amanda were present, but they weren't as close to the family and so they didn't feel as comfortable dealing with these mother/daughter squabbles, which at times escalated to all-out throwdowns. Leslie had the ability to calm the fires between the two women. There were many times during the planning of the wedding she had to direct the fighters to their respective corners because of differences of opinion. But when it came to Natalie's nuptials, she knew, just like Natalie, that she didn't want to tell her mother that she could leave the church and didn't have to participate in the wedding day activities. It wouldn't be the same without her, for anyone. Yes, Natalie was appreciative of all of Dreama's guidance, but this one thing, this only thing, she couldn't give in on.

Natalie could see into the chapel. She watched as each bridesmaid walked down the aisle, making sure to stay in time with the music. And then there was Leslie, she couldn't simply walk; she sauntered down the aisle making sure that she had all eyes on her.

"That child!" Natalie knew that Charlotte had struggled with Leslie in trying to get her to be respectful. After all, she was in a church and not in a disco trying to trap a man. Those two women battled as if they had known each other for years, but in the end Leslie did what she wanted. By the end, they both had a greater appreciation for one another.

Natalie waited behind the sanctuary doors with her father. Charlotte rushed back to her side. Peeking through the stained glass windows, Natalie watched Anderson wipe his brow. She nudged her father in the side.

"Daddy, look." She let out a soft laugh and directed his attention to Anderson with the index finger of her right hand. Her French manicure accentuated her tanned skin. Natalie and Leslie spent the weekend before the wedding enjoying the sun and shopping in South Beach, Florida. "Anderson has the nerve to be nervous. He talked so much junk about being calm, cool and collected. Look at him. He's sweating like a pig." She watched Anderson wipe his forehead with the handkerchief handed to him from his best friend, Sydney. Sydney caught Natalie's eye through the glass of the door and they both had a silent laugh at Anderson's expense. His sweating was exaggerated by all the alcohol he consumed the night before at his bachelor party, despite Natalie's intense arguing to discourage the event, not altogether, but at least to change the date to a week or two before the wedding. The party took place the night before the wedding and thusly, Anderson looked like hell.

Natalie wondered how the night went.

"Where's the alcohol?" Anderson asked. He was ready for the night that was planned in his honor. He was the first through the door of the St. Mark's ballroom.

Sydney Charles, his best man, planned the extravaganza, from the food all the way down to the ladies invited to entertain.

"Whoo hoo! Bring it on!" Anderson commanded, eyeing the tables of food and the fully stocked bar. The music filled the room, the bass reverberating off the walls. Anderson moved to the beat, a drink in each hand. The smile never left his face and, in fact, it widened as he eyed the seductive ladies of Dancers for Hire slyly moving toward him.

"Hey, big boy," the dancer, Sunny, purred in his ear.

"What's up, baby? Are you here to make my last night as a single man unforgettable?" He smiled and ogled her nearly nude body. "Hey, Sydney!" Anderson called across the room. He slapped another dancer, Honey, on the behind, and called to his buddy, "I love you, man!"

Honey pulled up close to Anderson, touching him in places that a respectable woman would never ever dare to. Their bodies connected. She flaunted her nakedness, pushing it all up in his face.

Anderson's hand was never without a drink. He gulped one after the other, barely able to keep his eyes open. He held onto her as the night went on, keeping her close.

As the room began to clear, Honey whispered in his ear, "I need you, baby."

"Whatever you need, I've got it, baby."

"Okay, Anderson. I think you've had a long night. Let's go. I've got to get you home." Sydney came over to separate the two. Honey sat on Anderson's lap.

"I'm good, Syd," he slurred. "I'll see you in the morning. I need to take a dip in a little Honey." Anderson laughed and slumped in his chair.

Sydney laughed. "I don't think so, man."

"I said I'll see you in the morning." Anderson slowly rose from his seat and wrapped his arms around Honey as she guided him to the exit of the ballroom. He had very little recollection of the night.

He awoke, in a hotel room with Honey lying next to him. He rubbed his head, the pain almost excruciating. They were both nude. Honey tried to initiate more of what Anderson was sure happened the night before by rubbing on him under the sheets. He angrily pushed Honey's hand away, pulled himself out of the bed, and began to dress.

"Anderson!" He heard Sydney calling his name from the other side of the door.

He looked back at Honey lying seductively in the bed, turned his nose up at her in disgust, and left her alone in the room.

Natalie knew what the outcome of a bachelor party the night before her wedding would be. She prayed that her soon-to-be husband had enough will power to abstain from the promiscuity that often happened at those events. She hoped she'd never have to say to him, "I told you so."

But something had come over her. Under different circumstances, she would have fussed at him until he thought his ears would bleed. Today it took everything in her to restrain herself from running to him. She couldn't wait to walk down the aisle to become Mrs. Anderson Kelley.

Natalie watched Charlotte run back and forth, making sure all the little things were ready. Monica and Dreama sat side by side. They whispered back and forth. Natalie was happy that they were both getting along. She watched Monica throw her head back and laugh, her body shaking with amusement. She was sure Dreama was cutting up, joking about one of their guests.

"Thank you for everything, Daddy. I am so happy!" They both smiled. He held her hand and gave it a squeeze.

"Are you two ready?" Charlotte asked. Her forehead was sprinkled with tiny drops of sweat.

Natalie nodded, her arm looped around her father's. She carried a small white handkerchief in her hand and dabbed at her eyes under her veil.

In unison, they said, "Let's go!"

The music began to play and Babyface sang, "You are so beautiful." The chapel doors swung open, and there he was, Anderson Dallas Kelley. At that moment, nothing else mattered. Nothing, not what he had done in the past, not what he had done the night before that she wasn't even aware of. She had even let what transpired between her and her mother before the wedding drift from her thoughts. They were starting anew.

CHAPTER SEVENTEEN
MONDAY MORNING

The rattle of pots and pans in the kitchen rustled Natalie out of her sleep. She rolled over hoping to see her husband, then realized that it was he who was disrupting the quiet.

Entering their bedroom with a large glass of orange juice and a muffin, Anderson barked out a bright and cheery, "Good morning, sunshine!"

"Good morning, Anderson," Natalie replied, massaging her temples. She hated when she awoke to a sinus headache. She rubbed her eyes and pushed herself up, leaning back against a large king-size pillow.

He handed her the juice and the muffin. She could almost taste both. Her stomach growled. She couldn't remember if she had eaten anything the day before after lunch at Kimberly's.

"What's on the agenda for today?" Anderson asked as he pulled his sneakers on. He was dressed in a T-shirt and sweatpants. Natalie knew that that meant he was on his way back to the gym. It was getting to be a seven-day-a-week job. He spent so much time away from home. But he would say that he warned her that it was going to be that way. Still, he had said it would be that way *only* in the beginning, while he was trying to establish himself. Natalie wondered, when was he going to be established, if ever. She hated to nag at him, but something needed to be said. She wasn't sure about how, when, or where. She, again, thought about following him. She wondered if she could be inconspicuous enough to trail him without getting caught. Maybe she should hire a professional to do what she was too inexperienced to do.

With her mouth full of muffin, she said, "Anderson, you know I have a bunch of stuff to do today. Dreama's new gardener and…." She paused to finish her bite. She started to explain to him about Leslie's request for them to meet. She had forgotten to mention it the day before when they were all together. It was Natalie's desire to try to prod her for information by phone today about what was so important.

Anderson cut her off. "Well, I've got some things to finish up at the gym. I've got a new client." He continued to move, neglecting to look at Natalie.

"Let's do dinner tonight?" she asked, hopeful. This could be her opportunity to breach the subject of his spending too much time away from his family. The kids were growing so fast, she was fearful that he would miss it.

"Sure, sounds good." His answer wasn't very encouraging. He could easily break these plans with a call claiming, "Something just came up." He leaned down, kissed her on her forehead, grabbed his wallet, keys and cell phone, and ran down the steps. She heard him humming a tune, but couldn't decipher the song.

"I'll see you later," Natalie called after him, stuffing the last bit of muffin into her mouth and then washing it down with the juice. She slumped back down, pulling the covers around her, grabbed the remote control, and surfed the channels for something good to watch. Thinking about the mess in the living room, Natalie pulled the covers over her head.

After dressing, Natalie made the drive to Dreama and her stepfather's house. The scenes were beautiful. She envied Dreama for what she was able to see daily. Natalie tried to duplicate it to the best of her ability with her very own garden, but this landscaping was in a totally different league. It took a long time for her to realize that Dreama actually appreciated such beauty. She, in fact, had planted roses since the girls were small, but Natalie would stake money that the only reason she did it now was for competition's sake. She loved to win and she was good at gardening. She had a green thumb and knew how to work her roses. It was something that came with ease for Dreama and if a prize came along with it, that was gravy.

"Good morning?" Natalie spoke to a man in blue jeans and a tan tank top. His gaze was fixated on the trees, big and small, outlining Dreama's front yard. Natalie, seeing him from behind was taken aback when he turned to face her.

"Good morning," he said back. He wiped his hands on a small rag he pulled from his back pocket and then extended his right hand to shake hers. "James. James Martin."

"Hi." Natalie found it difficult to speak. "Hi, I'm Natalie Richards, I mean Kelley. Richards is my maiden name." *Idiot*, she reprimanded herself. Too much information. Natalie felt like a schoolgirl all of a sudden.

James Martin was nothing like she expected. He was tall, his sun-soaked arms glistened in the morning light. He was muscular, about her age and the hair on his head was dark, thick and wavy. Natalie lost herself in it. His smile was brighter than the actual sun and his teeth were straight and perfect. This was a *man*! Natalie loved how he had cut the arms out of his T-shirt and how the tight material accentuated his powerful biceps. His jeans boasted a number of well-placed holes, worn from many washes, Natalie assumed. They hung low off his torso, the fabric following the line of his behind. She could tell that his thighs were well developed and she was sure that his calves were as muscular as the rest of him.

Natalie began to perspire. She wasn't sure if it was because of how quickly the day had heated up or if it was because of the energy radiating off of this fine specimen of a man. She could feel herself floating away on her thoughts. Stopping, Natalie pulled herself back to the here and now.

"Well, was there something in particular your mother wanted me to look at?" he asked with a smile on his face.

Why? Why? Why does he have to be so fine? Natalie asked herself. She wished Leslie was here. She could see Leslie trying to do him right here, right in Dreama's front yard.

"Natalie?" he asked.

Embarrassed, Natalie realized she had a silly smile plastered on her face. She cleared her throat. "It's back here," she said, pointing. Leading him around to the back of the house, Natalie fidgeted with the keys on her key ring. "Dreama wanted me to give you a key." Finally separating the keys, she handed the single to James Martin. Their hands touched and sparks flew.

He smiled, diverted his eyes and said, "Thanks." He tucked the key in his front pocket.

James Martin walked away, surveying the landscape. "It's nice back here." Looking at the plants, inspecting each and every leaf, the flowers, the trees, James knelt to check the soil and bent down to examine the sod.

Natalie's imagination wandered where it hadn't in a long time about another man besides Anderson. She could see herself leave her body and join James Martin on the grass. As he knelt, she bent down beside him. Pulling his T-shirt over his head, she ran her fingers across his strong chest. She leaned into him, kissing him, tasting the salt from his sweat. She smiled, removing her tank top, unbuttoning her khaki pants, and letting them drop to the ground. He kissed her stomach, her moans drowned out by the chirping birds. The wind rustled the leaves in the trees and the blowing air whistled the song to their lovemaking. He removed her bra and panties, throwing them into Dreama's rose bushes. Bare, she stood facing a man that wasn't her husband. James Martin buried his head between her full breasts. She breathed deeply, exhaling, following where he led.

They lay side by side, his fingers touching each strand of her hair. He took her all in, smelling her hair, her skin, breathing deeply then exhaling. She touched his face, the stubble from his beard piercing her fingers, but the pain was good. His skin was clear, beautiful. Natalie outlined with her fingertips his high cheekbones, his well-defined jaw, running her hands up onto his head. She pushed her fingers through his hair, his dark, thick, wavy hair.

Barely containing herself, she pulled his heavy body down onto hers, allowing her hips to move and gyrate. She begged him with her body to take her, to use her. She cried in his ear, "Please, I am yours. I am yours."

And before she could finish, she was startled out of her fantasy. "Ma'am?"

Again embarrassed, Natalie noticed that she was sitting in the gazebo, the smile still present.

"I am *so* sorry," she said, laughing. If only he knew what she was thinking. Never before had Natalie even thought about being with another man while married to Anderson. Maybe this was the repayment she needed to give him. Repayment for cheating on her. For not spending time with her. It would be so easy.

"Well, I'm done here. Can you think of anything else?"

"No. No, that's it. You have the key? I guess we're done."

He followed her out the gate and around to her car. He climbed up into his truck, honked his horn, and drove away.

Natalie blushed. She fumbled through her bag, searching for her cell phone. She wanted to call Leslie to tell her about her morning. To her dismay, Leslie's cell phone went straight to voice mail. She tossed the phone back into her purse and drove to her next destination, embarrassed by her thoughts of infidelity.

CHAPTER EIGHTEEN
MONDAY MORNING

Natalie navigated her sports utility vehicle through her old neighborhood. She passed her old high school and smiled when she saw the spot she first kissed Anderson. He had come to the school to pick her up after cheerleading practice. She maneuvered the truck down the road, sped up to catch the light, and turned onto the main street to reach her destination. The parking lot was pretty empty. This was the best time to make her weekly visit to the hair salon. She realized that there was a lot less drama on Mondays than on Saturdays.

"Hey, Lisa!" Natalie called out on entering the building.

"Hey, Natalie, I'll be ready for you in a minute."

"Sure." Natalie walked through the salon, poured herself a cup of tea, and grabbed a bagel. She grabbed a magazine, found a seat.

Not liking the atmosphere of the salon Dreama frequented, Natalie went to Lisa's Designs. While Lisa had a lot of younger girls who came in to gossip about who's baby's daddy was doing who, she was good and fast and that's what kept Natalie coming back.

"Okay, Natalie, I'm ready," Lisa called from behind her station. "I'll meet you at the washbowl."

Natalie gathered all her goodies and made her way to the washing station. On her way she saw two sets of eyes following her every move. The two young ladies sat huddled together under the hair dryers. Natalie had no clue who they were, but she wondered what they were gossiping about. A little unnerved, she dropped her magazine. Bending down to retrieve it, their eyes still glued to her, she smiled, trying to ease the situation.

It had always bothered her wondering who knew her business. Because of the small amount of fame Anderson had, she had no idea who knew her and who didn't. She wondered if they knew about his infidelities and wondered if they were questioning her sanity for staying with him.

"Lean back," Lisa instructed.

Natalie let the hot water burn her head. She felt she deserved the pain she was receiving. Pain for the impure thoughts she had earlier and pain for allowing such pettiness to invade her thoughts.

Lisa massaged her scalp, Natalie's eyes rolling back into her head. The smell of the citrus shampoo was scrumptious and Natalie began to float out of her body. She couldn't wait to get into Lisa's chair. Having her hair done always relaxed her.

"Well, what's going on, Natalie?" Lisa asked as she began to comb through her thick coif.

"Girl, same old craziness. The kids are with my stepmother and dad. So I have some welcomed time to myself."

"I know how that is. Girl, three kids and one more on the way."

Natalie turned around, wincing as Lisa was still holding onto pieces of her hair. "Oh my God! Congratulations!"

"Shhh." Her voice was a whisper. "I haven't told anybody here. Girl, I wanted to kill Marty." Marty was Lisa's husband. He was a schoolteacher. "Where are we going to get the money to raise four children? Girl, it's all too much for me." She smiled, turned Natalie back around in the chair, and began to comb through her hair again.

"When are you due?" Natalie asked, now whispering, too.

"I'm only about a couple of months. Girl, I haven't even been to the doctor yet. Let's talk about something else. Maybe if I don't think about it, it'll go away," she said with an uneasy laugh. "So, how's Leslie?"

"Girl, still crazy. I have to meet her later on. Hey," Natalie began. The girls had gone to the area on the opposite side of the salon. "Who were those two women that were under those dryers?"

"Huh? What women? Girl, I don't pay any attention to these girls. I try to take care of my business and stay out of all the other stuff that goes on in here. We got some new stylists on the other side. I'm not even sure."

Lisa began to blow-dry Natalie's hair and her eyes began to get heavy. She sat in the chair and drifted off. James Martin's face appeared. She smiled and wished she could continue her daydream where she left off.

"Natalie…" Lisa nudged her. "I'm done, girl."

Natalie looked up, staring at her reflection in the mirror. She rubbed her eyes. Pleased with what she saw, she pulled from her pocket the cash to pay Lisa and rose from the chair.

"Thanks, babe." Lisa tucked the money in her bra and smiled. "You are the only person I know who can sleep through getting their hair done."

"It's so relaxing. And I'm still so tired." She smiled, looking down at her watch.

"Tell Les I said what's up!"

"I will. See you next week." Natalie hugged Lisa, patted her belly, and they both laughed. She rushed to the exit and out to her car.

Natalie made her way through the parking lot and pointed her car in the direction of her next destination. At Sycamore Street, Natalie wheeled around the corner and into the entrance to McGovern Cemetery. She followed the winding road until she spied her sister. Andrea sat perched on top of a tombstone and her bleached hair hung down past her shoulder blades. She had her knees tucked under her chin and her arms wrapped around her legs. Natalie didn't notice the bleach job when she saw her sister a couple of nights ago. If she would have known, she would have told her sister to meet her at the hair salon instead.

Andrea looked as if she could have been a child mourning the death of the person lying under the head stone she sat on. However, her over-processed hair, ripped up T-shirt exposing her nearly bare breasts, and the Daisy Duke shorts that halfway covered her behind cancelled out the innocence of a child. Natalie felt a sharp pain in her stomach and pressure in her head. She hated seeing her sister like this. She was so different from the way she used to be.

Once upon a time, Andrea had taken such pride in her hair, pride in her whole appearance. Andrea's wet hair blew in the wind. Even though the day was humid, a cool breeze chilled the air. Exiting her car, Natalie could feel chills on her head that she was sure Andrea was experiencing right at that same moment. The goose pimples raised on Natalie's arms. She looked around her. She and Andrea spent a lot of time in this very cemetery. Natalie looked at the names on the tombstones and greeted each familiar title silently. "Good afternoon, James Spencer who died in 1863. Good day, Terry Secrest who died in 1978." And the one who bothered Natalie the most, Richard Mathias, who died when he was merely twenty-two months old. She spied a few new names, Oscar Mattox, Lamar Reynolds and Mariah Sanderson.

Each tombstone told Natalie a story. It was odd how the girls spent so much time in this cemetery. As a child, Natalie was extremely frightened of death. She would have anxiety attacks about dying. Her breathing would accelerate and her heart rate would quicken as she pictured herself lying in a casket, watching all her loved ones cry and moan at her demise. But she felt a strange peacefulness overcome her when she visited this cemetery. She still hadn't accepted the fact that she was going to die someday, but she was able to ignore the fact, somehow, when spending time around others who had gone on.

Natalie and Andrea would always meet at Agnes Stillman's gravesite, Agnes who died in 1903. When they had had enough of Dreama and her opinions on why women shouldn't wear dress clothing with tennis shoes or whatever her obsession of the moment was, the girls would meet here to get away.

When Natalie thought about Andrea, it was the fact that she had changed so drastically that hurt her so much. Andrea used to be so bright, so intelligent. She thought quickly on her feet and she could debate any fact. It was that sister, the Andrea of old, that Natalie lamented for. Natalie knew that Andrea blamed Dreama for her change in lifestyle. Hell, Andrea blamed Natalie. But whom else could she blame? She couldn't very well blame herself. No, she couldn't do that. But there did seem to be some correlation between the time that Andrea and Dreama had their big falling out and Andrea's transformation.

Andrea blamed Dreama for her father leaving them. She said it was Dreama's egotism, her spitefulness and selfishness that ran him away. And Dreama countered with it was Andrea's laziness, her lack of focus and her viciousness. They went on and on, almost coming to blows. And so Andrea had to go.

Andrea stopped caring when she thought her mother did. But that couldn't be farther from the truth. Dreama cared about Andrea. She had gotten to the point where she didn't think she could have any more influence on her. All the teaching that she was capable of doing to mold Andrea for her future was going in one ear and out the other. It hurt Dreama to put her eldest daughter out. It hurt her so deeply that she felt she had failed as a parent. In Dreama's eyes, she had had no alternative. Andrea had played her trump card when she pushed Dreama's hand, and Dreama wasn't one to play scared, so she called her on it. And Andrea was gone, sent packing, put out on her ear.

But where had Andrea gone wrong and what in her path led her down the road jam-packed with drugs, prostitution and destructive behaviors? She missed her calling as one who leads and jumped in line as a follower down a dark, spiraling tunnel of deviant and defiant behavior. The family had, at the beginning, dismissed her actions as a "phase," but once a child hits a certain age, the idea of a phase is shelved and they are forever known as lazy, rebellious slackers. Natalie would often question Andrea about her choices. What was so intriguing about her chosen lifestyle that would make her distance herself from those who loved her most? Andrea would answer that she never really felt loved. She was sure that those whom Andrea felt loved her most were merely putting up a front when she was younger, conforming to what the system dictated. They had to provide for her, they had to love her. Excuses, they were all excuses to act out. Natalie could see it, even when she was a teenager. Andrea punked out because she was too scared of becoming what Dreama wanted her to. And that was only a productive part of society, not her clone.

"Hey, baby sister!" Andrea's speech was slow and drawn. The sight of Andrea startled Natalie. Andrea's eyes had sunken into her head, the circles under them had darkened and grown larger. Natalie went from being startled to experiencing fear. She feared for her sister's life. Tears formed in her eyes. "I know I look bad. I'm sorry, Natbo. I know I've disappointed you. Please don't be too disappointed in me. I need you to help me." She lowered her head in shame.

Could Natalie deny her sister the help she obviously needed? Natalie had once before used some of her money to help Andrea, only to have been played for a fool.

Anderson rolled over, cursing the ringing phone and moaning at the thought of who may be on the other end. He lifted the phone, still a little irritated. "Yeah?"

"Anderson, it's me, Andrea. Anderson, can you hear me? It's me, Andrea."

Anderson dropped his head back down on the pillow. The rain outside the window pounded on the cement driveway.

He was annoyed by Andrea's inconsiderate behavior. "What do you want with Natalie?"

Awakened by hearing her name, Natalie rolled over, rubbed her eyes, and held out her hand for the phone. Believing that it was Dreama with one of her many crazy ideas, she prepared herself.

"Hand me the phone, Anderson."

"Natalie, I'm tired of her disrupting this house."

"My mother?" She had never heard him refer to her mother in that manner and she was taken aback.

"Not your mother, your sister."

Her expression changed from annoyance to concern. "Anderson, hand me the phone, please. I don't expect you to understand. Please trust me and hand me the phone."

That night, Natalie found herself standing on Andrea's porch banging on her door. The rain pounded down on her head, and although she had the hood of her jacket covering her fresh relaxer, she could still imagine the damage the weather was inflicting on her hairdo. Despite her attempts to erase four-letter words from her vocabulary, Natalie cursed her sister for calling her over to this unsafe side of town in this weather. Andrea had said she was, *"tired of the lifestyle I've haphazardly chosen for myself."*

"Damn it, Andrea, open this damned door!" Natalie pounded on the front door. Natalie stepped back to check the apartment number, making sure she had the correct one.

Leslie sat in the car, shielded from the rain. That night, she showed that she was truly a good friend. Leslie was extremely concerned for Andrea's well-being, too. Leslie laid on the horn, which startled Natalie. She whipped around. "Leslie, stop honking that damned horn!"

A look of surprise washed over Leslie's face and then she smiled.

"Oh, Miss Natalie, finally growing a couple of cojones, huh? Look at this neighborhood. No one is asleep out here. You forget I came from a housing project not too different from this one. I may see some of my dudes out here tonight. These people will stay up all night. Look at all these lights on and it's twelve o'clock in the damn morning!" She hollered up into the air, "Andrea, if you are in the damn apartment, bring your damn ass down here now!" And she honked the horn again.

The window to the apartment next to Andrea's slid open. "Honey, I haven't seen that girl in two days. I'm pretty sure she isn't in there. Who are you?" The woman's voice was pleasant and reminiscent of someone's grandmother.

It was obvious the woman was hard of hearing. Her voice echoed through the streets, awakening the curiosity of some of the straggling teenagers who were out way past their curfew. What happened to the time when children had to be in when the streetlights came on? Natalie wasn't that old, but she could remember seeing children scatter home when they heard the buzz of the lights threatening to brighten the darkening streets. "I'm her sister, Natalie. Andrea called me and asked me to come and get her." Natalie tilted her head up toward the window and tried to speak loud enough so that the old lady could hear her. Her neck began to ache. She rubbed it with her right hand. The massage eased the pain only momentarily and now that pain was joined by a throbbing in her head. Not to mention the fact that rain hit her in the face and soaked her hair.

Natalie raised her hand to begin to pound on the door again. Before she could reach the door with her balled fist, the neighbor's door swung open, exposing the silhouette of an elderly lady whose frame had been bent by her many years. She exposed a toothless grin. She gave Natalie a calm feeling, but with it came an eeriness she couldn't explain. Natalie blinked to keep the rain out of her eyes.

"Do you want to come in out of the rain, dear? By the way, my name is Mrs. Ballentine. There used to be a Mr. Ballentine, but he's no longer with us. The good Lord decided it was time for him to come on home. Did you say you wanted to come in and wait? Your sister is such a lovely girl, considering." Mrs. Ballentine looked off into the air as if she were trying to remember what Andrea looked like.

"Considering what, Mrs. Ballentine?"

"Well, that fella she's staying with sometimes, he, well, he may hit on her. You know, he tells her he loves her, but then he smacks her around, you know trying to get his point across, or at least that's what he tells that nice police officer when he comes. You would think someone as lovely as her wouldn't have to take that from a man, she could have any man she wanted. You're her sister, why don't you find a nice man for her? You have a husband, huh?"

"Hurting my sister? Look, if I give you my number, could you call me if you see anything like that happening again? Let me run to my truck and write it down for you."

Mrs. Ballentine called after her. "That's a pretty fancy truck you got there, girlie," she commented more to herself than to Natalie. "Seems if a girl could afford that kinda ride, she could get her sister away from this place."

"Did you hear that?" Natalie demanded of Leslie when she opened the SUV's door. "Did you hear what that old lady said?"

"Nah, what did she say?" Leslie turned up the radio, singing along to "Ain't Too Proud To Beg."

Natalie snapped her head around to face Leslie. "Did you hear what that woman said? She thinks that because I have this truck, I should be able to get my sister out of this situation. Is it my responsibility? Should I be doing more?"

"Natalie, why stop now? You always think everyone is your responsibility. You are always trying to save the world. You have three people you should be concerned with, and one of them is a grown-ass man. He can fend for himself. You've done all you can for Andrea. And look how she does you. It's twelve o'clock in the damn morning and we—yes, I said we—re out in the rain waiting for someone who had no intention of coming with you in the first place. You could learn something from Dreama. Let Andrea go. She has used you enough. I'm tired for you, Nat."

Natalie sat in her captain's chair and stared out the window. The rain made it difficult to see out the windshield, but she could still see the flicker of light coming from Mrs. Ballentine's apartment. She grabbed a stray piece of paper from the console and began to jot down her home phone number.

"Natalie, have you lost your mind? You're not giving that old lady your phone number, are you?" Leslie tossed her head around and looked out the passenger side window. "Anderson is going to have a fit. What do you want her to do, call you when Andrea gets here?"

"No, call me if she needs me. She said that guy she's living with is hitting her."

"Is that all?" Leslie acted nonchalantly. "What makes you think she will know?"

"She makes me believe that she is a neighborhood busybody. You know, sort of like your grandmother." Natalie laughed and opened the car door. She slammed the door closed and jumped back over the puddles on the sidewalk, handing Mrs. Ballentine the piece of paper. While standing there, two black cats brushed up against her legs and ran inside the apartment. The scene was too eerie for her. An old lady, black cats, a stormy night—the makings of a horror movie.

"If that guy hits on my sister again, Mrs. Ballentine, please call the police and then call me. And just because I drive this car," Natalie pointed to the vehicle behind her, "it doesn't mean that I am able to take care of a grown woman who has chosen to live like this. Please do not assume anything. I am a housewife and rely on my husband for most of what I have."

"Sure, sure dear. I should know better than to make those assumptions." She stared down at the paper and then back at Natalie. "Do you want me to call you when she comes back tonight? If she comes back?"

"No, I'm not coming back out here tonight. But remember, only call if it is an emergency, Mrs. Ballentine."

"Of course, dear. You go home and get out of those wet clothes. And I'll keep an eye out. Yes, indeed, I'll keep an eye out."

Mrs. Ballentine turned to close the door and continued to talk. Natalie assumed it was to the cats that inhabited the dark apartment. Natalie sneezed. She wasn't sure if it was because of the weather or the cats. She was allergic to cats, and that was alright with her because she couldn't stand the little hairy things anyway.

For the last time that evening, she jumped back over the puddle and settled into the leather seat of her SUV. She turned the knob to the defogger and turned up the heat. Even though it was warm outside earlier that day, the rain brought a chill.

Leslie stuck her hand out of the window and used the water from the rain to smooth back her hair. She adjusted the band holding back her ponytail and smoothed down her eyebrows.

"Leslie, we are going home. I am not going anywhere else. I need to get home and try to smooth things over with Anderson." Natalie readjusted the rearview mirror.

"Oh, come on, Nat. Let's go get a drink, you know you could use one!" Leslie attempted to coerce Natalie by using her sad face.

"Leslie, look at me!" Natalie pulled back the hood of her jacket, exposing her matted hair that was once so perfectly done.

"Ooh, alright, I guess you're right." Leslie turned back in her seat and the two rode back to Natalie's house in silence. "You are going to do something with that hair, right?"

"Andrea, you do remember the last time you asked me to help you, because you were," Natalie used her fingers as quotation marks, "tired of your situation? I stood outside in the rain for how long waiting on you? And if I remember correctly, I did get a bad cold..."

"I know, I know...look, I apologized for that. I wasn't in my right mind then."

"Oh, and you are now? And how would I know the difference?" It was hard for Natalie to hide her sarcasm. She had been forced to relive that night all over again, and she wasn't falling for the same ol' okey dokey. Andrea would really have to be serious about making a change. But how do you make someone in her situation stick to their decision? Could she make her sign something? Natalie was at a loss.

"Look, Natalie, *are* you going to help me or what?"

"Are you giving me attitude? You want my help and you're giving me an attitude. And this is supposed to make me want to help more? What do you want, Andrea? What do you want me to do? You know you can't come to my house. Anderson isn't going for that. I've already caused too much trouble to my marriage trying to help you and for what?"

"Because I'm your sister." Andrea slid off the headstone and began to push the loose dirt on the ground around with her right shoe. She made a figure eight. She couldn't even look Natalie in the eye.

"You know, you've got some nerve. For years I thought you should be there because you were my sister. My wedding, the birth of my children, times when I needed you the most you weren't there, because you were thinking about yourself. Feeling sorry for yourself, trying to take the easy road. Who'd you think you were punishing, Andrea?" Natalie walked closer to her sister in an attempt to grab her chin so that she could make her look at her. Andrea pulled away and put distance between the two of them.

"Forget it then. I told you all along that you didn't care. It wasn't my fault. What was I supposed to do?" Andrea screamed at the top of her lungs and stared at her sister, hoping she was making her feel guilty for not jumping to her aid. The cemetery caretaker who was tending to a grave a few rows over looked over to see if his assistance was needed. The girls knew his face, but not his name. He had been caretaker as long as they had been frequenting the cemetery.

"How selfish of you!" Natalie shot back. She stomped her foot on the loose earth. Her anger forced her to regress back to her childhood. She couldn't think of any other way to get her point across. Tears welled up in her eyes and began to stream down her cheeks. "All our lives I neglected myself to help you. I took the blame for all the trouble you caused. And now you have the nerve to blame everyone but who's at fault? You have torn our family to shreds, causing everyone unnecessary pain and grief worrying about *you*. You know, if you want to forget it, that's fine with me!" Natalie looked at Andrea for what she thought was one last time. She turned her back on her, and at that point, she thought it was the hardest thing she had ever had to do in life. She began walking to her truck. It seemed as if it were miles to where she had parked, as opposed to the few feet that it actually was. Natalie missed Andrea already. She kept thinking, *She's going to stop me, isn't she? She can't have that much pride.*

Natalie slowed down her walk, hoping that Andrea would call her name, throw a rock at her, anything to let her know that she wanted her to stop. She wouldn't even have to apologize. Natalie really wanted to help her sister get back to her old self. Finally making it to her vehicle, Natalie unlocked the door, lifted up the handle, and opened it. She paused momentarily, to make sure that what she had heard wasn't her sister's soft voice calling her name. Why couldn't Natalie turn around and tell Andrea that she would help her? She had forgiven worse. There was something stopping her and Natalie could only attribute it to God. He was telling her that if Andrea didn't make the conscious decision on her own to make the change, she would continue to slide backwards every time. Natalie knew that to be true. Every time Andrea conned someone, she would go back to her old ways. She would disappear, not to be heard from for days, weeks, months even. Natalie continued to get into her car. She slid the key into the ignition and fastened her seat belt. Her cellular phone began to ring. Hunting for it, she pushed papers, tissues and makeup out of her way in the bag trying to follow the sound of the rings. By the time she located the cell, she had missed the call, but what she did find when she looked up was her sister standing next to the door of her truck. If this were a made-for-television movie, the music would swell and the girls would embrace each other for what seemed forever. But Natalie needed to hear Andrea say to her what her intentions were. This time everything needed to be put out on the table, things needed to be spelled out, and Andrea had to agree to certain arrangements.

Andrea had to know that this was the last time that Natalie would bail her out. If she wasn't a willing participant and one who was able to make some sacrifices, Natalie was cutting her off. And for good. Andrea had to know that Natalie could not and would not put her life on hold or in danger searching for her sister in blighted areas of the city in the middle of cold and rainy nights anymore. This was it. Andrea either needed to shit or get off the pot!

"Wait a minute!" Andrea called out to her sister through the closed window. Natalie hit the button and the electric window rolled down. "I'm sorry, Natalie!" Andrea's voice was shaking. Was it because she was nervous or was it because she had missed her dose of her drug of choice? She continued, "You don't know how hard it is to come to your little sister for help. I'm supposed to be the one taking care of you and now you have to bail me out of all my trouble. I know you're thinking how can someone in my situation have pride. Well, I'm still Dreama's daughter… and that should say it all." The girls laughed together, which was probably the first time in years that they shared anything.

"Well, Andrea, this is it. If this little intervention doesn't work this time, I'm done. And regardless of what you think, that would be one of the hardest things I would have ever had to do, but I swear, I'll do it. Do understand?"

Andrea swatted at a fly and followed it along its course through the trees. "Yeah, yeah, I hear you." She neglected to look at her sister when answering her question.

"Now, how sincere was that? You better show me something a little better than that." Natalie tried to smile and play it off as if she were joking. However, she was never more serious about anything in her life.

Andrea turned to look at Natalie and stared her right in the eyes. "Okay, I know that this would be it. I *am* ready to change. What, do you want me to beg?"

Lightheartedly, Natalie chirped, "Nope!" She bounced in her seat. "Let's go, I know you're hungry. I'm starved."

"Yeah, I guess I could eat, something."

"Well, get in. I have an appointment a little later, but let's go by Kimberly's and make out a game plan."

"Natalie, this isn't going to be easy. You know I have a problem."

"I know, I know, we'll work on it. Hurry up, get in." Natalie unlocked the door for her sister and looked at her cell phone to see if she recognized the call she missed. It was a private number so she chalked it up as a loss.

Once Andrea was in the car, Natalie ran the dangers of riding in the front seat of a car without buckling her seat belt. Hesitantly, Andrea buckled the belt, wondering what happened to her sister. She had become an overcautious soccer mom. The girls were now ready to take the future on full steam. Natalie looked behind her to prepare to back up and she was shocked by a smell that burned her nostrils.

"What is that smell? Is that you?"

Andrea didn't respond.

"Oh, girl, you are ripe!" And again, the girls shared another laugh together.

Natalie waited in the middle lane of Jefferson Parkway so that she could make a left turn into the parking lot of Kimberly's. Her stomach growled with hunger. The small breakfast had worn off.

The bright midday sun shone through all the windows of the SUV, causing Andrea to squint her eyes to block out the unexpected light. The look caused her to appear even more perturbed than she probably was. Since they were young girls, she hated it when Natalie would join in on her solo, and Natalie did it then and now just to annoy her. A woman collecting money for a children's charity walked through the rows of stopped cars on the street. Natalie summoned her over to the car. She was closer to the passenger's side and she tapped on Andrea's window. Startling her, she looked over at her sister who was pulling dollar bills out of the ashtray that was stuffed with money.

"Andrea, roll down that window and give her this." Natalie balled up the few dollars in her hand and gave them to Andrea. Doing as she was told, she pressed the automatic window release and handed the stranger the money.

"What are you doing that for?"

"Since I'm able, I try to do all I can to help those who may be unable to help themselves. I've got it, I kinda want to share the wealth."

"Do you know what charity that was?"

"I don't know, why? It really doesn't matter, anything to help kids I try to give to."

"Girl, please, you don't know that woman. That could be a big scam. She probably collects money all day from you goody-goody people. You know, you guys think you can change the world by giving a few cents a day and she is taking that money back to some pimp or going somewhere to buy some blow. I've seen it happen before. One day you'll learn." Andrea let out a long sigh. She rolled her eyes up into her head at the thought of someone so close to her being so naïve.

"Well, my intentions are good. I can only hope that the money is going to the right place, you know, where it's needed. Your problem is that you've been hardened by what you've seen. Lighten up." Natalie turned the corner and parked in the closest spot she could find to the door.

"I like to think of it as being educated and not being blind to what type of society we really live in. I may not have a formal education, but I am aware. Looks like your big sister is going to have to teach you a thing or two about the real world." Andrea let out a little grunt and rubbed the tip of her nose with the back of her hand. She pulled down the sun visor. She tried to make her hair look more presentable, but it was shamefully obvious that she hadn't seen the inside of a salon in years. Natalie knew that, right now, Andrea needed help kicking her habit.

"Oh, I know the real world. I just haven't been hardened and am not so cynical to the point that I believe there is wrong in everybody, that no one can be trusted. There may be something to what you say, but believe me, I'll be alright. I'm not foolish. I like to believe there are some good people still left in the world. Now let's go."

CHAPTER TWENTY

The two jumped out of the SUV, and Andrea followed Natalie into Kimberly's. Natalie stopped at the maitr'd station and scoped the restaurant. Andre wasn't in his usual position, so the girls waited. Natalie appreciated the time, she liked to see who it was that she would be dining with, regardless of the fact that she probably didn't know half the people there, unlike Leslie, who knew everyone. It was really unusual to go somewhere that she didn't know anyone.

Today the crowd was small, just as she suspected. The lunch rush tended to end around two-ish. Natalie glanced behind her to see her sister rocking back and forth from her right foot to her left. She continued to brush the tip of her nose with the back of her hand and despite the fact that the room was especially chilly, she seemed to be sweating.

Natalie whispered to Andrea, "Are you sure you're up to this?"

Defensively, "What? It's only lunch, right?"

"Yeah, okay," Natalie shot back.

Unfamiliar with the behaviors of someone who was addicted to mind-altering substances, Natalie wrote Andrea's attitude change off to the lack of whatever it was that she had been consuming for so long. If she knew one thing to be true, Andrea hadn't taken anything for the last two hours at least. So she could have been feeling the effects of withdrawal. But if she said she was fine, then who was Natalie to dispute it?

Continuing her perusal of who was in Kimberly's this fine afternoon, Natalie noticed Kimberly dictating commands to her kitchen staff. The room boasted an opening to the kitchen in the shape of a fireplace's hearth and customers were able to catch glances of the restaurant's staff preparing their meals. It made for a more personable atmosphere. At least it did for Natalie. She felt comfortable that the chef knew that a patron might be peeking over his shoulder to see how their meal was prepared. And when she did, it was to ease her mind of all the rumors about kitchen staff contaminating customer's food. She knew it had a lot to do with her paranoid anal demeanor, but she didn't care.

Andre walked toward Natalie with his arms extended and the biggest "cat ate the canary" grin on his face.

"What?" Natalie questioned, exposing her suspicion.

"Girlfriend, this time it's not your world. I was on the phone with my boyfriend and he is feeling the after-effects of Hurricane Andre. He doesn't know that his time is limited." Peeking around Natalie, he added, "Where is Leslie? We had a spa day scheduled and that hussy stood me up!" Andre wore his alternative lifestyle like a dress. He draped it all over his body and wrapped it around his head like a turban. It wasn't something that he tried to hide. He was proud of it and even thought he was God's chosen homosexual. He was sent here, on earth, to represent all those who have accepted that they are different. That was his theory.

During his conversation with Natalie, Andre, peeked around her to see who it was that she had brought with her today. He had never seen anyone with Natalie that wasn't at their best. "Soooo, Natalie, darling, who do you have with you today?" His question wreaked of elitism. Luckily for the three of them, Andrea was so consumed with her inappropriateness in this establishment that she hadn't heard the snobbish remark.

But Natalie heard it and didn't appreciate it. She didn't mask her disapproval. "Oh, Andre, I know you are not raising that reconstructed nose of yours? It wasn't that long ago that I was beseeched to go on an expedition searching for your behind. Because of one of your boyfriends, you had holed up in some nasty hotel for a week or two taking every drug you could get your little hands on. We have all had our down times, so let's not judge, lest ye be judged, darling. Now get me a booth in the corner. Can you do that?"

Not taking too kindly to being put in his place, Andre grabbed two menus and escorted Natalie and Andrea to their table. As they were sliding into their seats, Andre smirked. "We do have a dress code." He flipped his imaginary hair and walked off.

Calling after him in her sweetest Southern drawl, "Don't you worry about the dress code and while you're at it, sweetie pie, over there doing whatever it is that you do, ask Kimberly to come over. Thank you, sugar!"

Andre stopped cold in his tracks, spun around, cut his eyes at Natalie, and stood there frozen for about thirty seconds glaring at her. He twirled around, causing his beige gauzy shirt to catch the breeze and make his dramatization even more elaborate. Andre was such a drama queen. Natalie knew that Andre really meant no harm, but she couldn't let him get away with his disrespect. She wasn't sure if she would have done the same thing if he had made his comments to someone other than her sister. All she knew now was that he had better watch his mouth. Kimberly put a lot of stock in Natalie and her opinions of certain things and people. One word from her and Andre could be history.

Kimberly was one to give those who weren't usually privy to chances from society as a whole the benefit of the doubt. Yes, she had been burnt many times, but she thought that everyone was deserving of an opportunity to prove themselves. But it was only one chance they were given and if you screwed her, you were gone. The turnover rate was high in her restaurant, but the staff that remained did so for years and they were good and trustworthy. And Andre happened to be one of the good ones. He had fallen on hard times at some point in his life, but he managed to turn himself around to be one of the most sought after "can-get-you-anything-you-need" men in the city. And Kimberly paid him well because of that. Normally he was very professional and courteous. But he had explained to Natalie what his problem today was, and she accepted this different Andre because of it.

"What's up with him?" Andrea questioned, still oblivious to what really went down. The hairs on her arms were standing on end. The building was quite chilly, Natalie assumed to make up for the heat they had escaped from on the outside.

"Oh, that's just Andre. Look at the menu, what are you in the mood for?

Everything looks so good. Hey, I see you're cold, I think I have a jacket in the truck. You want it?" Not only had Andrea's goose bumps made an appearance, but her lack of a well-fitting brassiere made her erect nipples stand up and take notice.

Nervously looking around the eatery, Andrea inquired, "No, I'm fine. Where's the ladies room?"

Natalie wore her suspicion like a mask. She questioned Andrea's desire to leave the table and wondered whether or not she should join her in the ladies room to block any activity that may not be conducive with her goal. It wasn't uncommon for females to retreat to the comforts of the powder room together. Maybe Andrea wouldn't be very offended if Natalie went with her.

Noticing her sister's apprehension, Andrea reassured her, "Natalie, I have to use the restroom; that's all."

Natalie watched Andrea bounce off to the ladies room, still shocked by how she looked. Natalie mourned for her sister. She hadn't passed away, but her spirit had been broken. Natalie was stumped on how to repair it.

Andrea didn't have to use the ladies room. She just had to get up. Sitting in one spot for long periods of time was difficult for her. She didn't know if it was a result of withdrawal symptoms or what. But what she was sure of was that she wasn't going to disappoint Natalie, or anyone else for that matter. Hotdog, her pimp, bet that she couldn't stay off drugs for more than a few hours. She didn't care what he thought, but she had to prove to herself that she was strong enough to overcome the addiction.

Andrea pushed through the bathroom door. She peeked under each stall, searching for feet. She couldn't blame Natalie for not wanting her to come in here by herself. Andrea looked around the bathroom. It was remarkably clean. Andrea had been in a number of bathrooms. She had seen the inside of enough of them, bathing, shooting up, having sex. She liked the ones with the mouthwash and hairspray on the sinks that anyone could use. Those were the best. She usually came out a little fresher than she was when she went in.

Even though Kimberly's didn't have the free stuff in her bathroom, it was still clean and it smelled fresh. Andrea grabbed hold of the edge of the sink and stared at her reflection in the mirror. Her hands gripped the side so tight she noticed her knuckles turning white. She continued to hold tight.

Had she chosen this particular lifestyle because she was fearful of what would be expected of her otherwise? It was questions like these that Andrea felt needed to be answered. But how? She needed to talk to her sister, seriously talk to Natalie, but she couldn't do it now. She lacked the emotional strength right now.

Andrea stared at herself for what seemed like forever. She searched inside herself for something. She figured she could find it if she looked into the mirror long enough. She watched as her face changed shapes, her eyes grew darker, and her nose disappeared. It was something that she had never seen before. She shook her head and her original image snapped back. The bathroom door swung open. But no one came in. Andrea looked in the mirror, waiting to see who it was. The door swung open again. This time, she saw Andre standing in the doorway.

"Your sister is looking for you..." The door closed before he could continue. And again the door swung open, "What do you want me to tell her?"

Andrea watched all the action through the mirror. She hesitantly turned around and caught the door the next time it swung open.

"Why? Did Natalie send you looking for me?"

"She's talking to Kimberly," he said, looking around her. "What are you doing in there?"

"It's a bathroom, what do you think?" Annoyed, Andrea pushed past Andre and walked toward the table.

"Hey, hey, Miss Thing! Come back here!" Andre flipped his hair, bothered that Andrea wasn't cooperating.

Andrea stopped and spun around. Her white canvas sneakers squeaked on the Mediterranean-style tile.

"What?" She stood face-to-face with Andre. She was irritated by the game he was playing. Andre looked older than she, but he was still young enough to play silly little games. Andrea wanted to slap him back into reality. Whose life was really that great that they could waste time playing around?

"Follow me upstairs. You can shower and change."

Andrea didn't like being told what to do, especially by this, Andre guy. But her desire to get washed up and change into something that didn't smell of the stench of her old lifestyle—hmm, old lifestyle, now she liked the ring of that—took precedence. She followed Andre through the kitchen and up the stairs to a door. He jiggled the knob to test the door and see if it was unlocked. Unable to get inside, he began to search through his black linen pants pocket for the key. Finding the correct one, he unlocked the door and pushed it open. The smell of vanilla incense escaped into the hallway and invited the two into the room. Andre flipped on the light switch inside the door and walked in. As he passed the couch, he bumped the seat cushion with his right leg and headed to the window. He pushed the curtains open and light flooded the apartment.

The bright sunlight allowed Andrea to see what had been hidden before. She could work with a space like this. "Who lives here?" She toured the room, picking up knick knacks, inspecting them and placing them back.

"You do, for now. Over here is the kitchen, try not to burn it up. Over there through that door is the bathroom. There are clean towels in the closet and through that other door, leads to the bedroom. No men, no drugs and no loud music. You start in the kitchen tomorrow morning, so make sure you get a good night's sleep. Oh yeah, there are clothes in the closet. They should fit.If not, there are some safety pins in the drawer in the kitchen, pin 'em. Get dressed. Natalie and Kimberly are waiting for you in the restaurant. Look, this is your only chance, don't blow it." He looked at her stearnly "Oh yeah, I'm Andre. If you need anything, give me a holler." And he walked out the door.

She flopped down on the couch. She threw her feet up on the coffee table and then decided that that wasn't such a good idea. Who decided for her that this is what she wanted? Maybe this wasn't how she wanted to make her big transformation. The smell from her underarms was overpowering. She went into the bedroom to find a full-size bed, a chest of drawers and a small nineteen-inch television. It wasn't fancy, but it was cozy.

Andrea sat on the bed, and bounced up and down. It felt comfortable. She recalled the time she was so tired, so out of it, that she had laid down on a concrete tombstone. If she could sleep there, she could sleep anywhere.

Looking at the bedspread, she wondered how many people had slept on it. Had it been washed after the last person stayed here? It was Dreama that put those thoughts into her head. Her mother would check into a hotel, and she would ask when the comforter and blankets had been cleaned. If the answer wasn't right, she would demand that all the linens be sent out for dry cleaning.

She wondered if Natalie was as finicky and demanding as her mother.

Andrea rose from her seated position, left the bedroom, and closed the door behind her. She pushed the door back open, grabbed the clothes out of the closet, and then walked to the other door. Through the process of elimination, she knew it was the bathroom. She showered and changed her clothing. It was amazing how a little soap and hot water could improve a person's mood. She used a cup she found to rinse the dirt down the drain. It was symbolic of the old Andrea being washed away.

Once downstairs, she felt so much better. Out of nowhere Andrea heard, "Alright, now that's the Andrea I remember." Kimberly sounded sincerely happy to see her. She scooted around to the end of the booth and grabbed her. With Kimberly's arms wrapped around her, she had no choice but to stand there and take the hug. In a way, she felt bad about not reciprocating, but what could she do? At the conclusion of her bear hug, Kimberly placed a big kiss on Andrea's right cheek. She took a step back, still holding onto Andrea's shoulders, and spoke to Natalie. "Yeah, Nat, she's going to be fine. I've seen a lot worse. I'll work with her." Andrea felt as if she was a prisoner of the whole event. Yet, Kimberly's sincerity and concern sort of warmed her heart.

Finally, Kimberly turned her loose and invited her to take a seat. Andrea slid into the booth and Kimberly followed. Andrea grabbed a biscuit from the basket and popped a piece into her mouth. It was time to change. She had done too many things she wouldn't want anybody to know about.

"Alright, let's get to why we're here. Andrea, keep on eating. It looks like you're pretty hungry. Just come up for air sometime and try to listen, because this is all for you. If you have any questions, don't hesitate to ask. I want to make sure you have a clear understanding of what it is here we're trying to do. *Comprende*?" Kimberly smiled at Andrea.

Andrea mumbled her understanding and continued to move her food around her plate. She had stuffed damn near a whole biscuit in her mouth. Unlike the biscuit, taking orders from Kimberly wasn't easy to swallow. As Andrea recalled, Kimberly had been addicted to cocaine and was familiar with the ride Andrea was about to embark on.

Kimberly began, "Okay. Natalie asked me to help you because she loves you. We know why she felt I was able to help. Right?" She answered her own question. "Right."

Andrea thought, *Spit it out, Kimberly! What's this way? What is it that I have to do?*

Andrea now had bitten into her chicken fajita. She glanced over at her sister who was checking her voice mail messages. She probably already knew what torturous act it was that Andrea would have to perform.

"You stay here, in the apartment you changed in upstairs." Kimberly pointed to the ceiling. "You work in the kitchen and you attend some twelve step meetings. I'll be your sponsor. What do you think?"

Still unable to speak, Andrea nodded her head. She again looked at Natalie, who was now smiling at her.

"Now, Andrea, you have to understand. This is it. No more using. It all stops here now." Kimberly pointed her index finger down to the floor. "Screw me and it's over, you're out! I've done it before, you know, and I'll do it again."

Anticipating the end of Kimberly's lecture, Andrea resisted the temptation to put something else in her mouth. This time she would be able to answer. "I've got it. No more chances." The words were spoken with little enthusiasm. She was feeling mixed emotions. Right then, she wanted a hit. She wanted it so badly, she could literally taste it. Andrea thought back to her first time and how she despised the feeling. She couldn't understand how junkies were able to continue to put their bodies through such pain. But it wasn't long after her first taste that the feeling got good to her. Then, she couldn't go a day without it. It was Kimberly who first broke Andrea off a piece. That's why all this bullshit was so hard for her to fathom. She knew Kimberly when she was at her lowest. Andrea even stepped over her a couple of times in the basement of Hotdog's crib. Now all of a sudden, Kimberly was this expert on coming clean. *Whatever*, Andrea thought. *She ain't no better than me.* Andrea could feel the corners of her mouth rise into a grimace. She stared at Kimberly and disgust bubbled up in her stomach. "Yeah, yeah!" The words fell out of Andrea's mouth.

"What are you talking about, Andrea?" Natalie's question equaled the look on her face.

At a loss for a sensible answer, Andrea stuffed the last of her French fries in her mouth. Andrea had long outgrown being embarrassed by situations she found herself in. She had been in many uncomfortable circumstances. But for some odd reason these women took her down a couple of notches. She hated the feeling she was experiencing. It angered her. But what was she to do? She was at the mercy of the two of them. Andrea desperately wanted to stop pumping drugs into her system. If this was the only way to do it, then so be it.

Kimberly broke the silence. "Good. Finish eating and get some rest. You've got a big day tomorrow. Remember this. The doors are locked at night. You don't have a key to get in. So if you leave, you're out. There's nothing out there after dark but trouble. Can I get an amen?"

"Amen!" Natalie responded.

Andrea nodded in the affirmative. She had no enthusiasm left in her body. She felt her head begin to shake, the result of her many hours without drugs.

"And… no one but you in the apartment. I'm here for you if you need me. This will be one of the longest nights of your life. My number is upstairs by the phone. If you find yourself having a hard time, give me a call. We'll talk about it. *Comprende*?"

"*Sí!*" Andrea responded, holding her large glass of Sprite in one hand and a fork full of salad in the other. She smiled with contentment. Food always brought joy to the lives of the women in her family. She had outgrown her habit of singing while she was eating. When Andrea was younger, she would hum a little tune if her food was good.

"Well, you look a whole heck of a lot better. And you smell much fresher!" Natalie declared.

Andrea frowned at her sister. It was difficult carrying around a tube of deodorant and a bar of soap on the streets.

Sensing her sister's unhappiness with her wisecrack, Natalie quickly added, "Are you going to be alright here?"

"Do you think this is going to work?" Andrea moved green beans around on her plate. Answering a question with a question had always worked for her.

"It doesn't matter what I think. What do you think? Is this something that you're willing to work at? If not, you might as well go back to where you were last night." Natalie took the napkin off her lap and placed it on her plate. "If you're not willing to work with Kimberly, then tell us now. Well?" Natalie stared at Andrea.

Andrea knew that Natalie hadn't meant to sound condescending, but the tone was there.

Natalie waited for a response and Andrea still felt like a child; like when she was younger standing in front of Dreama. Her mother would gaze down at her, with her arms folded and her foot tapping.

"Yeah, Natalie! Yeah, I can do this." Andrea sat her fork down and looked right at Natalie. "What about Dreama?"

"What about her?"

"Are you going to tell her where I am? All she's going to say is that I can't do it, that I haven't changed. That you shouldn't waste your time on me."

"Well, if you don't want me to, I won't tell her where you are. Right now she's out of town. We'll wait until you've got yourself together and show her. Andrea, I love you. You know that, don't you?"

"Yeah, Natbo. Thanks for everything, and I mean it. I promise, I'll make you proud of me. Soon, I'll be your big sister again." Andrea grabbed her sister's hand and squeezed it.

Natalie slid out from the booth. She gathered up her purse, keys and cell phone. She pulled Andrea close to her. Her wet hair smelled of coconut conditioner. Natalie buried her face in the long black and gold curls that covered her sister's head. The hair hid Natalie's tears. She finally regained her ability to speak. "I know you appreciate what it is everybody is doing for you. And I'm proud of you now for making this first big step. I can't wait to go to Dreama and show her the new you." Natalie pushed Andrea away. "Now finish up all this food and go get some rest. You've got a big day tomorrow."

"What's so big about tomorrow? You guys are scaring me."

"Tomorrow you start working. And no spitting in the food like you used to do when you worked at Burger King. Come to think of it, that was your last job, wasn't it?"

"You're right." Andrea thought back to when she was sixteen years old and she and Leslie had a job working fast-food. That lasted all of two months. They got fired for initiating a food fight in the kitchen. There would be no more of that.

"Okay, Andrea. I've got to go. I'll call you tomorrow. Love you!"

Andrea slid back into the booth. She wasn't about to let the rest of the food go to waste. But she did notice an increase in the number of people at the door of the restaurant. The dinner rush was starting. She rushed through the rest of her meal, looking up every so often to see a well-dressed man and woman being ushered past her by Andre. Kimberly stopped in front of her. "Hey, let's hurry it up. I need this table for paying customers." She smiled, but Andrea could tell she meant business. "I'll see you down here tomorrow at nine o'clock sharp. That's nine o'clock in the morning, not nine-fifteen, not nine-thirty. Let's start this thing off right."

A Mexican man in his late twenties came over to the table and began to clear away the dirty dinnerware. That was Andrea's cue. She got up from her seat, looked behind her to make sure she hadn't forgotten anything, and went up to her new home. She decided that this was as good a time as any to say a prayer. It was the first prayer she had said in some time.

"Dear God, this is Andrea. Do you remember me? I know it's been some time." She walked and prayed. "Well, God, I'm calling, well, I mean asking, for strength. I know that this is something that I have to do. I mean, I'm sure that You want me to, to, to You know, stop all the, all the stuff I've been doing. I mean, I couldn't have lived long doing all that stuff, huh?" Andrea heard footsteps behind her. She jumped as someone touched her arm.

Andre apologized, "Oh, I'm sorry. I didn't mean to startle you, Ms. Thing."

He moved in front of her. "Here, I've got to let you in. The door locks when you close it. I've got to go, dinner hour is a bitch. See you tomorrow and good luck. Get a good night's sleep." He ran down the hall, his black mules hitting against the floor and the bottom of his foot.

Andrea continued her prayer. She decided to ask God for forgiveness for the thoughts she had previously about Andre. He turned out to be a pretty good person. "God, okay, I'm back. Now, I guess I was pretty much done. Give me strength to get over this big hurdle that's coming. I know it's been a long time since I've gone this long without using. And You know what? I don't really feel all that bad. But who knows how I'll feel tomorrow. Well, I guess You know, and if You can do something to help me, I would really appreciate it. Thanks for getting me this far, God. I know that if it weren't for You, I wouldn't have made it. I love You for who you are, God, not for what You do for me. Amen." Andrea crossed herself, even though she wasn't Catholic. She figured it couldn't hurt. By the end of her prayer, she was in her new home and lying on her bed. Sleep came quickly. She dreamed about being clean and sober. She couldn't wait for it to be her reality.

Natalie sat in her car and waited for the air conditioning to kick in. She felt as if she had cried entirely too much lately, especially today. She swore that she wouldn't shed another tear if she could help it. But right now she was so overjoyed at the progress Andrea was making. It was hard to hold in her emotions. It hadn't been more than a couple of hours that, she was sure, her sister hadn't used any drugs. But to make the commitment she had just made had to have taken an enormous amount of strength. "All praises to God!"

The car was finally cool enough and Natalie began her journey to her next destination. Her sunglasses slid down her nose. The humidity caused her to sweat. She pushed them up with her middle finger, hoping that no one would think she was being rude. People were so sensitive these days you never knew what someone driving in the other car was thinking about you. Natalie hated that the world had changed so. Why couldn't everyone mind their own business?

The moistness under her arms forced Natalie to change her route. She had to swing by the house to change clothes. She had been in the same thing all day and the heat had taken its toll. She teased Andrea about her underarm alarm going off, when she was feeling less than early-morning crisp and clean now herself.

Natalie drove through traffic feeling somewhat invincible. She had accomplished something today that had been attempted so many times in the past. Natalie felt as if she were on top of the world. Things were finally starting to come together. Her sister was on the road to recovery. Her children were healthy. Leslie had a plan, no matter how much she disagreed with it. Right now, Natalie also saw a bright and promising future with her husband on the horizon.

Natalie caught herself smiling. She pulled the rearview mirror down so she could get a glimpse of what happy actually looked like. It had been some time since she felt this good about anything. She wanted to see it first hand. She could imagine how silly she looked. She was certain people thought she was crazy when they caught her smiling to herself while driving down the street, so she promptly put a lid on her giddiness. Besides, she had noticed a car full of black male teenagers staring at her. It seemed as if they had watched one too many rap videos. They had taken their look straight from the pages of the hip hop magazines. Their music was blaring, she could make out the words to the rap song, even though her windows were rolled up tight. Her face turned red at the derogatory words spewing from the rapper's mouth. Right then and there, Natalie promised to make her friends and family solemnly swear, cross their hearts, that if they ever saw Kendall looking ridiculous with his pants hung low, they would reprimand him on the spot and send him home to change. It most definitely took a village to raise a child. And if her children were going to be productive members of society, it would require all the people who cared about them to make it happen.

Natalie smiled at the boys. She hoped that she was able to pass on some of her joy to that car full of young men. Society beat them up so, they needed a positive word every now and then. Natalie had had a positive effect on Andrea today. She knew deep in her heart that she had the ability to influence others.

The light changed and Natalie left those boys in her dust. Their small economy car couldn't compete with the power she had in her sports utility vehicle. Natalie's jubilant demeanor was intensified by the music she heard on the radio. It seemed as if the disc jockey was aware of her happiness and played into it. Song after song was a testament to her good mood. "Dang, things can't get much better than this. I've got my sister back…well almost.

This is great." She gripped the steering wheel and shook it with glee. Natalie so desperately wanted to spread the news, especially to Dreama. She sung and hummed along with the words, sometimes at the top of her lungs.

The feeling Natalie was experiencing couldn't be destroyed today, by anything or anyone. She steered her truck into the crescent moon-shaped driveway and placed the vehicle in park. She took one last check of herself in the mirror. The smile was still plastered on her face. Even though she tried to tone it down, the feeling took her over. She thought to herself that it wouldn't take long to run a little hot water over her body and change clothes. The weather had been so sticky and humid that the feeling to be a little fresher was overwhelming, Natalie decided to sacrifice being on time to her next appointment.

Before unlocking the French door, Natalie checked the mailbox. The horn from Mrs. Wallace's car, her old nosey next-door neighbor, startled her. She managed a friendly wave and smile. Natalie continued to separate the mail, Anderson Kelley, Natalie Kelley, occupant, resident and Mr. and Mrs. Kelley. Deciding what was the most interesting of all the correspondences, she slid her finger through the envelope that looked like an invitation. Snatching back the index finger of her right hand, she winced from the pain. She noticed a thin line of blood and knew instantly it was a paper cut. The worst pain in the world. She stuck her finger in her mouth to ease the pain and continued to open the letter. She read aloud... "You are cordially invited to attend the union of Shalonda Matherson to Phillip Hatcher...Oh no! He finally got himself a sistah!" Of course Natalie was happy, ecstatic for them. Phil deserved the best. He was a good man. What could Leslie say? He was the one she threw away. It was a mistake she was going to have to live with. Again. Leslie couldn't have thought that he would sit around and pine for her the rest of his life. Anderson hadn't mentioned that Phil was seeing someone else. Natalie wondered if he even knew.

Natalie stacked the piles, one on top of the other, put the key in the lock, and pushed the door open. She punched the alarm code to disarm the signal and kicked the door closed behind her.

The coolness of the house sent chills up her sweat-soaked back. It amazed

Natalie how quickly sweat formed on her skin. It was a phenomenon that started after the birth of her children. Natalie was not happy with most of the physiological changes in her body as a result of her pregnancy. Most of them only reminded her that she was aging all too quickly. Her once perky breasts now started to sag; her once taunt skin was now plagued by marks that favored the lines on a road map. Now, with only the slightest hint of heat, she would sweat like a pig. The price we pay for our children.

Natalie cocked her head at a sound she heard coming from the back of her house. Knowing that she was the only one home, an eerie feeling sent a new set of chills up her spine. She always expected the worst. Every possible scenario entered into and exited her overactive mind. Maybe she missed the warning on the early morning news that a crazed maniac killer had escaped a mental hospital and was last spotted in her neighborhood. Maybe he had crawled into an unlocked window and was waiting in the den to chop her to pieces. Or maybe her husband had come back, knowing that she was going to be away. Maybe he brought some woman, to have his way with her in their home. Both scenarios caused fear and panic to overcome Natalie. She wasn't sure which one she was most fearful of.

Since she was young, Natalie had the ability to imagine what would happen as a result of any action she took. At times, it was a good thing. But times like this, it only made her overactive imagination dangerous. She couldn't count how many times she had dialed 9-1-1 only to find out that she had mistaken a noise in the attic for just that, a noise in the attic. But, maybe this time, there was something to be concerned about. There was someone waiting for her and, instead of calling for help, she let her fear of being embarrassed overwhelm her. She could be slaughtered by some serial killer or, if it was the latter, her husband would certainly need 9-1-1, to save him from Natalie's rage. *What am I thinking about? How could I be so foolish?* She tried to calm herself.

Natalie sucked up her nerve, but not being totally naïve, she armed herself with one of Anderson's golf clubs from the hall closet. Once prepared, she headed off down the hallway to investigate whatever it was that was causing her fear. She hesitated with the sound of something smashing to the floor and the low, muffled giggle of a female. Her worst nightmare was coming to fruition. "Please, Lord, protect me from whatever it is that I might find when I round this corner." The sound of her tennis shoes padding against the thick carpet sounded louder than the actual noise she was investigating.

She knew that the giggles had to be coming from Anderson and his guest. She remembered that he said he had a number of things that he had to do today, a number of errands to run, but he must have remembered that she had said the same. The sounds grew louder as Natalie carefully made her way down the hall. She knew for a fact that she heard a women's voice; it was unmistakable. And the voice pissed her off more so than scared her. The sounds were all too recognizable, all too familiar. The sounds of two adults being intimate. Natalie cringed. "How dare he!"

At the end of the hallway, Natalie raised the club high above her head and planted her right foot, ready to swing.

Natalie thought about it. If she were to physically harm the female who belonged to the voice, she would have to face the consequences. These events could ultimately take her away from her children for a very long time. She thought about it and figured she'd get off. A crime of passion usually gets sympathy. But whatever punishment would be worth it. She had to release the built-up aggression that had plagued her for so many years. The smile had long left her face. It now was replaced with the smug look of a woman scorned yet again. The adrenaline floodgates had been opened and Natalie's heart was beating at what seemed to be a million times per minute. Her shirt was now soaking wet with a new coat of perspiration. She was now adding to the funk she had acquired being out in the heat all day. Her hands were moist and a small trickle of sweat slid down the right side of her face. She was going to pummel the hussy. It took all she had in her to stand still. She wanted to run screaming out of the hallway, out of the house. But she knew she had to confront it all. Especially confront her man. He would most definitely get a taste of the ass whoopin' that was waiting on the other side of the wall from him.

It seemed as if hours had passed since Natalie first heard the noises, from the room at the back of her home. But in all actuality, it had only been seconds. And now that Natalie had thought about it, she only heard the female's voice. Where was her husband when all this was going on? Natalie couldn't believe that he had been so quiet through this entire episode. How could he do something as deplorable as this? Inviting another woman into their home—the house where they lived as a family, as husband and wife, and especially the house where her children lived. The house where Kendall and Kayla took their first steps. Spoke their first words. So what if it had been a couple of days since they had actually been there. Did that negate the fact that this was their home, too? They still run wild through this house…this domicile. It was funny, just then Natalie was unable to refer to the building as a home. It suddenly lost its hominess. Natalie pictured her two children playfully jumping up and down, of course, on the couch in the family room and then pictured that "other woman" resting her fat ass on the very same sofa. Instantly, the heat of anger rose from the pit of Natalie's insides and up to her head, causing an intense sharp pain at her left temple. It was a pain she had never experienced before. She closed her eyes, bracing herself against the wall. The heat coupled with the pain, caused her to lose her footing momentarily. She leaned against the wall and prayed that it was all in her very vivid imagination. But what Natalie knew to be true was that she heard something. She hoped that she hadn't lost her mind, or had she? Was she at the point where she was hearing things?

Natalie figured this was as good a time as any. If she was going to confront her fears, she might as well do it now. She raised the golf club, took a deep breath, and rounded the corner, only to be confronted by…

Natalie's face heated again, only this time as a result of embarrassment. She couldn't believe her eyes. She had fallen prey to the feminine wiles of a television vixen. She had allowed a scene from a popular television show cause her to question her husband's fidelity. Well, he did that one on his own years ago. But she couldn't believe it. Her paranoia had gotten the best of her. At least she hadn't called the cops this time. She humbly slid over to the television and punched the off button. A tiny giggle left her mouth as she passed the sofa she had suspected another woman of lying on. The sofa she had suspected her husband of having… Natalie shuddered at the thought. It was all too much. She had other things to accomplish this day, other things to mark off her to-do list.

Without hesitation, Natalie increased her speed and began walking to the door of the family room. As she rounded the corner, as quickly as she had when she entered, she bumped her left shoulder on the door jam. The pain radiated through her body. Momentarily stunned by the smarting, she continued on her mission. If anyone else had the opportunity to see the bruises that painted her body, they would believe that she was a battered wife. But that was one thing that she would not tolerate. Oh, that was out. She had accepted much of Anderson's emotional abuse, but physical, oh no! It was funny how she was able to justify one as being acceptable and the other as being out of the question. It was like comparing evils. But that was something that she would have to deal with another time. Right now she still had a mission to accomplish.

CHAPTER TWENTY-THREE

T aking the steps to the upstairs level two at a time, Natalie pulled her
clothing off one piece after the other. By the time she reached her
bedroom, she was completely nude. Glancing quickly at herself in
the mirror, she pulled back the shower curtain to find a tub full of grime.
Disgusted by the unpleasant present her husband left her as a result of his
morning bathing routine, Natalie decided that she had neither the time nor
the inclination to clean up his mess. Normally, remembering the teachings
of her mother, she would have quickly pulled out the cleaning supplies and
began her regimen of scouring and disinfecting the bathtub. But, for the
sake of time, she bit the bullet, turned on the hot water and hesitantly
stepped into the stall. She made believe that the steaming liquid would save
her from the grime, the tiny granules of dirt, beneath her feet. Every grain
of dirt she felt was a testament to how much she despised her husband's
trifling ways. She squirted one of the many bottles of scented bath gel into
her sponge and lathered the soap over her body. Whose bright idea was it
to give the scented lotions, bath gels and candles as gifts? Natalie decided
right then and there that if she got one more gift basket full of those scented
"treasures," she was going to scream in the face of the giver, "Keep it!" She
had at least one big drawer full of the stuff and she had given Leslie's little
sister, Jasmine, bags and bags full.

Natalie's mind jumped from one idea to the next. Her next big task was
finding something to wear. Despite disliking the feeling of jean material
next to her skin when the temperature was so high, she knew that the only

thing she had in her closet pressed and ready to wear, that wasn't too dressy for the occasion, was a pair of jeans. The material was heavy, much too heavy for the heat that accompanied this spring weather, and besides it made her legs sweat. She always misconstrued the moisture between her legs with the beginning of her period. But at this point, she really had no choice. She was in a hurry. She jumped out of the shower, made her way to her chest of drawers, and searched for a bra and panties. She had a number of matching sets. Anderson loved them all, the lacy ones, the silk ones, the thongs. He was aroused by the mere sight of them. Anderson took joy in watching her march around in her bra and panties. He thought that it was so sexy and who was she to deny her husband that pleasure? Stopping to reminisce about one of their wild escapades, Natalie smiled momentarily.

Upon taking one last look at herself in the bathroom mirror, she approved of what she saw. It wasn't her best, but it would have to do for now. She made her way back down the steps, grabbed her car keys from off the table, and headed out the door.

Once in her car, Natalie carefully thought about her destination. In her head she mapped her route. The reason why she was to be there was still unclear, but instead of arguing the point, she gave in. It was simply one more thing to add to her busy day.

Natalie made sure everything was in place, her seatbelt, the mirrors, the seat position, everything, and started on her way. She pushed the buttons to change the station. Natalie was irritated by excessive talking of radio personalities, especially those who thought they had a slick style and used their so-called fame to make their listeners look silly. Finally finding a station without talking, she recognized the song and decided that this was as good a song as any to start her on her journey. The young and oh-so-sexy male singer pushed the right buttons. Natalie remembered the first time seeing the music video that accompanied this song, and the gyration of his hips, his soulful crooning and his fine looks caused her to have hot flashes on what she recalled was a cool day. It shamed her that someone she didn't even know, and particularly someone that much younger than herself, had the ability to conjure up such thoughts. His romantic lyrics made her envious of the woman, or women, he was singing about and to. For so long, she had convinced herself that she didn't need romance, but was it because she never really was privy to it or did she really not need it? Anderson wasn't really the romantic type. Their lovemaking consisted of one of them making a move on the other, clothes coming off and boom, bam, it was over. Not real romantic but extremely efficient. She was able to satisfy her husband, most times herself, and still had enough time to clean the house, cook dinner and tend to her children. For some reason, Natalie had the overwhelming feeling that she was missing out on something, but she couldn't quite put her finger on it. She figured that the saying was true that if you never had it, how could you possibly miss it?

"Man, how did I get this far from home?" Natalie knew that it was dangerous thinking about other things while she was driving, but it happened often. There would be many times when she would end up at the shopping mall or the grocery store without even knowing how she had gotten there, and many of those times her children were in the car with her. She had scolded herself for having such a bad habit but in her defense, she rationalized that she was so preoccupied with so many other things she couldn't help it. She thanked God that to date she hadn't had an accident as a result of her careless behavior. She was lucky, until today…

CHAPTER TWENTY-FOUR

The sound of metal scraping and bending was the most terrifying noise Natalie had ever heard. Her luck had most certainly run out. She found herself right smack in the middle of a mixture of metal and glass. She had no recollection of how she had gotten to where she was. Checking out her surroundings, Natalie deduced that she was merely blocks from the gym.

She was confused about what had happened and still wasn't quite sure whose fault the automobile accident was. Natalie remained in her truck until she was absolutely positive that she could feel all of her appendages and that nothing was broken. But what she was most concerned with was whether or not she was still alive. Having assured herself that everything was okay, she pushed the SUV door open. As her foot hit the glass and car-part riddled concrete, the tears of an emotionally draining day escaped her. There went the promise to remain tear-free. Natalie lost what little composure she had hidden within and despite the fact that no physical harm had been done to her, she was emotionally wounded.

She was bombarded by concerned people who claimed to have witnessed the collision.

"Girl, are you okay?"

"He came out of nowhere! Are you alright?"

"Girl, you'd better get you a good lawyer!"

She was guaranteed that it wasn't her fault, but it still was all too overwhelming for her. She cried, unable to hold in her emotion.

Accepting the big, muscular arms that came out of nowhere, Natalie released again. Disregarding her embarrassment and nearly depleted of tears, she sniffled and hiccupped herself back to a semi-composed state. But what really snapped her back to the present was the wailing sound of the ambulance getting closer and closer to the scene. Realizing where she was and what had happened, she was finally able to focus. She stared at the dark brown, tattooed, brawny arms of a man who had the scrumptious musk and citrus smell that calmed her frazzled nerves and sent her on a high dangerously close to cloud nine.

The closeness felt good. Maybe a little too good. This was the time she was supposed to be comforted by her husband, who was, as usual, nowhere to be found. It should have been his arms.

Realizing that she was floating a bit too high, Natalie distanced herself from this stranger who held her, secretly hoping that the package was complete. Was it possible that he looked as delicious as the rest of him? Backing away, not sure what she was going to see in terms of Mr. Muscles or her vehicle, her prayers were answered. He was fine, extremely fine. Unfortunately, she wasn't able to say the same about her car.

"Are you okay?" he asked.

Hold up, wait a minute! Stop the music! Something did not compute. Natalie was sure that she was caught in a bad comedy. The voice that flowed from the full, juicy lips of this muscular chocolate God was not what she expected. He was certainly a victim of steroid abuse. Finding it impossible to hide her disappointment, Natalie was certain her face had contorted to show her inability to understand how it was possible that a man so fine, so sexy, could possess a voice so void of masculinity. His high-pitched falsetto negated the whole visual. Realizing that she was exhausting too much energy into something that had no relevance, Natalie peered behind the brick wall of a man to see the mangled front fender of her SUV. Despite the fact that it was an inanimate object, she felt a small pang of empathy for the vehicle as a result of the fender bender. And she could practically hear the disappointed voice of her husband, who had some strange relationship with all the family cars. She swore sometimes she could hear him in the garage some nights tucking them in.

"Arnez! Arrrr-nez!" The unforgiving shrill of a female voice cut Natalie's thoughts short. "Who is this woman and *what* is her problem?" Her piercing voice cut into Natalie and caused her to cringe. The two fit together perfectly. They were both so indescribable that Natalie knew she would have difficulty reliving the events for Leslie and Anderson.

"What the hell is going on here?" The voice and the woman came closer and closer to Natalie. The fear of being assaulted by her was real and Natalie prepared herself. There were so many women she had wanted to smack around as a result of her husband's infidelity. She knew exactly how this girl must have felt. But Natalie's violent rages would have been justified. This, on the other hand, was all a big misunderstanding. Usually, confrontation was something she shied away from whenever possible. Most times she could tell right off who she had a chance battling with. Then there were those who had nothing to lose. This woman looked like the latter. She came much closer than Natalie was comfortable with.

Arnez's big arm pushed Natalie to the side. She stumbled, but quickly regained her footing. He must have been in similar situations in the past and knew what this woman was capable of.

"Bernadette, Bernadette, baby, calm down. It's not what you think, baby." He used his large hands as a barrier between the two women.

He was as big a punk as his voice led Natalie to believe. *Grow some balls*, she thought. But when she got a full glance at this man, she noticed that balls were the one thing, or rather two things, that he was not lacking. Arnez's black and purple biker shorts put all his business on display for everyone to see. And now Natalie figured out what the attraction between Bernadette and Arnez was. Boy, was he packing!

In Bernadette's attempt to see the female Arnez was hiding behind his back, she nearly knocked him to his knees as she laid a right hook to his left jaw. "Arnez, I'm tired of this shit! What's going on with this bitch!" Her hand slipped between Arnez's right arm and his cut-up abdominal muscles. The acrylic nail from Bernadette's right index finger flicked off and slid across Natalie's face, nearly jabbing her in the eye, but leaving a burning sensation she was sure would show as a bright red skid mark on her face. She surprised herself at her quick moves. Those boxing classes she signed up to lose fifteen pounds, following the birth of her children, were certainly coming in handy this day. Arnez was all brawn and no backbone. He let this woman bring him to his knees and make him look quite foolish in front of the crowd.

"Ma'am, are you okay?" In the knick of time. Natalie thanked God that a police officer was on the scene. He saved her. She wasn't sure what Bernadette had in mind for her, but the Calvary had come and intervened.

"Yeah, I think so. I'm fine, but I guess that's more than I can say for my truck." She tried to add humor to the situation, but she was the only one who saw the funny side. To keep from crying, she had to laugh. The officer took her statement. The fact that he handed Arnez a ticket was confirmation that he believed Natalie's account.

"Wait a minute! What about Miss Thang! Don't she get a ticket? It's not all his fault." Bernadette found it hard to swallow the fact that her man was the only one at fault.

It was obvious that the officer was preoccupied by his traffic duties. "Look, lady, Mr. Lewis accepted fault for the incident…and based on my investigation of the facts…"

"You're going to accept that? Ain't you gonna do an investigation? You ain't done no investigation!"

Turning his attention to Arnez, "Sir, will you please take your friend away before she gets this situation blown out of proportion!"

"His friend, you mother…" Arnez picked Bernadette up while she screamed and flailed her arms. He covered her mouth with his hand to stop her from looking more foolish than she already did. He carried her off to her car. Arnez's car was damaged to the point that he wouldn't be able to drive it away from the scene of the accident.

The officer began speaking to Natalie, "Mrs. Kelley, do you think you're going to need a tow truck?" He assessed the vehicle, looking at the damage done by the Cutlass Oldsmobile owned by the other driver. "Can you try to start it? I think you can still drive it."

Natalie stepped over the parts to her SUV that lay in the street. Sliding into the driver's seat, she recognized the alert signal to her cell phone. She knew she was being summoned. She was now nearly an hour late. Her first attempt to start the truck failed. The officer lifted his head and mouthed the words, "Try it again." The second time the truck hesitantly fired up. He made his way to the driver's side window. Waiting for what he had to say next, Natalie rolled it down.

"You can't drive it far, but you will be able to get home and probably to a repair shop. Take your time and you should be fine." He faked a smile and turned his back on her, not waiting for a response. Natalie was going to thank him for saving her behind from the deranged, over-jealous black woman, but it was obvious that he wasn't trying to hear anything other than her driving away from the intersection that had now become congested with rubberneckers.

Putting the truck into drive, Natalie decided not to push her luck. She turned off the air conditioner and the radio. From being outside for as long as she was, it seemed as if it had cooled off. She sat still for a moment, took a couple of deep breaths, and collected her thoughts. Routing her path in her head, she looked behind her to see the biggest semi-truck she had ever seen. It whizzed passed her newly damaged truck, shaking the vehicle as if it were taunting it, saying that she had no business on the street with such a monstrosity.

CHAPTER TWENTY-FIVE

B eing sure to take her time so that she wouldn't have another incident, Natalie drove slower. Finally reaching her desired street,
she turned on the right turn signal, not sure if it was actually working due to the damage. She turned into the parking area of Hoop Dreams
and was met by the demonic glare of Leslie West.

"Where the hell have you been? I've been calling you…" Natalie could
read Leslie's lips through the front windshield of the SUV and her words
smacked of irritation and impatience. And then Natalie could tell by the
confused look on her face that Leslie noticed the damaged front fender
of her car. Her irritated expression turned to concern. She rushed to the
driver's side window to assess the situation, particularly to make sure that
her sister-friend was in good health.

"What happened?"

Surprised that there wasn't another release of tears, Natalie unhooked
her seat belt, opened the door, and slid out of the truck. Without a word,
she pushed past Leslie and walked to the front door of the building. Once
inside, she glanced up and down the hallway, searching for the drinking
fountain she was sure was near the entrance. Finally finding what she was
looking for, Natalie bent over the fountain for what seemed like an unusual
amount of time. Leslie repeated her question, "What happened to the car?
Were you in an accident? Are you alright?"

Slowly turning to face her friend, Natalie answered her question while
wiping away the excess water with the back of her hand. "Yes, Leslie, I am

alright. Trying to rush to get here to you. Why *am* I here? Where's Anderson?" Natalie looked behind Leslie to see Trent. Dr. Trent Gentry was one of Anderson's exercise physiologists. She nodded at him, not really wanting to take part in the pleasantries they usually exchanged. She was exhausted and had a killer headache. She rubbed her temples.

"Doctor." Natalie smiled. "Do you have a couple of aspirin? My head is killing me."

"Of course. I'll be right back." Dr. Gentry had a bit of a lisp.

Natalie followed him with her eyes as he entered his office and returned with a bottle of water and two aspirin in a small cup used to dispense medication.

"Thanks so much," Natalie responded after she swallowed the pills and took a long drink of water. "You're a lifesaver."

"Not a problem," he answered. His movements were quick and his response was brief. Usually, Dr. Gentry sat and discussed with Natalie her children, but today she sensed an urgency in his demeanor.

Natalie always wondered why Leslie hadn't pursued Dr. Gentry in her usual manner. Although he wasn't polished, he had the cash she so deliberately looked for when choosing her men. And he did show an interest in her.

Dr. Gentry would try to engage Leslie in conversation, despite her curt answers. He would buy her lunch, even though she wouldn't eat it with him. And she avoided his numerous requests for her phone number. She was way out of his league. But Natalie credited him with persistence. And she figured that was worth something. She felt pity for him, even if Leslie didn't.

Leslie liked them flashy and on point. His docksiders, fanny pack and short shorts were not her style. He would most definitely require work effort that Leslie wasn't willing to expend.

"Leslie, what happened with Stephen Walker? Where did you two end up last night?" Natalie asked.

"Huh?" Leslie was caught off guard with her question. "Oh, girl." She began swatting Natalie on the hand. "Girl, he was crazy. He tried to use my toothbrush this morning." Leslie howled. Her laughter disrupted the calm of the entryway. "You know, that's a big ole no!" she barked, nudging Natalie again.

"But that was strike number two. You know most times I can work with a brother, but he had as much charisma in the bedroom as a wet blanket. His moves were lame." She laughed again. "I almost fell asleep."

"He couldn't have been that bad," Natalie reassured.

"He was worse. I had to think about someone else to get off."

"Stop!"

"Yeah, stop is what I wanted him to do. And what makes it worse is that he thought he was doing something. Girl, he had the nerve to ask me how he was! You know I couldn't wait for this morning. I wanted him out of my bed. Out of my house! And once he was gone, I had a date with my trusty friend Brutus." Leslie smiled mysteriously.

Brutus was the name Leslie had given to a special friend she kept in a box under her bed. He was accompanied by handcuffs, instructional videos, lotions and creams. Leslie encouraged Natalie to get her own box, but the introvert in her turned down the offer.

The two laughed. Natalie was feeling a little better.

Trying to get back on track, Leslie began, "Well, I didn't want you to run someone over to get here. I knew you couldn't drive, but damn!" Leslie jabbed Natalie in the arm. "What a lot of damage done to the car?"

She smiled. "Just the fender but I sure don't want to hear Anderson's mouth." Her headache began to lessen. "I didn't know you were still going through your physical therapy." Leslie was required to participate in a series of physical therapy sessions for injuries she had sustained while on a date with another man she was trying to impress. The man was Harold Reynolds, an attorney who had mentioned to her that he enjoyed mountain bike riding. So, in true Leslie form, she lied and claimed to be an avid rider herself.

But then deciding that if she could ride a regular bicycle, how much more difficult could mountain bike riding be, she kept her date. Never one to ignore an opportunity to go shopping, she purchased all she could find to impress her new man. She got the outfit, the shoes, all the gear necessary to look the part in style.

The day of the date came and Leslie was dressed to the nines in her clothes, shoes and all the hiking accessories. Dr. Reynolds and Leslie headed to the mountain and instead of using the time in the car to muster up enough nerve to confess her ignorance of riding, she used the opportunity to profess her attraction to him. Leslie made it about a third of the way up the mountain, and with one wrong turn, she slid back down. She not only bruised her ego, but she had to be transported to the hospital via helicopter. Fortunately for her, she hadn't broken her tailbone, but she had bruised it so bad that sitting caused pain. Leslie's prognosis once she was evaluated at the county medical center was that of amazement. The paramedics expected her to be damaged much more than she was. They referred to her as a medical miracle. She broke her right fibula, chipped a bone in her left patella and sprained almost all the muscles in her right arm. Her injuries were not severe enough to require a hospital stay, though she begged for drugs to ease the pain and time away to nurse her broken ego. Her many injuries required that she go through extensive physical therapy.

Anderson courageously accepted the responsibility of rehabilitating Leslie. Leslie was a horrible patient. She caused grief to most who tried to help her and Anderson wasn't any different. She challenged every instruction given and questioned the benefit of each exercise to the point. She even accused Anderson of giving her such difficult and strenuous activities as punishment. Sometimes he confessed to Natalie that he did. Most were to strengthen the muscles she hadn't used because of the cast on her right leg and her inability to use her left. They fought like cats and dogs, like brother and sister.

As a result of the time Leslie was required to put in at the facility, she became privy to information. She had waited patiently over the last few months to make sure her sources were correct. To her dismay, they were, and it was time she shared the information before the deception went on any longer. "Natalie, I wouldn't have asked you to come here today if it weren't important. This is something I thought long and hard about and decided you should be with me in person to hear."

Leslie knew she had to approach this situation with caution. Natalie assumed the worst with everything and even though what they were about to discuss wasn't good, she had to make sure that Natalie did not stop listening, as she so often did when things weren't going her way. Leslie needed her to be attentive.

"Leslie, what are you trying to tell me?" The sweat began to build at the base of her neck. Even though the building's air-conditioning system blasted cold air, she began to experience the sweat associated with nervousness. She felt a bead slide down her back and stop at the strap of her bra. Leslie had her attention, however her mind did wander. She wondered how her children were and when she would see them again. It had only been two days, but it seemed so much longer, especially now. She didn't handle bad news well and she should have guessed by the events of the day that it would end on a sour note. The sun was going down and the rays shown through the glass doors of the lobby, causing her to squint.

Seeing her difficulty in paying attention, Leslie moved in front of her to block out the glare from the sun and to make sure that she helped Natalie focus.

"Okay." Leslie let out a breath of air in preparation of what was to follow, "Now you know I have been here for a while now." She swallowed, and continued, "You know getting my therapy and all? And…" This was the first time either woman could recall Leslie being tongue-tied. She always had the ability to speak her mind and there were times it wasn't all that eloquent, but she got to the point. "Well…" Leslie's words trailed off as her eyes left Natalie and followed a woman who had entered the lobby.

The female passed by the two who were seated in the hunter-green leather lounge chairs in the front waiting area. Natalie told Anderson that the chairs were a bit ostentatious for a workout facility, but he insisted that they made the exact statement he wanted his facility to portray—upscale, classy. Once the female was out of eyesight and what Leslie thought was hearing distance, Leslie cleared her throat to continue her thought, only to be interrupted once again. This time by the thunderous crash of a clipboard to the floor. Leslie would have put money on who had made such a clattering noise. She knew the culprit without even turning around to see.

"Natalie. Baby. What are you doing here?" Natalie slowly turned around and rose from her seat. Anderson planted a kiss on her cheek and hugged her, pulling her into him so that she got a good whiff of perspiration mixed with soap. He smirked at Leslie, not sure what to think of the two sitting there, alone, for an undisclosed amount of time. "You didn't tell me you were coming by here today. What's going on here? You two planning on working out?"

Not being sure how to breach the subject so that she could get to the bottom of all this secrecy, Natalie decided to dive in headfirst, "Why am I here, Leslie?" Her question was directed to Leslie, but her eyes stayed on Anderson.

Anderson's heart melted as he gazed into his wife's eyes. He could tell that she was hurting and it all had to do with him and his actions. He stared at her and tried to comfort her for whatever it was she was about to hear from her best friend. He could almost guess, hell he knew, what it was and decided that he wouldn't fight it. He knew the news needed to come out and since he wasn't man enough—there, he admitted it, he wasn't man enough to break the news himself—he would leave the task up to Leslie.

"Anderson, who's that woman you were following?" Leslie's question stabbed him in the heart. Natalie could almost see the dagger enter his chest. "I've seen her before? Who *is* she?" She now turned the dagger. "You two look like you know each other." She stabbed, pushing it in farther and farther.

Natalie had seen her before as well, but she couldn't figure out where it would have been.

Her words weren't cruel; they weren't meant to be mean. Leslie intended to answer all the questions she knew for sure that Natalie would have. It was about time Natalie was able to see the demoness who haunted her and her marriage.

Anderson's eyes left Natalie's. He turned his back on her and it was so symbolic of their whole relationship. He knelt down to begin collecting the clipboard he dropped. Unable to concentrate on the task at hand, he stood back up, attempting to avoid the stare of his wife.

"Who is she, Anderson?"

Natalie maneuvered her way around him so that she was able to look him in the eyes when she asked the question. It hurt his heart even more to hear Natalie ask. And there she was, the woman in question. She appeared in the doorway. Her long legs were shapely. She was thin and very athletic looking. The black and white lycra tank and short set hugged her body and showed the small pouch of a belly it was obvious she was there working out to reduce. She tilted the water bottle in her right hand and poured the liquid into her mouth, being sure not to touch the opening of the bottle to her lips. She swallowed and called out…

"Anderson?"

All six pairs of eyes focused on her.

"Who are you?" Natalie questioned.

"Anderson?" Again, she questioned. But he didn't answer. His thoughts were disrupted by the sound of small feet padding quickly down the carpeted hallway.

"Mommy! Mommy!"

With Natalie's chiding, Anderson had a daycare center placed in the facility. Natalie rallied that he would get more people in to workout, especially those who had children, if there was a place they felt was safe enough to leave their children. Safety was key and Natalie took it upon herself to overlook the process of hiring and training the person who would be in charge of the center. Anderson knew that he wouldn't be able to dodge this issue, Natalie had her heart set on it, so when Hoop Dreams was days from being completed, plans had to be redrawn to include a daycare center. Natalie could kick herself this day for being so persistent.

"Yes, baby!" The mother and child reunion warmed Natalie's heart. She only saw the back of the baby's head, but she could tell that the child was similar in age to her own children, maybe only a year younger. Previously, Natalie thought of the woman as cold and distant, but the connection she saw between the two changed her perception. Mother and child exchanged words. Natalie starred at the two cooing and oohing over the goldenrod paper, covered with the erratic drawings of a child. Still only able to see the curly brown hair of the child, Natalie wasn't even able to tell the gender. The sweat clothing that covered the small frame could have been for a male or female seed.

"Natalie, let's go to my office to talk." Anderson reached for Natalie's arm.

Right then the little girl who hung from the arms of her mother turned to face Natalie's husband and let out a cheerful, "I wanna go to Daddy!"

It was something that Anderson couldn't deny. The child was an exact replica of the pictures Natalie had viewed at Anderson's mother's house many, many times before. From the large locks of hair to the large hands on to the eyes. That child had the very same flowering eyelashes and the dark, large pupils that a person could lose themselves in. The cleft chin and skin color were exact replicas. She looked even more like Anderson than her own children did. It made her question the bloodline of the twins.

Anderson's mouth dropped open as he witnessed all the color wash from his wife's face. She was his wife now, but how long would that last after this revelation of his infidelity. Not to ignore the child's request, he bent down, smiling a warm, endearing smile Natalie had believed he reserved only for his children, their children, and he scooped the girl up into his arms.

"Gracie, go back to your mother." *Gracie, he finally got his wish.* Natalie's shoulders dropped a little. Her exhaustion was evident so much more. Anderson wanted Natalie to name Kayla Gracie after his grandmother. However, she put her foot down that she wouldn't curse a child with a name she viewed as being synonymous with old age. He pleaded with her. However, she wouldn't give in. Anderson had finally gotten his wish, just not with a child from his wife. "We'll go play later." Anderson placed her back onto the floor, tussled the curls on top of her head, and gently guided her back to her mother who had remained frozen in time in the doorway. "Sandy, can you take her? I'll be with you in a minute."

"Oh, how cute, Sandy and Andy!" Leslie's sarcasm was released into the atmosphere. She wasn't letting Anderson off as easily as it seemed Natalie was with her silence. Her breathing and heart rate began to quicken. To steady her herself, she grabbed for the side of the chair she once sat in. Reaching to assist her, Anderson offered his hand as security. It was something that she didn't want from him, not now, not ever again. Then she questioned herself, *Had I ever really had it anyway?* She felt betrayed. She *had* been betrayed. If looks could kill, the rigor mortis would have already started to set in. Natalie pushed his hand away from her as if he possessed the plague that destroyed a nation. She sat there unable to speak. She stared into the eyes of her best friend begging for her to ask the questions, to get the answers she was unable to find words for.

"Well, Anderson, what do you have to say for yourself?"

"Leslie, look, this is between family…"

"Oh, which family? I am family, and it's obvious more so now than ever. Family? Family would never do anything this crooked. You used to always tell her that her worries were in her head, that she was crazy or something. Your ass was trying to cover up all your shit. You are *so* wrong, Anderson! So, how old is Gracie?"

"Look, Leslie…"

"Answer the question, Anderson!" Natalie demanded.

He lowered his eyes. It broke his heart. "She's almost two." His words were almost a whisper. And then his voice grew louder, directed toward Leslie. "You couldn't wait to run and tell. That's why you don't have any business of your own, you're always in everybody else's. You don't give a damn about anybody but yourself!"

Natalie groaned. She did the math and realized how recent his indiscretion was.

"Oh, no, you didn't! You cared more about satisfying some urge to have sex with someone else than about your wife's feelings. Anderson, this ain't some silly high school shit! Run and tell? Your shit is out now, and now what? You want to blame everybody but who's at fault. You are foul!"

What could he say? Leslie was right. He had destroyed the one woman who loved him more than anybody. Anderson wasn't even sure that Sandy cared about him, or better yet that he cared about her. He loved his daughter and now that she was here on earth, he would never give her up. He wasn't sure if he wanted everything that came along with the mother. He supposed he should have thought about that before.

Natalie sat there and listened to the exchange of words. All eyes were on her, especially Anderson's as he waited for the other shoe to drop. He awaited the scolding that he would inevitably get from Natalie. But her silence made him feel even worse. If she would say something, anything, he would know what it was that she was feeling. And then they could get started with counseling or whatever it was that couples do. But, would she ever forgive him? Was he selfish enough to want her to accept his indiscretion and move on? She had before.

It took Natalie a second to regain her composure. This was the event that warranted a breakdown. The breakdown she warned herself not to have unless something horrible happened. But she didn't want to give him the satisfaction. She took a couple of deep breaths to prepare for whatever she decided to do next.

"So that's what, or who's, been occupying your time? So when I thought I, or we, the twins, were the last thing you thought about before you closed your eyes each night, it was always someone else. What are your plans now, Anderson?"

"Nat?" He moved closer to her. His hand extended.

Moving back out of his path, she pushed his hand away. "Don't touch me," she warned.

"Please, can we talk?" He tried to remain calm, deciding that it was the right way to proceed.

"Talk? Talk about what? *Now* you want to talk?" Natalie's voice rose until she was screaming at him. "You should have been talking years ago!"

Gym patrons walked back and forth watching the drama unfold. Sandy had since removed herself and her daughter from the situation. Natalie looked around for her. Although this needed to be dealt with, she didn't want to expose the child to it. Gracie didn't ask for it.

"I didn't want to lose you." Tears began to fall down Anderson's face.

"Don't give in, girl." Leslie whispered from behind Natalie.

"Shut the hell up, Leslie!" Anderson screamed.

Talking to herself, Leslie muttered, "Oh, this is a trip." She shook her head back and forth.

"Please, Natalie, let me explain."

Natalie ignored his pleas, reached for her bag, pushed through the door marked exit, and headed for the parking lot.

She wondered where her strength came from. She turned her back on the man who had done the same to her so many years before. It was obvious to her now that he only pretended to be in love with her. He was in love with the idea of being in love. She had put together a lifestyle that anyone in their right mind would want. No, she wasn't crazy. All her suspicions and worries were dead on. She had never been more sane in her life.

Natalie put the man behind her who had caused her so much anxiety, pain and turmoil. What seemed to be so difficult all those many times over the course of their relationship seemed to come so easy to her all of a sudden. She never believed that she was a strong person, but today she proved to herself that she was one of the strongest women she knew. She didn't look back.

CHAPTER TWENTY-SIX
TWO WEEKS LATER

Two weeks later, after many meetings with attorneys, a real estate agent and numerous goodbyes to family and friends, Natalie sat alone in the living room of her house. The cordless phone sat in her lap. She'd been on the phone most of the night with Anderson arguing about her decision to leave him and the city—with their children.

"If you think I'm going to sit here and let you take my children away from me, you are *so* wrong!" His words were sharp and bitter.

"It doesn't matter what you want, Anderson." Natalie was calm, cool and collected. It was distinctly different from her demeanor once she made it home from Hoop Dreams that day two weeks earlier.

After Natalie left the gym, she drove straight home, identifying the number to a locksmith while en route. Joe from Joe's Locks met her at her house, where she changed every lock there was. Not wanting to destroy Anderson's clothes and other belongings, Natalie packed up everything he owned, placed it all in boxes and sat them out on the curb, not caring whether he or someone else collected them.

Tears streamed down her face as she chastised herself for putting up with his philandering ways for years while taking him back after each indiscretion. She knew that he believed she didn't have it in her to leave him. He doubted her ability to live without him.

"How vain could one person be?" Natalie questioned. "Could he really believe that he is such a great catch?" And her answer was a resounding, "YES!" He had lived his life that way. Ignoring other's feelings for his own. Natalie balled her fists and shook them.

She felt for a long time that she was dependent on him, for everything. She had invested all of herself in this man who toyed with her life. And she knew this time couldn't be like the other times. He had to be taught a lesson.

"Uggg! How could you be so stupid?" She stomped her feet, regressing back to her childhood. "How could *he* be so selfish?" Natalie screamed at the top of her lungs. Throwing herself down on her bed, she kicked her feet and screamed into a pillow, "I gave him everything he wanted! How could he do this to me?"

Crying for what seemed like forever, Natalie pulled herself together and continued her work. Her eyes were red and her throat ached from the strain. Again, the tears began to flow. And the phone began to ring.

She lifted the receiver, trying to muffle the sounds of her pain.

"Natalie? Natalie?" Leslie hollered into the phone. "Natalie, I talked to Monica. She'll keep the kids. Do you need me?"

"No," Natalie whispered into the phone, then disconnected the call.

She was pissed that Anderson hadn't even called to attempt an apology. "He's got some nerve." Satisfied that she had put out the trash, she remembered that the next day the garbage truck would come. Natalie took satisfaction in knowing that if he didn't at least come by to check on her, he would be without a number of expensive articles of clothing, shoes, jewelry, trophies, all he had. And she wondered if that that would hurt him more than life without her.

Natalie looked at the bags she had packed for herself and her children. They sat at the front door. She would be soon leave 25527 Windsor Gate Place forever. She would distance herself from her past, leaving behind the man responsible for destroying her emotionally.

Again, the phone rang and Natalie bet her life that it was Anderson. "What, Anderson?" she sarcastically hollered into the phone. "You know I don't want to talk to you."

"I'm not concerned about what you do or don't need or want." He had turned indignant, trying to turn it around as if Natalie was the one at fault.

"You've never been concerned about what I need *or* want. So why would I think this time would be any different?" She sat still, waiting to see if he had anything else to say.

"Look, Natalie, I'm not trying to fight with you." Seeing that she wouldn't weaken or break, he changed his tune. "Can we talk?"

"There's nothing to talk about, Anderson. As I've told you before, I don't know how many times before, my attorney will be in touch to discuss all we need to say to each other. I don't even think it's a good idea for us to be on the phone now."

"Wait! Natalie, please wait!" He got quiet. Natalie knew that he was crying. She heard him sobbing.

"Anderson, you destroyed our family. You tried to break me as a woman and as a person. Did you ever love me?" Natalie so desperately needed to know the answer to that question. It would be the question that would haunt her for the rest of her life.

"How could you ask me that? Of course I loved, I do love you."

"Liar! You are such a fucking liar!" she screamed into the phone. "You don't do what you did to someone you love! You are a liar and I hope you burn in hell for what you did!" She slammed the phone down, picking it up and slamming it again and again and again, hoping that the sound would hurt him as much as she was hurting.

Natalie regrouped after a moment. She started to pack the car she had rented and securely buckled her children into the backseat. She wasn't the only one making a change. Amanda called and told her that she had left Earl Walters. She had finally tired of the many phone calls from other women, the blatant disrespect. She was packing up her children and relocating to Arizona. Filling her in on her very own life-shattering predicament, Natalie and Amanda decided to heal together. They decided to meet in Phoenix and comfort one another.

CHAPTER TWENTY-SEVEN

Only 400 miles into her trek across country, Natalie was starting to decipher her past that was once too muddied by deceit, lies and betrayal. The silence that used to drive Natalie absolutely crazy had now become so soothing and peaceful on the long drive. It gave her space to think. She was able to concentrate on what was ahead of her and attempt to forget what she had left behind. The gentle snores of her children sleeping in the backseat comforted her; it encouraged her to process her situation, to plan for the future. There was a time when the silence between Anderson and herself was so disturbing that it was worse than the actual argument that initiated it.

Her cell phone sat in the seat next to her. It rang incessantly. The caller ID revealed that Anderson hadn't accepted her decision to leave him. But this time it was Leslie.

"What's up?" Natalie greeted her. Her tone was light and a direct reflection of the scenery that had led her West.

"Hey! You on your way?"

"Yeah, girl. We're on our way."

"Natalie, he still loves you…"

"Leslie…" Natalie tried to cut her off. She shook her head, indicating that she really didn't want to hear this right now. She was trying to put it all behind her.

"Before you say anything, know that he still loves you. I know you doubt it, and he sure as hell had a jacked-up way of showing it. But some people are not able to see what they really have until it's gone."

"So you're saying that this is all *my* fault? That if I would have left him years ago, showed him what he was in danger of losing, that he would have changed and we wouldn't be here today?"

"Would you cut it out!" Leslie screamed into the phone. "No, it's not *your* fault. He was horrible, disrespectful and selfish. He deserves everything he's getting right now. But Anderson has loved you from the beginning. And he hasn't stopped."

"Leslie, can I ask you a question?"

"Yes. What?"

"Do you think I was foolish for taking him back all those times?"

Leslie laughed. "I just figured you loved him."

"Yeah, but do you think I was foolish to take him back all those times?" she asked again.

"I wouldn't have done it. Girl, I've got one word for you, cattle prod."

"That's two words." Natalie smiled. "Thanks for not calling me stupid when I allowed him back into my life. I can't explain to you how much I loved him, Les. He was my world. I prayed for him."

"And how do you feel now?"

"I don't know. I'm really confused. I want to hate him."

"But you don't?"

"So what, I should go back?"

"Do you want to go back?"

"I guess I could, but then what. I don't think he's learned. He'd simply go back to his old ways. And how many more kids will we find out about in a couple of years. And then what, we could create our own football team, or better yet make a new movie with his, mine and ours." Natalie joked. She was now able to put humor to this situation. It also was a defense mechanism.

"Funny. No, don't go back. But don't cut him off permanently. You *do* have children together. Can you in good conscious keep them away from him forever?"

"They can see him, when they're eighteen. I'm not talking about this right now!" Natalie demanded, "If you want to talk, talk about something else, okay?"

"What do you want to talk about? It seems like I haven't seen you in forever. I miss you."

"I miss you, too, Leslie. Thanks for everything. Without you, I'd be somewhere with my head in the oven." She laughed. "What about you? Have you decided anything?"

"About what? Me and having a baby? I still want to have children and I want to get married. I'm not going to let *your* drama affect my decision. Maybe I'm a closeted hopeless romantic. Wonder where I got that from?" Leslie teased.

Unable to stay away from the original conversation, Natalie confessed, "You know what, Leslie, I miss him. He was my life for so long. But how much disrespect should I be willing to accept?"

"None. I'll say it again, he needs to be punished. Girl, handle your business."

"I know that anything worth having is worth fighting for and all relationships have their ups and downs. Love is never easy. But this is ridiculous. I was willing to fight, I did fight, but this was a TKO. Girl, he knocked me out with that last one. And it's going to take some time to heal from this."

"I feel you, girl," said Leslie. "So when do you think you'll be coming back?"

"I'm not sure. Amanda and I both need some time away. These men did a number on us." Natalie's car swerved, missing a car that tried to get into her lane. "Oh my God!" she whispered to herself, glancing back to make sure her children were still sleeping peacefully.

"What was that?" Leslie asked, hearing the car horn warning Natalie.

"Nothing," Natalie lied.

"I'm going to let you go. You be careful," Leslie cautioned. "I've got a date. Girl, ain't nothing changed." Leslie laughed. "Hey, Andrea is good. She's doing well. Don't worry about her. I'll keep her in check. Call your mother. No back talk!" Leslie demanded. "Be safe and call me when you get there. I love you, Natalie. See you." And before Natalie could answer, the call was disconnected.

Natalie smiled, recalling the conversation. And then her smile faded, remembering how a few weeks earlier she was traumatized with uncertainty. The repeat phone calls with no one on the other end. She realized now that it was Sandy. Natalie laughed, realizing she wasn't the only one bamboozled by his deceitful ways. Funny, knowing that someone else was feeling pain was somewhat comforting. And she said it again, "Misery really does love company."

Natalie's one consolation was knowing that she wasn't the paranoid person Anderson made her believe she was. It's a shame, she thought to herself, that she had to realize her sanity was intact at the expense of finding out that her relationship, the relationship she had staked her life on, was all a lie. But there were two things that weren't a lie—they were hers, part of her. Natalie's two angels, her two reasons for living, her children—they were what she held dearest to her heart, always had. Because of them, she knew she must make it. She was ditching the joker finally, the thing that was compromising her card game of life. So now it was time she continue playing with the hand she was dealt.

"Mommy?" A little voice from the backseat cut into her thoughts.

"Yeah, baby?"

"Where are we going?"

"Somewhere new, baby. Somewhere brand-new."

ABOUT THE AUTHOR

Playing With The Hand I Was Dealt will be Nikki Jenkins's first published novel. Nikki identified her passion for writing after receiving her graduate degree from The Ohio State University. It was at a time when most writers had been honing their skills for years. However, her passion for storytelling is so intense that she feels that she can overcome her lack of experience with her God-given talents. By using her ability to create realistic characters and captivating storylines, Nikki feels that she is on her way to establishing herself as a heavy-hitter in the writing industry.

Nikki's ultimate goal is to parlay her part-time writing into a full-time career. "I want to write children's stories, screenplays and scripts for television. I want to do it all! At times I feel as if my personality is too creative to be confined within the walls of an office building." In addition to being free to write, Nikki wants to spend more time with her family. "Not only am I writing to entertain, but I want to write to give my children opportunities that I may not have had because my mother was either working or too tired from working.

"I want to be known as a serious novelist. One who is clever with word choice and thought-provoking in delivery. The ability to take arbitrary words and put them together to create sentences that flow and are rhythmic, now that's what gets me going!"

Nikki lives in Reynoldsburg, Ohio with her two small children and her fiancé. Visit www.NikkiJenkins.com or email Nikki@NikkiJenkins.com

A Love So Deep

BY SUZETTA PERKINS

Prologue

It was early fall, and weeping willows bowed to sun-baked lawns while giant redwoods spanked the skies, casting a lazy-like setting about the Bay Area. Maple trees were adorned with leaves of gold and reddish brown while squirrels scampered up twisted branches in preparation of the winter months that lay ahead. It was an enchanting feeling—a movie-set backdrop. The summer was coming to an end, but its remnants were still very evident.

It was five in the morning when Charlie Ford, Dexter Brown, Bobby Fuller, with Graham Peters bringing up the rear, strode onto the Berkeley Pier, carrying tackle boxes, bait, chairs, and insulated coffee mugs filled with steaming coffee. The sun was not due to come up for another hour. The calm and peacefulness the water yielded was just right for the few fish that might nibble on their hooks.

Not much talk passed between the four men. This was to be a short trip— a two-hour excursion to help lift the spirits of a friend. Then it would be back to Bobby's house for his wife's hot, homemade biscuits with honey oozing from their sides along with a plate of soft-scrambled eggs, a couple pounds of bacon, and fresh brewed coffee to wash it all down. If they were fortunate to catch a few fish in the process, that would be alright, too.

Their poles were extended, lines laying in wait, birds chirping signaling the day to begin. An hour passed, and the sun rose like a yellow monster ready to devour the city. Its reflection illuminated the water a little at a time as it rose over the Oakland and Berkeley Hills to sneak a peek at the four men.

"Something's biting," Charlie yelled, reeling in a three-pound halibut. "Hey now, I got me a fish for dinner."

"Who you gonna get to clean and cook it for you?" Dexter chimed in. "See, I've got me a woman that'll clean my fish, fry it up in a great big pan, and serve it on a platter with homemade potato salad, collard greens, and hush puppies."

"But you don't have no fish for your woman to fry," Charlie countered, letting out a great big howl and slapping Bobby with a high-five.

"I wouldn't eat the fish from the bay anyway. Heard there might be mercury in the water," Dexter said. "These puny little bass and halibut out in this water are just for sport—test your skills."

"Amanda!" Graham shouted, jumping into the water, causing the other men to gasp out loud in alarm. Graham gasped for air, his arms flailing around like he was cheering on his favorite offensive end, Jerry Rice of the Oakland Raiders.

"My God, Graham. What's gotten into you? What are you doing?" Charlie shouted at the top of his lungs, ditching his pole and jumping in. Graham could not swim.

Dexter and Bobby threw down their poles and ran to the water's edge. Sixty-two- year-old Charlie was the only one in the bunch who could swim, and he was giving it his all in the cold, murky water to save the life of his best friend.

Three feet out into the water, Charlie's muscular arms grabbed onto Graham, pulling him up. Bubbles came out of Graham's mouth. Charlie gave him a quick glance while paddling back to shore.

Anxious faces looked down at Charlie as he neared the shore. Dexter and Bobby extended their arms as far and pulled him onto the bank.

Graham's body trembled as he stood facing the group. His wet clothing stuck to him like Saran Wrap. His teeth clinked together in rapid succession, making a chattering sound. Bobby took off his jacket and placed it around Graham's shoulders.

Graham appeared tired and worn as he stared back at the alarmed men who were unable to utter a word. He looked at each one individually—Charlie, Dexter, and Bobby—then shut his eyes, clasping his hands over his face. He let out a sigh and his shoulders slumped with the weight of his grief. Amanda's death had sapped the life straight out of him.

"What's wrong with you, Graham?" Charlie shouted out of fear. You could have drowned out there? Talk to me."

"Stop it, Charlie," Dexter cut in. "I know you're still hurting," he said, turning to Graham. "It's gonna take some time, but you hang in there, buddy. It'll be alright after awhile."

"Manda, Manda, Manda," Graham moaned over and over again, his tears flowing like a busted fire hydrant. He fell to his knees, shaking his head, unashamed of his outburst. Life didn't seem worth living now that Amanda was gone. Charlie held onto him. His crying was so uncontrollable that his body shook violently as if he had been injected with a thousand volts of electricity.

"It's gonna be alright, man." Charlie hugged and squeezed his best friend. "If I could, I'd bring Amanda back, but that is not humanly possible. I loved Amanda, too. I wish I could somehow drain the pain from you, but for now, you'll have to trust that I'll be there for you."

"I can't go on without my beloved Amanda," Graham wailed.

Charlie, Dexter, and Bobby sat down on the bank next to Graham and wiped tears away from their own eyes.

Chapter 1

S he was everywhere. Everywhere Graham turned and in everything he touched, she was there. Her reflection peered back at him when he looked in the mirror. She was a glimmer of light on a distant ocean. He felt her hand graze his while placing the oversized pillow on her favorite spot on the sofa. On the day he'd gone fishing, there she was in all her radiant beauty, staring back at him through the ripples in the water, and he had jumped in to try and save her.

♥♥♥

It was almost two months to the day since had Amanda died. Graham had not ventured out of the house except for the day he'd gone fishing with his buddies. He sat home day in and day out waiting for Amanda to return so they could resume their life together. But with the passing of time, his obsession left him scraping the bottom of loneliness.

Today was going to be a new day, Graham promised himself. Self-pity had its place, but now he was ready to rise from its shadow. As he lay on the couch trying to make good on that promise, he was suddenly twenty again—a young man recently come to the Bay Area from St. Louis to follow a dream.

♥♥♥

Graham's best friend, Charlie Ford, had arrived in the Bay Area a year earlier. Charlie's Uncle Roscoe, or Roc as he preferred to be called, had migrated to California after the war, finding work at the Naval Air Station in Alameda. Uncle Roc had invited Charlie to come out West after high school.

Graham and Charlie went way back. They met at junior high school. Charlie was one year older and seven inches taller than Graham, although Graham swore he was six feet tall when he had his Sunday-go-to-meeting shoes on. Charlie had coal-black, wavy hair that appeared an iridescent blue depending on the light. Graham had a thick crown of self-made waves with the help of a little Murray's hair pomade and a stocking cap. They were a pair. You'd rarely see one without the other. And yes, they could turn the charm on and were not accustomed to being without a girl wrapped in each arm.

Graham and Charlie played football in high school and were the main ingredient in a singing group they formed. Now Graham found himself in the Bay Area by way of Southern Pacific Railways with a shoebox filled with all his worldly possessions under his arm. Graham's mother, Eula Mae Perry Peters, had died suddenly of a brain aneurism, one short year after his father died. So Graham set off to see the world, leaving his two younger sisters behind with his Aunt Rubye to care for them.

It was Graham's first week in Oakland. The city was all abuzz—a little like St. Louis, except that there were more jobs for Negroes and maybe a chance to strike it rich. Striking it rich didn't seem to be a likely event in Graham's immediate future unless he accidentally fell into it, but he did like the feel of the place he now called home.

Charlie subletted a small room from his Uncle Roc and asked Graham to stay with him until he got on his feet. There would be no problem with Graham getting a job. Hire notices were posted all over the black community. Everyone was looking for young, strong Negro men to work in the Naval shipyard, lifting heavy cargo.

But this was the weekend, and Graham was ready to see the sights. It had been a long, tedious ride on the train. The bright lights of the San Francisco Bay were a wonderful welcome mat for a young kid a long way from home.

"Come on, Graham," Charlie shouted. "The show's gonna start in about an hour. Man, you and me will be back in business in no time—all the babes we want."

"Church, Charlie? You've gotta be kidding. All of those clubs we passed on the way in. I'm sure we can find some good-looking girls there. I'm ready to unwind a little, kick up my heels."

"Relax, Graham. They say if you want a real woman, go to the church house. There's a convention going on at this big church up on Market Street that's about three blocks away and in walking distance. My man, Curtis MacArthur, swore up and down that there's gonna be a lot of babes at the convention. They come from far and wide. Graham, man, you can take your pick—short ones, tall ones, skinny ones, fat if you like, but there's enough to go around for seconds, thirds if you want. There's gonna be good music, eating and even a little preaching, but this is the place to be if you want the cream of the crop."

"Charlie, you are crazy. You should have been a car salesman. Anyway, I don't have anything to wear."

"That's no problem. Uncle Roc got plenty of suits. They might be a tad bit too big, but they'll do for tonight." Charlie laughed and hit Graham on the back. "You're my buddy, and we're a team. Now what kinda friend would I be strolling with a fine babe on my arm and my best friend sitting back in the room all by himself?"

"You don't want me to answer that…?"

"Go on, tell me."

"What makes you so sure any of these girls are gonna even look at you? They're lookin' for preachers so they can become first ladies. No slick, jive-talking, unrepentant, tall, dreamy-eyed, dark-haired boy without an ounce of salvation got half a chance."

"I was counting on that tall, dreamy-eyed, dark-haired boy to do the trick." They both laughed until it hurt.

"You're right," Graham continued, "we are a pair, but you run on tonight. I'll catch you in church another time."

"Suit yourself, buddy. You're gonna wish you were there. And don't let me have to tell you I told you so."

"Get on and get out of here. I might take a walk later."

"Gonna try and sneak a peek, eh?"

"Catch you later."

Graham sat in the room contemplating life—what he was going to do tonight and then tomorrow. An hour had passed since Charlie left. It seemed the whole neighborhood had evaporated into the night—a hushed quiet that made Graham a bit wary. He jumped up and went to the window, but only the stars and the moon dared to stare back at him, the moon illuminating his face in the windowpane.

Graham grabbed his jacket off the chair and headed out the door. He wasn't sure where he was going, but he knew he needed to get out of that noiseless house—maybe hear a little music, ahh maybe some preaching, but he wanted to be where there was life and a little reminder of home.

He headed west passing a few couples out strolling. Then he noticed the cars—so many lined the street. He continued another block, and the cars—Buicks, Packards, and Fords, inhabited every available space on either side of the street. Yeah, he would own one of them one day. Then he heard it, felt it reverberate throughout his body. It reminded him of thunder, cymbals crashing. Yes, someone was having a good time, and it didn't sound like the blues they were playing back at Slim's in St. Louis.

As Graham neared the big church on Market Street, a flurry of activity surrounded it. The building seemed to sway on its cinderblocks, careful not to empty its precious cargo from inside. It was 10 p.m., and although there seemed to be a lot going on inside the church, there was a lot happening outside as well. Small circles of young people milled about holding conversations. Suddenly, Graham was converged upon by a sea of purple and white choir robes which dutifully stretched into a single line waiting to march into the sanctuary. Graham looked around, but Charlie was nowhere to be found.

As Graham inched closer, a beautiful girl in her late teens emerged from the fellowship hall. She was about Graham's height, give or take an inch. She wore the prettiest white silk suit and a white pill-box hat with a bow made of lace attached to the front. The ends of her hair were turned up in a shoulder-length flip that accentuated her nutmeg-colored skin. But it was the nut-brown legs that made Graham come from his hiding place. Graham stumbled over a workhorse that had been placed over an open manhole. He regained his composure and followed her right into church.

He'd forgotten for a moment that he was not dressed appropriately, but that didn't matter. Charlie was right; "the crème de la crème" resided here. Someone called "Amanda," and the girl with the nut-brown legs, waved her hand. What a pretty name. Graham would have to move closer if he was going to say anything to her at all. She looked his way and then quickly away, bobbing her head to the music as the choir marched in. She looked his way again, and Graham locked upon her gaze and didn't let go.

She seemed shy in a girlish sort of way, but Graham forged ahead. He pushed closer to her, the crowd unyielding until he was within an inch from touching her nose.

"Hi, Amanda," he said above the noise.

She sneered at him, wrinkling up her nose.

"Who are you, and how do you know my name?" Amanda Carter demanded.

"That's a secret," he said, even more mesmerized by her beauty. "My name is Graham." He extended his hand. "I'm going to be a preacher one day."

Graham saw the puzzled look on her face. "What does that have to do with me?" she retorted, leaving his hand in mid-air.

"Well…I. Would you like to go outside and talk for a few minutes?"

Amanda cocked her head back hesitating before she spoke. Her eyes cut a path down the length of his body and rested on his wrinkled khaki pants and blue peacoat that had doubled as a pillow on his trek to the West.

"Sure, why not," she said nonchalantly. "You seem harmless enough, but after this choir sings. They are so good."

Oh, if Charlie could see him now. Graham could tell Ms. Amanda liked the attention he was giving her, although she pretended she didn't. When the choir had finished singing, they quietly went outside. They made small talk, but Graham was transfixed by her beauty (eyes the color of ripe olives embedded in an oval, nutmeg-colored face) and those beautiful nut-brown legs that he wished he could wrap his own around. Actually, he wanted to reach out and touch her, maybe place a kiss on those fine chiseled lips of hers that smelled of sweet berries when he got close enough to catch a whiff.

There was something about Amanda that was different—unlike those other girls who stumbled over themselves vying for the chance to be his lady. Graham Peters became a different person that night—his heart ached for Amanda Carter, a girl he had just met. If given half a chance, he would cherish her until the end of time.

Chapter 2

Two hours had elapsed when the telephone's ring brought Graham out of his reverie.

"Who's wanting me now?" he said aloud. "Don't they know I just wanna be left alone? Shut up!" he hollered at the telephone as the caller made no attempt to give up its quest to be heard. Graham made no attempt to answer. "All people want to do is give advice and get in your business," Graham grumbled. And he was having no parts of it.

Graham walked listlessly around the house, finally retreating to his bedroom. "Why Amanda, why?" Graham cried out loud, throwing his hands in the air. He sat on the edge of the bed, closed his eyes, and shook his head. He would not fulfill his promise to himself today. *Maybe tomorrow*, Graham thought.

Graham stood up and ran his hand along the dresser where Amanda kept her things. There were photos of their two girls, Deborah and Elizabeth, now fully grown with families of their own. The pictures were taken when they were five and six years old, respectively. Sitting next to the pictures was Amanda's jewelry box. It held everything from precious gems to costume pieces. Many were gifts the girls or Graham had given her. Amanda cherished each and every piece and would often tell people she couldn't part with them.

Graham rifled through the box until his heart stopped where his finger had also stopped. In the midst of all those trinkets was the rose pendant Graham had given Amanda on their first date as a token of his love and affection. Graham picked up the pendant and twirled it in his hand. He clutched it tightly, finally bringing it to his chest. The memory was so vivid—that first date. Graham fell on the bed and let time take him to the moment when he knew for sure that Amanda was his true love.

♥♥♥

It had been three weeks since Graham set eyes on Amanda at the big church on Market Street. Amanda lived not far from Charlie's Uncle Roc, but it was difficult to see her. Since Graham worked during the day at the Naval shipyard, it was next to impossible for Amanda to meet Graham. Mr.

and Mrs. Carter kept a tight rein on their daughter. The best that Graham and Amanda could hope for was a phone call here and there.

As fate would have it, Graham got a weekend off and vowed to see Amanda. After giving Charlie what he owed for rent, Graham took five dollars from his remaining salary and set off to find something nice for her. A man bearing gifts had to amount to something. He'd show the Carters what he was made of.

There was an H. G. Grant store downtown that sold nice little trinkets; hopefully, he would find something befitting Amanda. He had called her the night before and asked her to meet him there for a fountain soda. Then he would give her the gift.

Graham circled the jewelry counter examining each piece. His eyes finally rested on the most beautiful rose pendant he had ever seen. He picked up the pendant and examined it thoroughly. A big, burly white woman peered at him from over the counter, sure Graham had no money to pay for the pendant. It made Graham's heart soar when he asked those steely-blue eyes how much the pendant cost. When she said $3.95, he handed her a five-dollar bill. It made his heart even happier when he saw Amanda walk through the door and head for the lunch counter.

Graham hoped she was as happy to see him as he was to see her. It was the longest three weeks, but sometimes things worth having took a long time to obtain. He saw her look around, then look at her watch, wondering if he would show. He picked up his stride, walked up behind her, and whispered, "Hi, Amanda. You look so pretty today."

Unable to contain her smile, Amanda blushed openly. Graham and Amanda stood at the counter and ordered floats, then sipped in silence. It was easy on the phone, but talking to each other in person posed a real challenge. Neither of them had felt this way about anyone else. They were both so young, however, nothing had prepared them for how they felt now. Graham sipped the last of his float and prepared to speak.

"I have a little something for you. I hope you don't mind."

"What is it, Graham?"

"You'll just have to open it and see," he said excitedly.

Amanda reached into the bag and pulled out the cardstock that held the rose pendant. Her smile turned to a frown. "I can't accept this, Graham. My parents would be furious."

"They wouldn't have to know; it's just between us. You can wear it whenever we're together. Do you like it? I picked it out special for you."

"Yes, I like it…I like it very much It's the best gift anyone has ever given me outside of my mother and father."

Graham was pleased with himself.

They sat staring at each other, each wanting a little more. A long A-line wool skirt now covered those nut-brown legs that Graham had admired. The wrinkled shirt and khaki pants Graham wore on the night he met Amanda were replaced with a red-and-white-striped, short-sleeved shirt that was tucked in a pair of starched blue slacks.

"I need to run home now. I'd like to see you again, though. Maybe we can meet in the park."

"How about tomorrow?" Graham said gleefully. "I have the whole week-end free. Mosswood Park isn't too far from here. We could meet about noon."

"I have to go to church tomorrow, but maybe I can get away around two o'clock."

"Okay, that would…"

"Graham, I have a better idea. Why don't you come to church tomorrow? That way, my parents would see you—even get to meet you."

Graham pondered this. Church was where he met her, but he certainly had no intention of venturing back there anytime soon. Graham saw the spark in Amanda's eyes, and somehow he knew that if he disappointed her, he would probably lose her forever. He must really be in love to agree to attend church services. There was nothing left to do but say yes.

♥♥♥

Graham was cute and even a little intelligent—well, maybe very intelligent in a weird sort of way. He was kind and attentive, although the extent of their casual relationship had been through the telephone lines.

Amanda's eyes searched the pews looking for Graham, not wanting to appear too anxious. He said he would come to the eleven o'clock service that had been in progress for the past ten minutes. Then she spotted him in the rear of the church. She slowly turned her head back toward the front, satisfied things were falling into place. She allowed herself a small grin—surprised by her own forwardness, her attempt to be a catalyst in bringing the two of them together.

She was in love and like a flower in bloom.

There were plenty of walks in the park after that day in church—the trip to the Santa Cruz boardwalk and many root beer floats were slurped from the counter of H. G. Grant. A few kisses were shared between them—sweet, tender kisses. And their bodies begged for more than Amanda was willing to give at the time.

There would be more than enough time for that, as Graham finally proposed to Amanda four months later, to the delight of both Deacon and Mrs. Carter. And to top it all off, Graham became a deacon in the big church up on Market Street—a place Amanda knew Graham had come to love. It wasn't just the people or the fact he met Amanda there, it was the love that transcended the place and how Graham was taken in among its members and made one of their own. And now he was going to marry the head deacon's daughter. He and Charlie could have never envisioned this back in St. Louis.

Graham opened his eyes. The house was dark and still. He must have lain there a long time, because the street lamps provided the only light that shone in his empty house and empty heart. It was then he realized that the rose pendant was still in his hand. He slowly rose from the bed and put the pendant back in the jewelry box, closing the lid gently. Another day had come and gone.